Praise for Emily Schultz and

Little Threats

"My new hero."   —Stephen King

"*Little Threats* hooked me from the first line. A gripping, haunting story about family, memory, and most of all, grief—this book is difficult to put down, and more difficult to stop thinking about."

—Rob Hart, author of *The Warehouse*

"At its heart, *Little Threats* is a devastating and elegiac novel about teenage friendships, sexuality, drug use, and ultimately betrayal. Emily Schultz is unflinching in revealing the way prison isn't merely a place but a feeling that can haunt a girl who grew into a woman behind bars. Freedom isn't absolution, and the answers are as painful as the questions in this heart-stopping, powerful story."   —Bryn Greenwood, author of
All the Ugly and Wonderful Things and *The Reckless Oath We Made*

"Emily Schultz gives us fierce, if damaged, Kennedy Wynn, a young woman returning home from prison, haunted by a crime for which she maintains her innocence and plagued by a legacy of pain and loss. Schultz has the reader eagerly flipping pages as secrets are revealed, while also pausing to consider Kennedy's poignant observations about trust and love. It's a pulsating mystery and a deftly rendered portrait of a family in crisis, where small details, like little threats, enlighten and illuminate."

—Lori Lansens, author of *This Little Light*

PRAISE FOR

The Blondes

An NPR Great Reads Selection of 2015
A *Kirkus Reviews* Best Book of 2015
A *BookPage* Best Book of 2015

"Wow!" —Margaret Atwood

"*The Blondes* is scary and deeply, bitingly funny—a satire about gender that kept me reading until four in the morning—and a fine addition to the all-too-small genre of feminist horror." —NPR

"Intelligent, mesmerizing, and fearless. An entirely original and beautifully twisted satire with a heart of darkness."
—Emily St. John Mandel, bestselling author of *Station Eleven*

"This frighteningly realistic nail-biter is as acidly funny as it is twisted."
—*People*

"Schultz spins an eerie tale with perspective into our cultural attitudes about beauty." —*Entertainment Weekly*

"What sounds like George Romero with a bottle of peroxide is surprisingly sensitive and contemplative . . . As classic blonde jokes acquire deadly hues, the novel's satiric color remains subtle." —*The Washington Post*

"A road story, and a feminist bildungsroman, and a parable about prejudice and reproductive freedom and immigration." —*Los Angeles Times*

"Those who enjoy Margaret Atwood should sign up for it. I did, and gladly." —*Dallas Morning News*

"The literary love child of Naomi Wolf and Stephen King."
—Helen Wecker, bestselling author of *The Golem and the Jinni*

"A nail-biter that is equal parts suspense, science fiction, and a funny, dark sendup of the stranglehold of gender." —*Kirkus Reviews* (starred review)

"Funny, horrific, and frighteningly realistic . . . A must-read."

—*Library Journal* (starred review)

"[A] ferociously clever, exceedingly well written variation on the pandemic novel . . . This canny, suspenseful, acidly observant satire cradles an intimate, poignant, and hilarious story of one lonely, stoic, young mother-to-be caught up in surreal and terrifying situations."

—*Booklist* (starred review)

"*The Blondes* is the book you can't put down; it's also the book you can't stop thinking about after you do." —*BookPage*

"Emily Schultz balances biting humor and thrilling suspense in a complex story." —*Us Weekly*

"A campy, King-inspired nightmare sure to satisfy the scream queens in the audience . . ." —*Bustle*

"*The Blondes* by Emily Schultz gives a twisted meaning to the phrase 'blondes have more fun.' I giggled and shivered."

—*Minnesota Journal Sentinel*

"Fast-paced drama, punctuated with humor . . . Schultz writes a subtle commentary on how discrimination operates around the globe."

—*Shelf Awareness*

"A wild and smart look at cultural theory, gender roles, and societal expectations." —*LongReads*

"With a lively sense of danger . . . and an absurdist but compelling feminist premise, the book has the enviable qualities of a smart page-turner."

—*Flavorwire*

"Corrosively humorous commentary on social, sexual and cross-border politics." —*Toronto Star*

"Skin-crawling, Cronenbergian satire." —*Rue Morgue*

ALSO BY EMILY SCHULTZ

The Blondes

little threats

emily schultz

G. P. Putnam's Sons
New York

◆ ◆ ◆

PUTNAM
— EST. 1838 —

G. P. Putnam's Sons
Publishers Since 1838
An imprint of Penguin Random House LLC
penguinrandomhouse.com

Library of Congress Cataloging-in-Publication Data

Names: Schultz, Emily, 1974– author.
Title: Little threats / Emily Schultz.
New York : G. P. Putnam's Sons, [2020].
Identifiers: LCCN 2020016460 (print) | LCCN 2020016461
(ebook) | ISBN 9780593086995 (trade paperback) |
ISBN 9780593087008 (ebook)
Subjects: GSAFD: Mystery fiction.
Classification: LCC PR9199.4.S394 L58 2020 (print) |
LCC PR9199.4.S394 (ebook) | DDC 813/.6—dc23
LC record available at https://lccn.loc.gov/2020016460
LC ebook record available at https://lccn.loc.gov/202001646
p.   cm.

Printed in the United States of America
1   3   5   7   9   10   8   6   4   2

Book design by Katy Riegel

For Brian,

my nineties, my now

We are all detectives walking around with our flashlights and notepads.

We all feel that there is more going on than meets the eye.

—DAVID LYNCH

little threats

⫿ ⫿ ⫿

FINAL ASSIGNMENT:
Write about your victim.

T HE DEAD GIRL never gets to write her own story. She never gets to shake her cramped hand after falling into the words for too long, like I get to do. The dead girl never gets to take a creative writing class taught by an instructor from the local college who is nervous and excited about being in a prison for the first time. The dead girl doesn't get to put up her bloody, leaf-encrusted hand when the teacher asks, "Does anyone know what *epiphany* means?" Her side of the story is always unwritten, and that becomes the secondary tragedy. She's the only one who knows what went down. Everyone else is a tourist in her resting place, even me.

This is what I know, and what I keep on imagining, happened.

In the woods she looked battered and sunken, like a tossed-aside doll. At first I thought it must be a game, an act. But Haley remained still where she lay with her legs in the creek and the rest of her on the sand. An Ophelia in Doc Martens. "Haley," I said, kneeling beside her. "Your mom is going to freak out."

I saw that blood filled Haley's transparent blouse. I tried to stand but my legs were shaky and my velvet skirt was heavy with water. Even then, I wasn't sure this was happening. The sand beneath the girl was dark, like an oil stain. I was coming down from the acid trip, and the air still felt scratchy as yarn and the trees waved in time like music. I reached out and pushed Haley's shoulder and thick blood poured out of her like she was a tipped cup. I sat back, trying to breathe.

Haley was my friend and now she was falling apart, becoming part of the ground. I couldn't leave her like this. I leaned forward and hurriedly rearranged her, crossing her hands over the wounds to hide them. There was dirt beneath the nails, as if she'd gripped the ground at some point. One hand had a wound through it, a place where the skin gave way. Under the swaying trees of Blueheart Woods, I fanned out Haley's hair, brushed it back with my fingers, trying to make her beautiful. The curls felt the way they always did, but why wouldn't they? Giving way to frizz, this reddish bush of it around Haley's face.

I thought about the boy, Berk—there is always a living boy to go with a dead girl. I did not remember anything between getting out of his car the night before and this moment now. I thought he could never have done this. I'd seen him care about her, sometimes I thought more than he cared about me. Berk had left us by the woods, angry at me. Then I was angry at Haley, because she left me alone on acid. I remember seeing her walk into the dark woods, singing "Feed the Tree" as the night lowered on her like a sheet. *Silver baby come to me. I'll only hurt you in my dreams.*

Then nothing, until I was in my room after the sun came up. I said, "Haley," and jumped out of bed, knowing that I needed to find her. And I did.

This would be Haley's burial, I reasoned, so I arrayed several twigs and branches around my friend's head, like a Renaissance halo.

I dug into my purse and found a pair of fold-up nail scissors. I reached out and took a lock of Haley's hair between my fingers. I apologized even as I snipped away a curl—as if I could apologize for the future, that it was no longer her story.

I tucked the trimmed hair into a side pocket in my purse, where it settled next to a tampon.

My sister, Carter, had always said that when something happened to me, it was like it had happened to her. Just one of those twin things. I knew she would call the police so I tried not to tell her about Haley. I was afraid that if someone could do this to her, he could do it to me. But then more terrible thoughts came, and really, never stopped coming. *What happened? Who did this?* In the end I wasn't good at secrets, not at that age anyway. I went back to the woods, and after I got home, I managed to keep my silence about half an hour.

Before I confided in Carter, I stashed the orange curl in between the pages of *Jane Eyre.* The strands became flattened and dull inside the book, like the hair a child might unthinkingly cut off a doll. It didn't stay together, pretty, the way I had hoped it would.

—*Kennedy Wynn*
Heron Valley Correctional Facility

Chapter 1

G ERRY WYNN HAD CHOSEN his daughters' names after presidents, so they would know anything was possible. If they'd been boys they would have been Jack and Jimmy, or more formally John and James. But thirty-one years ago they had been handed to him screaming, pink, and female.

The afternoon before his daughter's release from prison, Gerry finished preparing things for Kennedy's arrival. He walked out to his SUV and placed her old army jacket in the front seat so she would have something to wear when she came out of the Heron Valley Correctional Facility. He had commissioned Carter to arrange for a new wardrobe for her, but she had forgotten to buy her sister a coat. Already blouses, pants, belts, and boots were stashed in an upstairs bedroom. And it was Carter's job to bring the cake to the party, although she hadn't said yet whether she would come with him to the prison to fetch her twin.

Gerry thought that strange—Carter had dutifully visited her sister every week throughout her sentence but had stopped as the release date came closer. He had never understood daughters, much less twins. After he finished making up the room, he would call Carter, he thought, try again to convince her what a momentous occasion this was. With the exception of their mother, Laine, the family was going to be together again.

He was excited to show Kennedy the renovated house. Hers was the only room he hadn't redone. He stood in the doorway often but didn't cross into the space, as if it were still hers. Now it would be. As he went in, he discovered the bedroom had gathered dust. He remembered changing the sheets before her first parole hearing five years ago. She should have been let out then, given that the evidence in the case had been purely circumstantial. No weapon. No blood anywhere in the Wynn home. Only that goddamn lock of hair forced her into a plea. The Kimbersons had protested the release at a press conference that time, trotting out their living child, a boy. Everett was hardly old enough to shave then, let alone read a victim impact statement about what it had been like to lose his big sister when he was just nine. Distasteful, Gerry thought, to use a child that way. Kennedy had been denied that time. This time, they hadn't shown and Kennedy had been given the release date of November 7, 2008.

Gerry gripped the new set of sheets against his leg. He stared at the contents of the shelves: books, perfume bottles, and banners, ribbons she'd won, tennis trophies. Kennedy and Carter had played doubles until they were fourteen; on the tennis court, they'd moved like music. His favorite memories of Kennedy involved driving long-distance to sporting events—she and Carter were twelve, then thirteen, that little window of time before he would lose them. Even then, he'd known they would go: it was just that he'd thought it would be to school dances and sleepover parties.

Gerry walked over and opened the window, hoping to get some air into the room. The floor around the end of the bed was still strewn with old tapes, titled, personalized, and annotated with a story known only between the gifter and the giftee:

EXTREMITIES, DIRT & VARIOUS REPRESSED EMOTIONS FOR KENNEDY

Side One
Screaming Trees: Nearly Lost You
Dead Kennedys: Goons of Hazzard *(I had to!)*
Dinosaur Jr.: The Wagon
Sebadoh: Wonderful, Wonderful
Killing Joke: Love Like Blood
Soundgarden: Flower
Soundgarden: Big Dumb Sex
  (Don't play when your parents are around!)

Side Two
Radiohead: Creep
Bauhaus: She's in Parties
Lush: Nothing Natural
Jesus and Mary Chain: Reverence

Echo & the Bunnymen: Killing Moon
Jane's Addiction: Summertime Rolls
Nick Cave: Straight to You

Kim Gordon's Silver Hot Pants for Berk, xo

Side One
Nirvana: Come As You Are
Suede: Animal Nitrate
Concrete Blonde: Tomorrow, Wendy (*Kennedy reference
    back at you*)
Sisters of Mercy: This Corrosion
Cure: Lovesong
Sugarcubes: Leash Called Love
NIN: Something I Can Never Have

Side Two
Skinny Puppy: Chainsaw
Thrill Kill Kult: Sex on Wheelz
Smashing Pumpkins: Rhionceros
L7: Pretend We're Dead
Pixies: Here Comes Your Man
Iggy Pop: Candy
Siouxsie and the Banshees: Kiss Them for Me
Pavement: Summer Babe

He kneeled down and looked at them. He detested Berk
Butler. Until Haley's death he hadn't even known his daughters

and their friend had been involved with him. Gerry had to admit to himself how distracted he had been that summer, with he and Laine working through things.

The hand lettering on the tape case from Kennedy to Berkeley was loopy and doughy, the *o*'s and *a*'s almost square instead of round. The one from the young man to her had thin, tight lettering, as if he had forced himself to print neatly, pressing hard with the black pen. It didn't occur to Gerry that the fact that there were two tapes was an upset to the usual order—that Berk Butler should still have been in possession of the one she'd gifted him. That either she'd changed her mind about giving it, or he'd given it back. The song names held nothing for Gerry—they brought no winding ribbon of melody to his mind. For him, it was all teenage code. He gently placed the tapes back on the floor beside a milk crate that housed other homemade Maxells.

A woman from the cleaning service was the only other person who had been in Kennedy's room, but years ago, after Gerry had found some jewelry boxes and notebooks moved, the curling iron and the lava lamp all shifted around, he had switched services. *Everything has its spot*, he'd told her repeatedly. He'd told the new one not to bother with that room at all.

Now Gerry tentatively unmade the corners of the old bedding, working around the half-spilled crates of tapes and crammed racks of CDs. A button stabbed into Kennedy's corkboard read *Hope Not Fear Clinton Gore '92*. Earlier that day he'd been sure to take down the Obama/Biden sign, one of only two in their neighborhood, before he got a letter from the homeowners' association about the election's being over.

The duvet was dark violet with a spray of a lilac pattern across it. Everything had been purple that year.

He recalled the name of the little tub of trouble she'd used on her hair: Manic Panic violet. Kennedy had stained all the towels with each dye job. Gerry remembered Laine had cried over the steeple-gray Williams Sonoma ones blemished with streaks of violet; she shouted that Kennedy didn't respect her. Kennedy shouted there was more to life than money. He thought he'd have to draft a lawyer's letter to force the two women to communicate again. The tops of Kennedy's ears were violet for weeks, like she had a bad sunburn.

Laine and Gerry had hated their girls' style choices at the time, each new one cutting more, the short, bell-shaped dresses; the clunky, mannish boots; the distressed clothes from charity stores. What were they rebelling so hard against? He couldn't believe it when he started seeing the Salvation Army on the credit card bill. He took it as a slight against all that he'd worked for. The girls were honors students at the best public school in the county. Even if it had some lower-income residents from Longwood, Liberty High School had a great arts program and athletics, the kind of place that he'd dreamed of attending when he was a kid.

Gerry lifted the duvet up and smelled it. It didn't smell like Kennedy. The scent was musty, like old cigarettes, though he'd quit and no one had smoked in the house in at least a decade. He still had time to clean it. Gerry stripped the bedding quickly—years since he'd made a bed himself. How was this to be done? He stepped on a cassette case on the floor and felt it crack. Public Enemy, *Fear of a Black Planet,* the cassette read when he picked it up. He set it on the bookshelf. He tugged the new mauve sheet over the mattress. After years on a prison cot, a person deserved a well-made bed.

When Gerry was satisfied, he gathered up the old duvet and went across the hallway to his home office. He dropped the duvet in a leather chair and went to the phone on his large carved desk. He had Carter's cell number programmed into his speed dial, and although she almost always picked up, this time it went to voicemail.

"Carter, it's Dad," he said, cringing at his own adherence to tradition; she'd insisted on calling him Gerry since her days in rehab at twenty-two, when she said they needed to deal with each other on adult terms. "I really think you should plan to be here for more than the dinner. Come on the drive out with me. Just come by and we'll ride together. Leaving at ten." He hoped the deadline might work.

Gerry set the phone down and scooped up the duvet. Downstairs in the mudroom, he crammed the whole thing into the washing machine, but as he measured the liquid soap, he looked down and noticed a zipper ran along one edge of the purple cover. The cover should probably be separated from the duvet, Gerry realized. He yanked the bedding back out and unzipped the duvet cover, shaking and pulling. The white, fluffy comforter inside tumbled out. With it came a perfectly folded one-by-one-inch square of notebook paper, the end of it tucked inside so it formed a little envelope made out of itself.

Gerry stared at the shape of it against the porcelain tile of the laundry room. He left the bedding where it lay and picked up the tiny note. As he stooped to pick it up, he felt a burning sensation in his fingertips. His cardiologist had warned him about leaning over—avoid raking leaves, or taking the golf bag out of the trunk, the man had said, as if Gerry had had the nerve to show his face at the club in the last fifteen years. His fingers fumbled for the thin paper before grasping it. He breathed deeply and straightened. Holding it between his thumb and index finger, he peered at it like it was a fossil discovered on a beach. If the police hadn't found it all those years ago, Kennedy must have shoved it so far inside they'd overlooked it—or perhaps it had felt like a tag and they didn't pull it out.

He carried it across the hall to his office and set it gently on the desk, staring at the tiny white square shape it made there in the middle of the leather blotter between the stapler and the letter opener. He reached out and slowly unfolded it.

Chapter 2

K ENNEDY RODE WITH HER FATHER for an hour with the flowers he'd brought clutched against her chest, breathing in, smelling them. She had been surprised when she saw that Gerry had laid an old jacket of hers from the closet across the front seat. It had a cluster of round pins still clinging to the lapel—one for the band the Smiths, an AIDS awareness button, and one that she knew had made Laine and Gerry glare with worry: *No means no.* She pulled the jacket around her more than put it on. She'd wondered if there would be some sad polyester shirt or crushed velvet top to be returned to her upon release, but they had only her wages for her. Between the flowers and a McDonald's milkshake Gerry insisted was once her favorite, he was like an eager boy who had come to take her on a date.

The drink was a punch of sweet that delighted and then quickly nauseated her. Kennedy was overwhelmed. The smell of the daisies, the world flying past her beyond the window—it was all starting to seem like a trip: the point where the cresting acid would make the banal world beautiful. She gripped the inside of the car door with one hand. It was dizzying.

Gerry drove fast and talked fast. "I'm sorry Carter didn't come. I'm sure she'll be at the house."

But Kennedy said nothing. She didn't felt like speaking. She just wanted to breathe in the delicate air.

Gerry tapped some buttons on the BMW console and connected a call. Kennedy listened to the ringing, an ordinary thing that seemed alien to her, coming as it did from within a car. After the ringing, her sister's recorded voice came out of the speakers. "You've reached Carter Randall, I can't pick up." Then silence.

"Carter? It's me. I'm out," Kennedy said to the windshield of the car when Gerry nodded at her.

"Give us a damn call, how about it!" Gerry exclaimed.

Carter Randall. Kennedy had almost forgotten she still went by it. Carter had discarded their surname, *Wynn*, years ago, like a baby-doll dress. At the height of the media coverage it made sense to all of them for Carter to hide under their mother's name. No one in her family had thought any of this would be permanent. It would right itself like any other record-skip in suburban life, no more serious than a possum in the garage, a quiet separation, or a DUI. Her dad was a lawyer after all. He had told Kennedy all the charges would be dropped. He had told her the defense attorneys were looking into the possibility that the crime was connected to the Colonial Parkway Murders—a string of lovers'-lane murders a few years before that had never been solved. I-64 ran practically past the woods, he'd argued, and these victims were all young people too.

A year after Kennedy went to jail, Carter had brought in a

page from *SPIN* magazine showing Trent Reznor wearing a homemade "Free Kennedy Wynn" shirt during his Richmond concert. It was a rush, and for a minute Kennedy felt free from the not knowing—all the thoughts of *Did I do this?* But ultimately it only put murder groupies onto her family. People who clipped things from newspapers or, a few years later, found case details online. Those fans dubbed her "Dead Kennedy," just like the kids in high school had done. Carter tried not to tell her about the emails and phone calls that still sometimes made their way through filters. Men wanting to get in touch with Kennedy, others telling Carter, "You'll do," because of their resemblance.

Carter had once been a mathlete and won scholarships to Drama Summer Intensives, but Kennedy had attended more college inside of a prison than Carter had managed to outside of one. She often wondered what Carter might have been without her as a twin.

There was a faint scent of perfume on the collar of the shapeless black dress Carter had chosen for her, which Gerry had brought to the prison. Kennedy wondered if she'd tried it on.

She noticed that Gerry took a different exit from the highway, one she didn't remember. It meant they didn't have to drive down Smoke Line, past the woods.

"Here we are," Gerry said, pulling up to the house in Blueheart.

Kennedy hadn't realized they were there already: after fifteen years away, the neighbors' houses all looked generic to her. She saw their house was bigger and more ostentatious than she had recalled. The Wynn house was pale brick and stucco. The roof peaked in four separate places to imitate a Victorian skyline. The portico columns held up nothing. The front hall towered, the highest peak, even though it was an empty room used for little more than removing one's shoes. They always did remove their shoes, even in high school, when she and Carter wore Docs that could take a half hour to undo.

Gerry was gently cursing about the fact that Carter's car wasn't there yet, but Kennedy barely noticed. She opened the SUV door and got out, feeling suddenly shaky on her legs. She stared up at her old home.

"Where does she live now?" Kennedy asked. In all the visits over the years, Carter had mostly told her about Gerry, or about current music, films, or trends. The visits, she supposed, had been meant to distract her from her surroundings, and Carter had been good at it. She'd heard about Carter's boyfriend and sex life over the years, but they'd never discussed Haley. It was only at her final visit, six months ago, that Carter had brought her up. "I still miss Haley," she said, and when Kennedy only nodded, Carter pressed. "Tell me honestly . . ." Carter faltered and didn't ask, though her face said everything.

Kennedy reached for her mantra: "I don't know what happened that night."

"I think I'm a little tired of that line after fifteen years." Carter's visits stopped abruptly after that. She wasn't there for visiting hours the following weekend and had not returned since.

Gerry waved his hand. "She and Alex broke up. I don't get

it. She moved into an apartment in the Museum District. It's all right, they'll get back together soon."

Her father pocketed the keys and began to detail the afternoon plans: catered lunch, neighbors and family he'd invited to stop in. Plans. Plans were something she hadn't had in a decade and a half. She glanced down the cul-de-sac at the stately houses, their blank windows, wondering if people were watching her arrive home and if they'd really come by later.

Kennedy remembered how Carter had complained about their parents' need to impress after moving to Blueheart Woods from the city, how they were hippies turned yuppies turned people who yelled about welfare reform during the 1992 election. The girls' natural distrust of their parents had been inchoate until the night Carter made Kennedy watch *Manufacturing Consent*, the documentary about Noam Chomsky. Politics were always beyond Kennedy; she'd spent civics class with her head down, hair hiding her sleeping eyes. But when the double videocassette from the library and three joints were finished she saw her parents as one part of a larger, oppressive agenda. The word *hegemony* was stuck in her head for weeks, like a curse.

Now Kennedy gazed up at the dormer windows that had been hers and Carter's as girls. Gerry was already moving away from the BMW SUV, expecting she would easily walk back into this world, this affluence that wasn't understood and made no impact at Heron Valley. They'd sent her away because the state wanted to make an example of her, send a message that rich kids go to jail too. That's what their lawyers had told her and her parents. *They're threatening life no parole if we don't plea out.* After they'd been fighting for over a year it was Gerry who finally told her to take it. Even Laine had worn down.

Kennedy stood there so long that Gerry turned back, gave her a questioning glance.

In the garden in front of the dining room window the glass globe still shone atop its wrought iron stick: a recycled-glass sphere the size of a bowling ball, coiled with gold and teal strands of color. "I gave that to Mom for her fortieth birthday."

Kennedy remembered Laine had cried when she opened it. Although now she wondered if her emotion came from some other place. Both girls had known their parents were heading for divorce, that they had turned into Bill and Hillary, keeping separate schedules for everything from dinner to TV watching. Eventually, their mother had moved out, three months before her death, because only Laine Wynn would initiate divorce while going through chemo. Taking care of her had been Carter's job; taking care of Kennedy had been Gerry's.

"You're back, and she would be proud of you today," Gerry said decisively. He clapped his hands together as if dusting them off. Done with it. Done with a long-ago tragedy in that way in which men try to own death, deciding when and where it matters and how long to grieve.

"I made up your room," he said.

It hadn't occurred to Kennedy that anything would need to be done. She edged into the foyer, removed her shoes, a new pair of black Mary Janes purchased by Carter—a little-girl shoe, almost as if her twin couldn't conceive of her having aged in the time she'd been in prison. She noticed a wall had been removed between the foyer and the sitting room. The paint and furniture looked new: teal curtains, white paint, a textured brown wallpaper on the accent wall, and a long chocolate leather couch. Everything crisp, masculine. Like a luxury hotel where no object had meaning. She crossed the room and gazed at the new gas fireplace. Gerry came over, excited to tell her about the fuel efficiency and show her how to turn it on.

Above it, there was a large wood frame surrounding a photograph of Gerry just after Kennedy and Carter were born. His hair was longish, sandy, and he sported a mustache. He was holding a girl on each forearm, bundles light as loaves of bread. Kennedy had seen it many times, but in an old album years before.

"My decorator, Laura, found it, did some cleanup work on the print, had that specially mounted."

"Which am I?" Kennedy asked.

They both stepped closer, peering at the long-ago babies. The one that had Gerry's attention was crying. The other small face, only a few days old, was placid.

Gerry chuckled. "Laine didn't always mark the photographs with your names, because she thought it was obvious which was which. And it was to us, at the time."

He walked over to the sound system and flicked it on, keen to show her everything. He paused. "You looked identical, but you were different. She was born first . . ."

Ten minutes before her, but Kennedy was the more dominant personality from the start. Their mother said it was like that even in the womb—there was one side of her belly that kicked harder and she always implied it was Kennedy who did the kicking. Kennedy had always suspected Carter was her father's favorite too—until Haley Kimberson was found in Blueheart Woods. Then he'd turned his attention to Kennedy, and she became his project.

Kennedy saw her reflection in the glass frame as she frowned and said, "She stopped visiting me."

"I know."

Kennedy nodded. She'd felt abandoned by her in the last few months of her sentence. But that wasn't fair, was it? It sounded like her sister had gone through some things, if she'd really moved out from Alex's. Life had gone on and Kennedy had been a madwoman locked in a tower. *Who wants to deal with those bitches?*

THE CHAFING DISHES set up along one side of the dining room presented a buffet dedicated to Kennedy's favorite foods from age sixteen: lasagna, onion rings, fried rice, egg rolls, mini tacos, and mini samosas. There were ceramic bowls of dill pickles, egg salad, Chex Mix, and various sugared sour candies. The offerings would have been better suited to a kid's birthday party than a welcome-home party with a guest list of two adult women and a fifty-seven-year-old man. Gerry told her the rest of the family would be there at one thirty. Even though Kennedy was pretty sure he hadn't spoken to them in a decade, he'd apparently invited her mother's sister, Aunt Jackie, and the cousins from that side. She remembered when catered buffets had been a normal part of her life—now "chow" meant a cafeteria line with barely recognizable offerings.

Gerry walked up behind Kennedy as she stood in the dining area. He put his hands on her shoulders and pressed down, gently massaging her. She realized she had stiffened. In fifteen years of living and speaking only with women, no one had once touched her without asking. They heard a car in the drive, and Gerry's hands fell away.

"It's Alex!"

Gerry paced eagerly to the window. His belly had expanded slightly, pushing against his shirt buttons, and his hair had grayed—things Kennedy didn't notice when he came to visit at Heron Valley but that she saw now, observing him in contrast to the house and her memories of him there.

"If they're not together why did you invite him?" Kennedy asked, defending her sister even in her absence.

"He was family too."

"She said you never liked him."

"I like him. He's normal now." When Carter had first met Alex he was in a band and wore a leather jacket and eyeliner.

The bell rang and Gerry left. Kennedy could hear them making small talk in the foyer. She walked over and plucked one of the sour candies from the dish. In her mouth, it felt like the past, sugary and sharp.

She walked upstairs to her bedroom, drew in a breath, and lingered in the doorframe. She hadn't expected it to be the same.

As she slowly edged into the room, her gaze went immediately to the faraway boy handwriting on a cassette case on the floor. ***Extremities, Dirt & Various Repressed Emotions for Kennedy.*** Repressed. What had any of them repressed? She had loved Berk with an intensity she didn't understand, and he'd seen that love—bright and pure—and turned away from it. He'd loved, instead, her best friend. It was why Kennedy, even though she'd continued to see him, had never given him the mixtape in return.

There had been a creative writing assignment she'd done for the instructor at the prison about growing up in her home. Some of the other inmates wrote about trauma, moving constantly or in the middle of the night, being homeless, hunger. Comparatively, the piece Kennedy scribbled was light and full of adolescent longing, and she realized now that she'd painted the past with an optimistic brush. She had forgotten how the walls of the Wynn house could feel like they were leaning toward her. "Close your eyes," the instructor, Christina, had said. "What do you see? What do you smell?"

Kennedy suddenly leaped over the detritus, catlike, onto the purple duvet of the bed. She stared up at the posters, and between them the blank spots where investigators had taken others they deemed "objects of interest." The movie poster for *Basic Instinct* had been removed by police because it was about a serial killer. Laine and Gerry had objected to the image of Sharon Stone's fingernails tearing into Michael Douglas's back. There was another poster their parents detested that had gone too: the Red Hot Chili Peppers, naked except for tube socks they wore over their penises, as though having a teenage-sized amount of desire automatically made a person suspect. The detectives had seized Kennedy's diaries. The copy of *Jane Eyre*. Some poems she had written. They'd taken school textbooks from both girls with graffiti inside the covers that had been scrawled by numerous hands over the years, hoping to divine secret plots out of the palimpsest of *sluts, gross, penis-breath, love him* (with hearts), and *hottie*.

One officer had held up a CD by My Life with the Thrill Kill Kult as though it were evidence, exclaiming in his rural accent, "Woo boy. Got something here." The album was *Confessions of a Knife* and it was not a good look.

The week of the killing the investigators had shown Kennedy photographs to try to jolt her: the wounds blunt, flat, with dark bruising around them, as if they'd been punched into Haley. "Now, who did this?" they asked, waiting for her to implicate herself or Berk. She spat tears, not words.

At the pretrial they did their best to find a fiction that would support Kennedy having a motive. The prosecutor even read aloud from her copy of *Jane Eyre* after dramatically taking it out of evidentiary plastic. He called Haley a "Christian martyr, like Helen Burns in the book. And like Helen, Haley died at the hands of a sick, evil cult." He read Kennedy's own annotation in the book, blown up and projected onto a slide. "'Haley is our Helen, methinks.' That, Your Honor, is the defendant plainly grooming a sacrifice."

Kennedy always felt she had written it to show that Haley was her best friend, that they would stand up for each other, the bond unbreakable. But she never got to tell them that. They were already preparing another slide: a page where she had circled Lowood, the name of Jane and Helen's school, and written in *Longwood* beside it, the suburb where Haley had lived.

The defense attorney rose and argued: "Your Honor. We're prepared to have several scholars from UVA testify that interpretation of *Jane Eyre* is without merit and simply ridiculous. The character of Helen Burns died of consumption, no violence whatsoever. The works of Charlotte Brontë should not, cannot be entered into this trial's evidence.

"If Haley is Helen, then please tell me: who in this scenario is Rochester?" her attorney railed. "Find Rochester and you'll find her killer!"

Even at that young age, Kennedy had realized what lawyers did: waste a lot of time.

Now Kennedy jumped off the bed and dodged across the room for the bathroom. She made it to the toilet before the dry heaves began. After, she rinsed her mouth with Scope and went back in her room and lay down, shivering. Foolishly, she'd thought the crime would be gone after serving her sentence, but finally being in her teenage room didn't bring freedom, only frightening reminders.

Chapter 3

Everett Kimberson leaned his elbows on the sill of the bedroom window looking out at the downtown. It was one of the only condo towers in the city, sleek, shiny, and modern amid the wide white-pillared historical buildings Richmond prided itself on. He'd bought it with the money from the civil suit against the Wynns and gotten the key half a year before. In his early twenties, every time he'd planned for an apartment, or a room away at school, it had somehow gotten short-circuited. As move-in day grew closer, Marly Kimberson's face would take on that behind-glass look, as though parts of her were being permanently pinned down. She never told him not to go. She would say that if Haley's death meant her surviving child could live a better life, then Jesus meant for something to come out of the pain. That method was more effective and he always pulled out, angering his friends and losing deposits.

The condo was something she'd been able to come to terms with gradually—his mom could see it unfolding in a solid and predictable manner, the amount of time it took for them to finish the building while Everett showed Marly photos and conceptual renderings on a website. It didn't mean his departure was really permanent.

He used the apartment more as a clubhouse with friends than a living space, a place to drink and let off steam. It was furnished, but the drawers and closet were half-empty, as he often returned to his mom's house in the suburb of Longwood. For the amount his family had struggled to get what they deserved for their suffering—the long duration of the civil suit against the Wynn family had driven his parents finally apart, if Haley's death hadn't done that already—it did seem like he ought to have been able to bring more happiness into the place. Everett had had a Budweiser flag as a curtain on the large window—it was his only decorating decision—but the condo association had made him take it down. There was really no other use for the condo, except sex. But that he felt worse and worse about.

"Don't go," Everett said over his shoulder to the woman in his bed. He knew she wasn't asleep even though she'd been lying there for over an hour. "I don't want you to."

He heard her stir, the rustle of sheets as she sat up. A moment later she was standing behind him, her arms around his waist, one hand on his chest. She'd come the day before and stayed over, something she hadn't done yet. Everett could feel the smooth touch of her underwear and the warm press of her against his back. She left a kiss low on his shoulder blade as she put her face and her hair against him. Everett watched the white trail an airplane made across the steely November sky. He knew she hadn't meant to sleep over. Carter had places to be.

"Why shouldn't I go?" she asked. "It's what I'm supposed to do. I have to be with them."

Everett turned to face Carter. He put a hand against her light brown hair and looked down into her eyes. "Once you go, you go."

Carter stood on tiptoe and reached her arms around Everett's neck, kissing him on the mouth. When he pulled away again she sat down on the bed and began to tug her jeans on.

"Do you know when we were young I used to have her dreams?" Everett watched her retrieve a pale pink bra from the floor and put it around her shoulders. It was a front-loader, and she pushed her breasts into the cups and secured them. "Not her dreams exactly. More like things that had happened to her that day, even if I wasn't there for them. Sometimes stupid things. Her playing with a neighbor's dog with a rope knot, or writing something on the chalkboard and the class laughing. She peed her pants in first grade because she'd been holding it in; she was ashamed to use the bathroom because they had fussy locks and she thought someone might walk in on her."

"I don't think I want to hear about Kennedy's dreams."

Carter was seven years older than he was, and her body showed it. She was attractive when dressed, but when naked her torso and hips showed a quilt of weight wars won and lost—lovely but also loose in places. So why did he feel overwhelmed every time he looked at her? He adored her to the point where even her faults fascinated him. The shiny, pale white stretch marks on her outer thighs seemed more like mermaid scales.

Everett remembered when she and Haley were friends, just

glimpses: the way they used to walk past him playing in the yard and head up to Haley's room, or the times Kennedy was there too and the Wynn twins would bet him ten bucks that he couldn't tell them apart. He always could—their voices, their hair, their different-colored tiny backpacks were all giveaways, though they never paid him for his discerning eye. That was kid stuff, forever ago. At the time, Carter had had dyed black hair and pimples along her temples, a rebelling sterling silver ring in her nose where now there was only a freckle.

He remembered too that there had been a choreography to their interactions. The girls would finish each other's sentences in a way that he and Haley couldn't. He'd watched the twins speak for each other, and although they were infinitely different they were also the same: gleaming, confident, righteous.

Carter zipped up the jeans. She always wore jeans when she was around him, tight low-rises that hardly covered the hip, as though it could close their age gap. The difference was that even her jeans were 7 For All Mankind and cost $300. He'd tried to step up his game in the months they'd been seeing each other—to spend more, dress better—though he still felt like a redneck kid from Longwood, the poor relation to Blueheart Woods. This city, he decided, was where all kinds of Americans came together to politely dislike one another. Everett sat down on the bed beside her and almost asked if she ever dreamed about Haley. Since they'd begun sleeping with each other they had avoided the names of their respective sisters.

"What if I don't let you go back to them?" Everett said. He didn't like to think about her away from him, becoming a family with the people he hated most. And then, although he knew he shouldn't, he grabbed Carter by her wrists and pushed her backward onto the bed. He gripped her hard but kissed her softly, feeling the moment her lips parted. He loved her teeth, so straight and white. Expensive teeth. He ran his tongue over them, which he knew drove her crazy.

"You weren't supposed to happen," Carter said into his face. Her lips curled up on one side, like she didn't trust the words even as she spoke them.

Everett didn't answer her because it was an argument they'd been having for a long time, ever since he ran into her at the bistro around the corner, Heritage. She'd gone and broken things off with her live-in, Alex, but Everett knew she still wasn't his. He didn't feel it, not yet, and maybe never would—not with either of their families.

Everett kissed her again and unbuttoned the jeans she'd just done up. He licked her smooth belly, downward. He knew she wouldn't say no.

AFTERWARD, they lay again on the bed, Carter with a soft look on her face as she gazed up and out into the sky, the sunlight brightening into afternoon. She had asked him to stay inside, which they didn't usually do.

He rolled on his side. "Did I tell you I tried reading *Jane Eyre?*"

"You didn't."

"I did. I am. I use Google for the weird words."

"You're using Google to read *Jane Eyre*?"

"Trying."

He had been so young during the preliminary trials, it was hard to recall all the details. He'd never been brave enough to go digging into them as an adult until he started sleeping with Carter. What Everett remembered was his father turning to stone, his mother into a pile of sand.

The one thing he remembered was the stuff about *Jane Eyre*. Because it was more like a story they were telling and less about his sister's being gone. The prosecutor kept insisting the girls were embroiled in an elaborate fantasy, a day-to-day kind of game that had led to Kennedy's obsession with Haley.

When the prosecutor had to admit to the judge that they had not found the murder weapon, Everett saw his parents shake with disappointment. Despite assurances from the lawyer that people could testify Haley carried a pocketknife with her at the time, and likely her own knife had been used against her, Everett began to sense the case was getting weaker and weaker as the preliminary hearing went on.

CARTER SAT UP. She breathed deep. She stopped talking and pulled hard on her hair, twisting it around her hand. "My sister was dropping acid every week. She wasn't sane. She was sick."

"My pa was a drunk. Yours too. And I can't stop you from talking about your coke days when you get going about them."

"What are you saying?"

"A hit of acid didn't kill Haley. You're making excuses."

Carter let go of her hair and it fell around her face. "I can't make it better, what happened."

"You're not her." He sat up with her. "I know that's simple, but it's true."

"It's not that simple."

"You should check your phone," Everett told her as he shrugged on some clothes and checked his own cell, though no one had called him. "Didn't you hear it?"

Carter found the phone in her purse. There was only one number, but it had called three times. "Gerry. Shit."

She'd known her father would call, Everett pointed out, and she said she had but that she just couldn't stand him—his nervousness and his controlling nature, which canceled each other out, leaving behind an inertia. In their youth he'd been a partner in a small law firm, but after years now of working from home, Gerry Wynn had acquired the habit of running dialogue, she said. Like a toy car that had been wound up and let go, he possessed a tight energy that came from the tiniest mechanism inside him. She didn't think he knew when he was doing it or what he was saying. She got up off the bed and went into the shower.

"You've made a mess of me," she said as Everett got in with her.

The shower was covered in tiny chocolate-colored tiles and was the same size as the entire bathroom at his mom's place. Before he stepped into the shower with her, Everett glanced into the mirror and saw, for a second, a shadow of his sister in his own face, something about the way they both held their mouths. As Everett joined Carter he said to her soapy shoulders, "I think I miss her but then I think I barely knew her."

Haley had had hazel eyes like his, almost green, but he'd turned out dark haired and olive in complexion like their father and she'd always been pink, with their mother's kinky auburn hair. Occasionally Everett caught himself making a certain face—he didn't need to see it, would just feel it forming—and he knew it was an expression he'd picked up from his older sister. Other times, the memories seemed to be getting further and further away, in part because he was older now than she'd ever be, yet in his mind she was still somehow older and more knowledgeable. Everett wondered if she would dress like Carter now, the way she'd always tried to when she was a teenager.

Carter had shown up in their lives, whipped out a credit card, and bought Haley things the Kimbersons could never have afforded. Like magic she came home looking like someone else and showed everything off to him, saying, as she always did, *Don't tell Mom.* As if their mother would overlook the Ray-Ban sunglasses, the tickets to Lollapalooza up in DC, the ten-hole Doc Martens on Haley's feet. The Wynn twins convinced her to get Glamour Shots done with them at the mall. To them, it was ironic and hysterical. To Haley, she could put on earrings and find the glimmer of everything she'd never had. The photo showed her with a hand hovering near her hair, a scrunchie half-ponytail on top of her head, and a large gold-link necklace, her lips painted with chocolate-brown lipstick. It wound up being used as her funeral photo.

He still thought of things they could do together if Haley

were alive, what kind of adult siblings they might have been like, but it was nothing more than a mental exercise, and trying to conjure her up made Everett hurt in a place that was deep in his body but also not his body at all, a kind of infinite pain like the universe was throbbing all around him.

When the mismatched couple had gotten dressed, Carter sat and phoned her father and Everett put frozen waffles into the toaster. He went to the espresso maker he'd only purchased that week. She hadn't noticed it yet. Everett realized he didn't know how to use it.

Carter played a message on her cell, and Everett could hear Kennedy's voice. He hadn't expected it to punch him like it did. Carter's sister was there, breathing, talking, on the other side of the receiver. Today was as hard for him as it was for Carter, he thought, but all morning he'd wanted to take care of her and she didn't seem to grasp that. Everett listened as Carter called Gerry back. He gathered they were at the house in Blueheart Woods now. He listened as she explained she wasn't feeling well, that she'd been dizzy and almost had a car accident. The conversation only lasted a few minutes, then the toaster popped loudly, and she glared at him. She said she'd be there soon and she clicked off.

He knew the hurt showed in his face because she avoided looking at him and focused instead on her new iPhone.

Everett watched her finger flick over the screen. She hadn't signed up for Facebook, saying she had no interest in reconnecting with the past after running from it for over a decade, so what was it she found to look at on that thing? The photo on his profile was a selfie he'd snapped in the condo with her in the background. But she wasn't recognizable so Everett didn't think she'd mind. It was just her bare knee and her hand, the tips of her golden-brown hair. She'd seen him take the photo but hadn't thought to ask if he would post it. Why had he done it? She wasn't his girlfriend, he told himself, though his friends suspected he had one.

Finally he asked what she was looking at, and her answer surprised him.

"My sober app."

"What's an app?"

"It's like a computer program but on your phone."

"You need a program to count your program?"

"Five months, ten days."

She didn't tell him that it provided inspirational quotes too. She set down her phone. Her glance flicked over the kitchen and settled on the De'Longhi. "When did you get the espresso maker?" She stood up and went to examine it, touching it reverently. "You got the kind I told you I used to have?"

Her ex had managed to keep it. Her mouth twitched at the corner and he couldn't decide what the expression meant. Did it make Everett an idiot that he'd run out immediately to get something she wanted as if he could win her? He'd gone out with plenty of girls, but none who made him want their approval. She looked exactly like the girl who had killed his sister—but that was a thought he was good at pushing away.

His phone rang. It was his mother, and unlike Carter he knew better than to speak to her now. He didn't like to hear

Marly's voice while looking at Carter's face. Their face. He already knew what his mother wanted: him to come back to the house in Longwood, only a five-minute drive from the one where Kennedy would be soon with Gerry and Carter.

Everett had been inside their house once.

WHEN HE WAS TWELVE and Haley was three years gone, Everett had walked over to Blueheart Woods. He went to the Wynn house at night and observed its stillness. There seemed to be no one left. When he worked up the nerve to look in the bay window he saw Mr. Wynn sleeping in front of an episode of *Friends*, the one with the cat. Breaking and entering wasn't like on TV, it had turned out. Everett didn't need a mask or crowbar or to disarm the alarm system: he just opened the door and stepped in. Everett crept up the stairs and opened both the girls' rooms.

Carter's room was the empty one: the half-bare bookshelves told him that. There was a wicker basket of mixtapes left in the closet and that was all. An old sweatshirt or two. He later figured out she had already left for her attempt at college. Carter was the twin he'd always thought about as a kid. Once he'd fallen off his bike and scraped a long line of red down his forearm. Haley and Kennedy stood there staring, but Carter took him inside the Kimberson house and held his arm under a stream of cold water. She put antiseptic on it while he bawled, and asked if he wanted her to blow on it, *even though it doesn't really make it feel better*, she said. He'd nodded.

He'd felt bad invading her space and gone into what was

obviously Kennedy's room, where there was a collage of photographs she'd made on a poster board, pictures of the twins
together and with their friends. Berk Butler, Kennedy's old
boyfriend, shirtless with a mop of gold hair and a tattoo on his
shoulder that looked like a ship wheel. Haley was on there too.
It made Everett angry that they still had her in their house. The
girls' arms were looped about one another's shoulders. Kennedy
with purple hair flashing the peace sign. Carter leaning in to
be closer. *We are "Daughters of the Kaos," Lollapalooza '92*,
scrawled underneath by one of them.

He felt an itchy rage as he flicked open Kennedy's jewelry
box, pawing through the items. Then he saw the lava lamp. He
thought about taking it and walking back downstairs. He
could smash it over the head of Gerry, sleeping on the couch.
But he remembered learning about evidence at the preliminary
trial and thought about fingerprints on the glass shards. They
might be able to find them, even there, somewhere in the blood
and psychedelic wax blobs. He carried the lamp around the
room with him while he looked at other stuff. At the last minute he lost his nerve and ditched it on a shelf beside the door to
the room. As Everett made his way out of the house he noticed
the terra-cotta walls in the dining room and the white wain-
scoting that seemed to run around the edges of each room,
paneling them and sectioning them into little boxes for no dis-
cernible purpose. He felt a weird joy at having invaded the
space, although what had he really done? Kennedy had taken
his sister. He had taken nothing.

As Carter gathered up her things now to go, Everett imagined her moving through the big house in Blueheart and all its splendid rooms. Before she left, she pulled her coat on, glancing at him nervously.

"I need you," she said as she did up the buttons. "Please know that."

It was the most serious thing either of them had said and he didn't respond directly.

Instead he walked over and put his hand at the base of her throat, as if he were examining it like a doctor. He placed his thumb in the divot lightly, barely a touch.

"This spot is my country. This one inch. When you're away from me—it's still mine, do you hear me? I'm planting my flag right here." He tapped her skin lightly. Then he let his hand fall.

September 29, 2008

ASSIGNMENT 1:
Write about your mother or another
female figure in your life.

I T'S HARD FOR ME to write about my mother because in all
the novels I read the girls are orphans. When I look for her
face in my mind, the face I find wears an expression of disappointment. The trial did that. It wasn't always that way. When
I think of her name—*Laine*—it's like a loon's call out on some
mountain lake, forlorn and faraway.

MY MOTHER VISITED ME for the final time during the last
days of my girlhood. Can I call it that? *Girlhood.* It sounds so
antiquated, like something out of one of the Penguin Classics
that I've read in here. Almost eighteen, I was in segregated
housing until a bed opened up at Heron Valley. In three months
of isolation my skin and hair had turned the same color as the
cold, humming lights. Laine looked no better when she came
to see me. There were no visiting lounges in segregation, only
the Plexi window and phone. My mother struggled to stay
awake during the visit. She wore a wig to hide the chemo damage, but it was all wrong: it was piled high and artificial look-

ing, like the hair a Dixie widow might have, the kind she made fun of after we moved to Blueheart.

"This is the last time I can come," she said into the crackling phone. "They're not going to let me travel again."

I began sobbing, but my mother remained calm. She had accepted this and I had not. She put her hand up to the glass. I did the same.

"You have to wait for me," I pleaded into the phone. I didn't think about how long that wait would have been. It was the last childish request I ever made.

My mother shook her head slowly. "You're going to get out one day. Don't forget that. You're going to have a life. And Carter. She'll need you. You're the stronger one—you always were." Laine breathed deeply before going on. Her voice, like the rest of her, had weakened, but I heard every rasped word. "But don't build that life around men. Just . . . be your own person." Laine took her hand away from the glass, leaving a hand smudge, as if she were already a ghost marking its presence.

Even through the glass she saw I didn't understand and spoke more directly.

"I'm not saying all men are shit. But some of them want to destroy you. God, if we went to trial things would have come out about Blueheart. I've never liked it there."

My mother seldom swore, but I had heard this tone from her before. The same year my father's friends and clients began staring at me as I walked through the living room or down the sidewalk with the other girls. They offered Carter and me rides home in postdivorce Porsche Carreras, with mentions that their pool water was a perfect temperature and we could use it any-time. We never went swimming in their pools or got into their cars, but Haley did. When my mother saw her getting a ride in Doug Macaulay's new Lexus the spring I was sixteen, I got taken aside and was told that these were divorced men. It wasn't right and Haley shouldn't have been taking rides with them. Doug especially.

Haley lived her short life for men, and it may have been Berk who killed her. It could have been someone else she was seeing, a stranger, or some neighbor. Who knows? Maybe Doug Ma-caulay, whose face I don't even remember. The fact that I don't remember the night she was murdered also means I must al-ways include myself as a suspect when contemplating the truth.

My mother died a week after the visit, and I wondered whether they buried her in the wig but couldn't bring myself to ask.

—*Kennedy Wynn*
Heron Valley Correctional Facility

Chapter 4

CARTER HADN'T MEANT TO BE SO LATE. She thought of her sister alone out in the world and felt, for a second, short of breath, but she inhaled her way through the panic and managed to open her car door. The same asthmatic feeling had happened when Gerry had asked her to go with him to pick up Kennedy. The color had seemed to go out of the world around her.

She pressed the key fob and got into her car, stuck the key in the ignition. Music bounced through the small space of the Honda with the suddenness of firecrackers. It was the Breeders covering "Happiness Is a Warm Gun." She quickly turned it down.

The dream she hadn't told him about: She was Kennedy; she was dragging Haley's body through grass, mud. Her blouse was transparent, yellowy. The hem was trailing and she had this urge to hoist it higher to stop it from getting dirty. The floral print on it almost matched the spots of blood. How did she know she was Kennedy? The way her hair hit her face (Kennedy had worn hers down, over one eye). Kennedy had always insisted she didn't move the body—she touched it, she didn't transport it, she said. There were other details that were wrong, yet it had felt so real.

Carter's fingers rested on the place on her neck Everett had stroked. She flipped down the visor and assessed herself in the vanity mirror. In spite of the makeup she'd dabbed on, her eyes looked cracked around the periphery and hollow. She'd plucked her eyebrows thin over the years, a subtle attempt to look like someone other than who she was. As she put the car in gear and backed out, her phone rang. *Rochester,* the call display read, though it was only a nickname and one she'd never told him about. She pulled back into the parking spot and picked up.

"I just wanted to say—" Everett began.

She knew. She'd almost said it herself upstairs. Five months, ten days; it was too early. "Traffic's really bad," she said.

"No problem. Just: good luck." He sounded relieved.

"You too," she said.

CARTER ALMOST FORGOT to push the brakes as she spotted Alex's Scion in the drive of the Wynn house in Blueheart Woods, bumping into it as she finally remembered to stop. She got out and inspected his vehicle, but there were many tiny nicks all over it already. The only damage to her car was a faint tear in the *100% Vegetarian* sticker. When she'd moved out he'd asked her if there was someone, and she'd just said that they'd been good for each other, but it was time to move on and they both knew it. He hadn't known it, he'd said, and so she'd said all the nicest things a person could say while still breaking a heart.

Gerry opened the door of the house—he'd been waiting. Kennedy wasn't behind him, and Carter instinctively glanced up at her old bedroom window. Gerry stepped out onto the concrete beneath the portico in his socks and closed the door behind him. Not a good sign.

She had practiced her line on the way over—*It couldn't be avoided*—but she didn't need it. Gerry was beaming.

"Kennedy's home."

Haley never will be, she thought, and wondered if she was becoming a Kimberson. Carter pushed past Gerry and placed her hand on the neck divot where Everett had touched her to cover it, hide it from her family.

Gerry followed after Carter, asking her, "Where's the cake? You were supposed to bring a cake!"

"I could have done a better job of today if you hadn't invited my ex."

By then they were in the living room and she wasn't sure if Alex had heard her. Alex set down his cup of coffee and came over and wrapped his arms around her. He thanked her for inviting him, even though she hadn't. He didn't break the hug when he should have and Carter had to step away.

Alex hadn't worked in almost a year when she finally broke up with him. Carter told herself this again to justify her actions. Alex was a computer programmer, but after his layoff he'd mostly just played World of Warcraft late at night, or noodled on his guitar in the living room after Carter had gone to bed. Since she'd left him, she had no idea how he spent his time, though she imagined it was much the same.

The house phone rang and Gerry left the room.

When he returned he said that the Cains were sending their regrets. Something unexpected had come up. Carter watched as Gerry began to pace, looking out the window as if he expected people to arrive, though they still had an hour. His stress could take over his body, tighten it into a coil.

IN THE SECOND-FLOOR BATHROOM Carter sobbed in a quick rush of tears and snot. After she sniffed and her red cheeks faded she turned the exhaust fan off and flushed the toilet, though she had not actually used it. As she walked down the hallway she saw a light on in Kennedy's room. The idea was as shocking as a haunting, that the room was occupied after all this time.

"Hey," she said through the ajar door. "Sorry I'm late."

Kennedy lay on top of the purple comforter, her black flats on the floor beside her, making an L shape just the way she'd toed them off. She was wearing one of the dresses Carter had tried on for her—black with a pleated front, almost like a tuxedo shirt through the chest. There was a design of small white and red twists or squiggles along the bottom and the sleeves. It fit a bit looser than Carter had expected. The diet in the jail had left Kennedy slim in the waist but puffy in the face, and pale. She was looking more and more like their mother. And a little less like her, Carter realized.

"Don't worry," Kennedy said, "I'm fourteen years late."

Carter saw that her sister stared up at a photo of the heavily lined eyes of Robert Smith: black hair that blossomed out around his head, lipstick red as fire. There was a disturbing beauty in the red smear. Carter remembered, vaguely, the waxy taste from an era when she'd kissed boys who wore makeup.

When Carter didn't respond, Kennedy raised herself up on her elbows and said, "That was a joke."

Carter walked inside for the first time since Kennedy had gone to prison. She wanted to be close to her, to see her as her sister and twin, but now they were alone—no guards and no tables bolted to the floor—and Carter felt suddenly apprehensive. She looked at the tennis racket standing in one corner of the room and remembered how much stronger Kennedy had always seemed on the court. *Strong enough to hurt someone*, she thought, then blinked the idea away. Carter gazed around at the posters, the dusty books and CDs, a shelf full of stuffed animals left over from childhood. "He wouldn't touch this room. I told him he should. It would be better for you."

She turned and sat down on the desk chair across from the bed.

"Have you ever heard about the Cotard delusion?" Kennedy asked. Carter noticed she spoke softly and low. A jail habit. She'd noticed it there but thought it was just to keep their conversations private. "It's a psychological condition where you're convinced you're dead, that your body is already decaying."

Carter bit her lip. "Can we not talk about death? It's not healthy."

"Are you glad I'm home? You don't look glad."

Carter managed a fake smile. "Of course! It's so fucked up that Dad invited Alex."

Kennedy got up and grabbed Carter by the hand. She pulled her onto the bed beside her. "Sit with me. We'll have to go downstairs soon."

Carter crab-walked back over the queen mattress so she could lean against the wall. She could feel an ache in her neck, and her hand crept up to massage it. All her muscles were stiff from the morning spent with Everett. Either that, or they'd locked up the second she saw Kennedy and her father afterward. Guilt came in a spasm.

"Are you in trouble?" Kennedy asked, her gaze locking on the hand that was massaging Carter's neck.

"Of course not." Carter let her hand fall, aware she must have looked stressed.

"You stopped coming out to see me."

She took a moment, pulled her hair to the nape of her neck, fastened it with an elastic she pried from her wrist. She knew she should cut it out; her sister knew she only pulled on her hair when she was anxious. "I've been seeing a therapist, but sometimes I think I'm happier not talking about things."

"You mean the murder?"

"Don't call it that."

"I have to call it that. I wasn't charged with a euphemism."

"But you didn't do it. You had to take the plea. Right?"

Carter remembered the morning Haley went missing, Ken-

nedy bursting into her room just after she'd returned from the
hospital with Laine, having been up all night. Gerry had driven
them home in the big white Cadillac DeVille instead of his
usual Acura, as if finding out about the possibility of cancer
were a formal event. Both their parents were shut in the bedroom, sleeping, when Kennedy came in, whispering again and
again, "I have no idea what happened."

Now Kennedy didn't respond. She pulled her knees up
against her chin. Carter watched Kennedy watching her, her
mouth suddenly firm. There was no arguing with Kennedy.
There never had been, really. Carter always knew what she would
say, so an argument was pointless. Carter heard the breath come
hard through her nostrils.

"I'm not a violent person," Kennedy said finally, as if she'd
had to assess all angles of the statement before deciding on its
truth.

"I believe you," Carter replied, not looking at Kennedy. It
was as practiced as Kennedy's saying she didn't remember anything. Though Carter couldn't admit it to herself until the last
visit, she had always doubted Kennedy. Gerry was an absolutist
about Kennedy's innocence, as much as the Kimbersons were
absolutists about her guilt. For Carter, doubt felt honest, liber-
ating. It was probably doubt that had brought her and Everett
together.

Carter scooted off the bed and walked out. She went and
retrieved the wicker laundry basket from the spare room—her
old room. She stood in the blank room and took three long

breaths, before she brought it back in and laid it down beside Kennedy on the bed. She told her Gerry had paid for them—wouldn't let her put them in the room, of course. Carter reached out and unfolded two blouses. She showed her sister the pants, which sat low; the thick belt, which could be worn with the buckle off to the side. Kennedy's eyes went from hard to dewy.

"These are nice," she said, reaching out to touch the sleeve of one of the shirts. It was the one Carter had known she would most like.

When Carter told her to try it on, Kennedy said maybe later, and Carter wondered if she didn't want to be naked in front of her.

"What are you doing for work?" Kennedy asked.

"Nothing real. Temping. Pharmaceutical advertising, but it's just answering phones really. Do you remember Ryan Whittles?"

"Ryan Shittles from your history class?"

Carter nodded. Haley had come to Carter's rescue in history class. That was how they'd all become friends. Ryan Whittles had been teasing Carter relentlessly, calling her tight-ass, asking why she couldn't be more like Kennedy.

Carter told Kennedy that at her last job some coworkers had gone out for nachos on a Friday. When she and her manager went up to the bar to order more food and beverages there was Ryan Whittles. In front of her manager he'd put his finger right in her face, drunk, and yelled, 'You can change your name, but you're still a fucking Wynn.'"

They didn't see Gerry standing in the bedroom doorway.

"What was wrong with being a Wynn?" he asked. The women turned. Neither answered him.

GERRY OPENED UP A BEER for himself and announced it was the one drink a day he'd negotiated with his doctor.

Kennedy exchanged a quick glance with Carter; they called it their radio: those moments when they had simultaneous thoughts. It was the first type like that to pass between them in years.

Gerry began to pace around the sitting room again as Carter asked whether they could eat yet. "You showed her the clothes. What should we do about her hair?"

Kennedy answered that she hadn't really thought about hair or clothes much. The biggest concern the other women had inside about fashion was how to hide their WP tattoos for their parole hearings.

"What does that mean, *WP*?" Carter asked.

"'White Power,'" Kennedy said as casually as if she were discussing a new movie. "But Heron Valley is easy time. We never had a big problem with the gangs. Just when country girls transferred in and caused shit."

Gerry looked at his daughters with horror. None of these words had been said in the Wynn house in any context before.

"What kind of shit would they cause?" Carter asked.

Gerry choked on his beer. He coughed and set the bottle down to thump his chest. When it had passed he said, "Don't talk about that stuff when the guests come. Talk about good things."

"What good things?" Carter asked, knowing it was what Kennedy was thinking.

"She got her diploma. Taught classes. Wrote short stories."

"It's not like I was a TA at Sarah Lawrence," Kennedy interjected.

"Just be Kennedy for them. Normal Kennedy."

Kennedy and Carter glanced at each other.

Kennedy tipped her head back and looked at the ceiling. "No one is coming."

Alex said, "I showed up."

Gerry gestured with two hands out, as if the young man's presence reaffirmed everything. "They're coming."

"To hang out with the reason they've been embarrassed of their name? No one is coming and I don't need them. You do," Kennedy said.

Carter watched the firm set of Kennedy's jaw. She could almost feel her back teeth grinding. It had only taken an hour for the breakdown to begin.

AS THEY ATE the now-tepid lasagna (one with meat and one without, for Carter), Alex said and did nothing but look at her. The only one talking was her father, a little louder than necessary to make up for everyone else's silence.

"It's a fine name, Wynn," Gerry argued, picking up on what they'd said upstairs. "I never understood why you took your mother's name. Nothing to be ashamed of. Now, Emmett Kimberson. That's a name to be ashamed of."

"You mean Everett." Carter touched her clavicle.

"What?"

"His name. You got it wrong."

Kennedy looked at Carter. Another radio moment that was a surprise for both of them.

Gerry jabbed at the air with his fork. "I'm just saying, here's a fool that's representative of the way this country is going. Do you know what he wasted the money on? Turned twenty-one, got one of these sucker mortgages, no money down, preapproved. That's not how you buy property."

The women watched Gerry cutting his lasagna with a knife even though it was so soft by this point it seemed unnecessary. He said Everett Kimberson was the whole damn reason the market was collapsing, people who think they can have anything and not work for it.

"Who are you, uh, talking about?" Alex said, possibly worried that Gerry was now talking about him.

"Haley's brother," Kennedy answered before Carter could respond.

Carter's phone began buzzing and she knew who it was without looking. She dug into her purse below the table with steady hands. She found the phone and held the buzzing thing— *Rochester*—between her legs, squeezing, trying to silence it.

Chapter 5

Berk Butler was never on time for work but that day he was meeting someone from TV. He parked outside the grocery store that bore his surname, looked in the rearview, licked his fingers, and smoothed his thick eyebrows. With his hair gone it was the last thing on his body he could remotely style.

He entered through the automatic doors and went to the office, though he mostly worked on the loading dock and only sometimes floor managed, taking care of cider displays, samples, and banners. *Come on, everyone, push them apples*, his younger brother, Wyatt, said whenever he did a walk-through at the store—their flagship and one of twenty-four in the state. With each repeated instruction about fruit sales from his boss, Berk imagined Sisyphus pushing a giant, soul-crushing apple up the hill.

He wanted Dee Nash, the host of *Crime After Crime*, to see him in the office. Wyatt was at this store only a couple of hours a day and would never know Berk had passed off this desk as his own. As he waited he played with his tie, which the younger guys had already teased him about. Dee Nash was punctual. At five minutes to one o'clock he saw her arrive on one of his brother's monitors. A black woman in a well-tailored pantsuit, she moved with a cop's authority past the registers and inquired with the floor manager.

Berk drew some papers to himself and picked up a pen as she entered the office. He had no idea what he was signing so intently when he looked back up.

"Mr. Butler?"

"Detective."

"Former detective. So it's just Dee now."

He'd watched one episode of Dee Nash's show. It began with a young woman, unmoving, in a pool of blood, the kind of image he would switch off if he could. The camera angle cut to a victim's-eye view, and they showed Dee Nash walking across a gritty parking lot toward the camera, police tape blowing in the wind. *I lost my sister to violence when I was ten. That's when I knew I had to dedicate my life to helping other victims. Time doesn't heal wounds. Justice does.*

The phone on the desk began lighting up and Berk realized he didn't have a plan for that. He let it ring.

"Berkeley," Dee began, "I don't believe in a lot of small talk." She glanced at the blinking phone lines. "And you're a very busy man."

"Twenty-four stores I run. Failing or succeeding because of the decisions I make every day. Lucky I even get to see my little girl at all at night."

Dee asked how old his little girl was, and Berk said four,

born after he'd met his wife, Serenity, and they'd wed in Vegas. His daughter was the best thing that had ever happened to him.

"We do it all for them, don't we?" she said.

"Sure as money is money." Berk leaned back in the chair, almost too far.

"And I want to thank you for taking the time to talk with us about going on camera."

He leaned forward in the executive chair. "So how much does this pay?"

"I'm sorry if there was any confusion. We don't pay interview subjects."

Berk made a sound like she'd slugged him in the gut. "Then I'm wondering what it is I can do for you. My memory might not be so fresh."

"You have a very personal interest in telling your story. You were closest to Haley Rae Kimberson."

Hearing her full name was like being accused of things all over again. "I wouldn't say close close."

"I'm not concerned about the age difference. Those were different times." Dee set her bag on the floor. She took out a small notebook.

"I'd feel more comfortable without that," Berk said, shifting in his brother's chair. "My words got used against me before."

Dee put the pen down. "Old cop habit. And after what they put you through I should have known. A good man like yourself. Never got to tell your side to a jury."

Berk nodded at the flattery.

"So what would you say was most important? If you were

trying to explain what happened to someone who'd never heard of Haley Kimberson or you or Kennedy Wynn, what would you tell them?"

Berk had brought a Polaroid of Haley with him to work that day, like a talisman. It was from the moment she'd walked into his off-campus apartment only a couple of weeks before she died. He'd tugged it out from hiding spots and looked at it over the years. It didn't quite capture how she could see right through his bullshit, that she knew his knowledge of philosophy and world religions would not stand up to the most basic interrogation. Or that he never read the books stacked on the floor in his bedroom. On their first all-night phone call he'd asked Haley what she was reading. She said W. S. Merwin. He laughed and said he wasn't into mom poetry. "Try some Bukowski. That's the real stuff."

She'd found the Merwin in the thrift store in Blueheart and it intrigued her. He knew she didn't have a lot of money to spend on new books. When Berk offered to drive her up to Washington, DC, to go book shopping at cool bookstores like Politics and Prose, she hedged.

"Everything ends up in a thrift store one day," she replied. "That doesn't make it less real. Just that everything had its time. Even your books."

She had touched his shallow soul by reading him poems all night on the telephone, and now the Polaroid was the last of her. Haley, full cheeks, light freckles, white tank top, necklace at her throat, her red hair spilling from a sloppy bun, her eyes slightly closed as she laughed, red-lipsticked mouth.

The only part of Kennedy in this photo was her hand, on Haley's upper arm. When he'd put it in his pocket that morning, he didn't know if he would show it to Dee or if he just wanted it near him. His fingers grazed its edge, then he took them away and put his hand back on the desk. It felt too intimate.

"I can see you're still a little hesitant, but I flew in from Los Angeles just so we could talk. I hope that shows how committed I am to telling the truth," Dee said.

He scoffed. "Hesitant? No, just thinking things through. That's what bosses do."

The phone began ringing again.

"You do know Kennedy Wynn was released today? We filmed her being picked up by her family," Dee said.

"That today? Didn't write it down in my daybook, I guess." Berk smirked.

Dee reached down into her bag and pulled out a camcorder, not much bigger than a pear. She set it on the desk in front of her, flipped the screen, and offered to play the video for him.

He could feel himself sweating through the collared shirt he wasn't used to. "Are you going to talk to Kennedy?"

"We'll talk to anyone involved who wants to tell their story. That's why it's important to tell yours."

Berk thought about what Kennedy would say about that summer. All the lies coming back. Maybe this hadn't been a good idea. "This is going to be like a documentary, right? Not an investigation?"

"We have some questions that we think weren't asked at the time."

"What questions?"

"Haley was stabbed nineteen times. Three of her ribs broken." Her voice was flat as she recited the facts. "Was Kennedy a strong girl? Tall? Maybe our height?"

Five-three, he thought, five-four maybe. Berk tried to remember, then realized where she was steering the conversation. "Not so tall. No."

"Those are the kind of questions we'll ask."

"Questions about height?"

"And other things."

Dee took out her notebook again and scribbled. When Berk glanced across to see, he thought it read, *little white vampire girl: not tall,* though it was hard to tell from his side of the desk. The office door opened. It was Liam, one of the peach-fuzzed stock boys. "Hey, Berkoff, what are you doing in Wyatt's office?"

"I'm having a meeting, can't you see that? And this is a shared office."

"Your wife's on the phone," Liam said.

Liam left and as Berk picked up the receiver he glanced at Dee. She held on to her notepad as if to say she would wait. Berk punched the line and the full force of Serenity's voice hit him.

"Are you an idiot?! You're meeting with those crime show people, aren't you?"

"We can talk about this later."

Dee heard the other side of the call, or could at least read

Berk's shame. She gathered her things and slid a business card across the desk to him, excusing herself silently.

"Stop talking," Serenity commanded him. "Go phone your dad. Now! Or get a lawyer. Jesus Christ, Berk. Leave the past in the past."

Chapter 6

ALTHOUGH MARLY HAD PHONED Everett earlier, she hadn't managed to make it out of bed or get dressed. Everett leaned into the bedroom and said, "I'm here," then went down into the kitchen, where he put the coffee on. There were too many times he'd wondered if he would walk in and see the shape of her under the covers, the blankets twisted up and her body unmoving, and he'd listen: breath. She was breathing.

He watched the kettle rasp. When Marly was younger, she was a different person. As he scooped coffee into the Bodum French press he'd given her, he remembered how, years ago, she'd spent three weeks bent over her sewing machine making him a pirate costume for a play. Every detail had to be right: the ruffle on the shirt, the embroidered velvet jacket. When she had it done, she boiled up some coffee. Everett watched as his mom poured pot after pot of coffee into a large plastic tub. She submerged his beautiful jacket and shirt—staining them. "A pirate is someone with fine things that have gone bad," she said. Everett didn't trust her—he knew how much she'd spent on the fabric, a whole week's grocery bill—but when she pulled it out and dried it and he put it on, he stood, four feet two, a real living, breathing pirate before him in the mirror. She clapped the loudest of anyone that night.

The kettle screamed and Everett reached out and turned the gas burner to off. He poured the water, watched the steam rise.

"Your dad called this morning," Marly said, and when Everett turned she was standing in the doorway in her bathrobe. His mother's eyes were sunken, dark. Marly Kimberson took things for the depression, but sometimes she went off them. Prozac, Zoloft, Lexapro, Lustral, Luvox: they all sounded so professional. She said they made her fat and forgetful. He never understood what his mom needed to remember though, or why she needed to be thin.

"Y'all never talk. Surprised he remembered the exact date."

She nodded. "Some things you don't forget. Judy was having herself a shopping day."

His mom had only met his father's new wife once but she made firm judgments. When his dad and Judy visited they took Everett and Marly out for barbecue. Judy wore fuchsia lipstick. She had dyed black hair and impractical shoes that meant she had to be dropped off right in front of the restaurant. She called his father *Teddy* in a high pitch instead of Ted, and she was always touching him, as if he'd get away if she let go for even a minute. Everett never really minded Judy though. He'd had to see her more than his mom had. Judy grabbed the hard edges of his dad and shook them out.

Everett put his palm on the top of the plunger. He squeezed the mechanism down, crushing water through the coffee slowly.

"He said that if I run into Kennedy Wynn in the supermarket, I should run directly at her, cawing and flapping my arms like a bird. Said the only way to deal with a crazy person is to pretend you're crazier." She laughed.

Everett hadn't heard her laugh in such a long time.

Marly put her fingers over her mouth. "Oh Lord," she said, and wiped a tear from the corner of her eye. "Your dad never played the same bingo card as everyone else. Haley was like that too."

She'd told him this about his father many times, but Everett never saw it. He saw the firm, unrelenting parts. In Ted's eyes, there was a way to squeeze a toothpaste tube, a way to make a bed, to tie a tie. Nothing could be out of place and he hated tardiness. It was probably why he'd called Marly early, just to see if Everett had arrived at the appointed hour. Even when Ted was a drunk, he'd been strict about the household rules—although he was the one who usually violated them.

"He's worried about you. Wants reassurance you're not spending through all that money too quickly."

Everett puffed his cheeks, blew out a breath. What did it matter? His family's finances had gone from dime-thin to swollen overnight, and the civil suit payout didn't seem to have disrupted the Wynns' balance sheet—Gerry continued to live in the same sprawling house and drive his red Acura on weekdays, and his other two cars on the weekends. Everett pulled the milk out of the fridge. As he closed the fridge door, a yellow-eyed Amur leopard gazed back at him, held up by a magnet from the Leukemia and Lymphoma Society. The door was covered in photos of animals from the World Wildlife Fund and children in faraway countries that his mother had sponsored. She'd spent her money as easily, though never on herself. Any charity that phoned could take her for an easy fifty.

"We shouldn't sit around the house," Everett said. "Let's drive out to Virginia Beach, walk on the boardwalk. Maybe get a pizza. Haley loved it there."

Marly nodded, both hands wrapped around a mug that read *World's Best Mom*. Haley had given it to her. "The neighbors' Labradoodle shit in our yard again. I was thinking we could pick it up in a plastic bag, drive it by the Wynns', and fling it at their house." Her mouth twitched in a way that wasn't exactly a smile.

Everett told her they'd do that on the way.

THEY TOOK HIS MOM'S CAR so she could smoke; he didn't want it to ruin his Mustang. Everett insisted he drive—Marly always went too slow, peering at the road ahead of her like a book with the print too small. As he backed her car out of the garage, he commented on the Spider-Man four-by-four he'd kept stashed there for two years.

The handlebars of the quad were positioned almost like a dog perking up its ears. There were two sets of headlights, round, alert. The whole machine looked eager, ready to go at all times—though it had sat in the garage for almost six months, since the last time he'd ridden it. It had a good personality for an inanimate object.

"I'm gonna sell that. It's kid shit, really." Everett felt hot as he said it, angry. He was surprised to discover the emotion.

"Oh, don't do that. You love zipping around here."

"I could get two thousand for it, twenty-five hundred maybe, enough for a trip. We should go somewhere, just us, like a family trip."

"There's no point. Every place is the same."

"What about Italy?"

Marly lit a cigarette and he put the window down. She glanced over and he knew she wanted it back up. His mother was always cold, even when it was fifty-five degrees.

"Italy. That's where you take your new wife, not your mother."

But he wanted to take his mother, he told her. He smiled. He tried his best. She was wearing an oversize hoodie that he'd bought for her from the college he'd attended for a year, its acronym puffed up over her chest. It was the one that everyone went to, the one that hadn't really required high SATs. She glanced at the window again, and Everett pressed the button and back up it went. He signaled and moved toward the expressway on-ramp. "I have been sort of seeing someone," he told her on an impulse. She didn't need to ever know the real story. He could always tell her it didn't work out later, that it was some college girl who had to move home, to North Carolina, or DC, or somewhere. He could see the lie like a thing of beauty.

"That is the fastest way to heartbreak," Marly said, lips drawing on her cigarette.

They drove along awhile and then she said, "Do I know her?

Is it serious? Will I get to meet her?" as if she'd only just realized what he was telling her.

Everett shook his head and said, "Probably not."

He knew Marly wanted him to be happy, get a girlfriend, get
a job, get married, give her grandkids. These were the things
she recited at him, as if reading from the script for the role of
the caring mom she'd once been. At the same time, she'd only
come to see the condo once. She was surprised to see it was a
tower; she said she'd thought a town house was more likely, and
he wondered how closely she'd looked at any of the pictures
he'd shown her in the months they waited for it to get built. If
Everett did any of that big life stuff, he wasn't sure she would
really care. She'd given up a long time ago, and bringing her
back was no easy task. Maybe that was why Everett didn't want
to go clubbing or meet girls through his friends, even though
they expected him to. They said he was the good-looking
one, the one who would bring the ladies scrambling toward
them. There was no point. Everett knew he could do all the
things a person was supposed to do, but at the end of the day,
just like his mom, he was a little dead inside.

With Carter, it was easy. He would get lost in a feeling that
didn't have a name—it was like a big wave carrying him forward.

"Everett! You're drifting," Marly said. "And you're driving
too fast."

He pulled the vehicle back from the outer line. He didn't
know why he'd said that thing earlier, to Carter about her
neck. Or why he'd phoned her right after she'd left. It was an

impulse. Stupid. "Italy," he said to his mother. "I was thinking of Italy."

"She has a name, this girl?"

"Of course, it's . . ." Everett squinted out the windshield. He took a moment to think as he reached for his sunglasses. "Jane."

"Jane. That's nice. Don't hear that name very much anymore. Is she older?"

"A couple years, yeah."

"That might be good for you, Everett." Marly nodded.

THERE WAS A TV on the back wall of the pizzeria near the beach. A commercial was playing for a crime show. "They've been calling," Marly said with a nod, and Everett followed her gaze. *Crime After Crime,* the spot read in large letters. *Tuesdays at 9.*

"Who?"

"You know these TV shows. I don't want to be interviewed again—not after what they did on *20/20* before the sentencing."

His mother insisted Stone Phillips had made her cry on purpose. But of course his mom had cried. She would have cried no matter who was interviewing her or what they asked. Everett never understood why she was so embarrassed by the segment. He'd found it on YouTube a while back, a small clip anyway.

Stone Phillips: The evidence is not that strong. The DA is now afraid to go to trial. A jury would never convict her. Do you think Kennedy did it?

Marly Kimberson: All I need to do is look that freak in her eyes and know the truth. She killed her. I knew something was wrong when I came home and they were hanging upside down off the bunk bed, arms crossed and hair straight down. I asked what in the hell? And that Kennedy said to me: practicing being vampires. Well, practice makes perfect, don't they say?

His mother ran her hand over her red hair—lately she'd been wearing it super short so she didn't have to deal with it. She squinted out the big front window of the restaurant. It was after two p.m. and the sun was streaming in.

He was about to ask if she wanted him to stand up and fix the blinds when she said, "I always thought we got a raw deal—shoulda been both of them."

The server came then and the pizza tray landed between them. Everett waited until the server left, then, as his mom lifted her slice up, he said, "What are you talking about?"

She chewed and didn't answer right away. He took a few bites, then picked some of the mushrooms off. They ordered them because Haley liked them.

"I'm not saying they're telepathic, but c'mon, secrets with twins?" She shook her head. "There ain't no secrets."

He felt himself flinch. What was it Carter had said that morning? *It's not that simple?* Did that mean she included herself in what happened? He thought about the dreams she'd hinted at.

Marly was chewing and staring out the window. "I always

thought Haley could've been a lawyer, or something like that. Wouldn't have been easy, the tuition. But she was so smart. Do you know what she got on her PSATs?" For once his mother didn't rattle off the numbers but bragged instead. "And she had an internship with Doug Macaulay. You know, a law firm ain't Arby's."

"Wasn't she a little young for that?"

"It was a school internship." Marly shook her head. "I knew we never should have taken her to that Clint Black concert. Too secular. That's when it all started with Haley—the makeup, the dancing."

They were finishing up when the TV played the *Crime After Crime* spot again. This time Everett caught the whole thing. A young woman lay, unmoving, in a pool of blood. At that moment he turned away but could still hear. The narration carried through the half-empty restaurant: "Time doesn't heal wounds. Justice does."

"Maybe we should do it, Ma." Everett threw some bills down on the table. "It might help you feel better."

"Nothing helps."

"That's what I mean."

"Well, maybe I'll talk to Haley about it." Everett knew that Marly went to the grave more than she said she did. It embarrassed Everett to think that she believed they could communicate with the dead. Prayer, he understood. Talking to a tombstone with his sister's name on it, he didn't.

They left the pizza place and walked along the boardwalk. He wandered away at one point and tried to phone Carter, but she didn't pick up. She was with her family—and they'd said they would never put each other at risk—but suddenly Everett didn't care. The tenderness he'd felt earlier was gone, replaced by jitters.

He went back and sat with his mom and listened to the waves rise and fall. Marly reached out and took his hand, something she didn't normally do. Everett asked if she remembered the time he was the pirate in the school play and she said, "Of course, Everett. I was so proud of you." Her voice warmed and she sat there, beaming at the water.

He wondered if she was still proud of him at all—what it would feel like if she were.

Chapter 7

KENNEDY PEERED OUT her window at Gerry below in the darkness. She had heard him shout *sonofabitch*. He was stacking the chafing dishes outside the door for the caterers to pick up in the morning and his hands were covered in lasagna splatter. She shut the window and lay back down on her bed. It was softer than she remembered beds ever being. Her bedroom and prison cell were the only two rooms Kennedy had known. She'd run back to the security of her room the moment Carter and Alex left. She was aware of the psychology behind her behavior immediately.

Part of her plan for the morning was to visit her mother's grave for the first time. Then she would start filling out employment search forms for her parole officer. Gerry had started his consulting company after he was semi-forced out of his law firm during the preliminary trial, and now he worked from home. Maybe she would find a coffee shop to do her employment work in. She wondered if the café they used to go to near Plan 9 Music was still in business. She and Carter had spent countless hours drinking cappuccinos, eating spanakopita, and staring out the large front windows at the shoppers and scavengers of Carytown, a mishmash of alternative kids who came for the used-book shops and bead stores, and affluent housewives who came for the craft shops and hair salons.

The summer of '92, Laine had said she thought Kennedy should keep busy and *push herself*, a phrase Kennedy had noticed was never applied to Carter. Laine had found Kennedy part-time work at a card shop that printed social stationery for the West End families. The store did calling cards, which were business cards without any details on them, as if you were automatically supposed to know where a person lived and why they'd come knocking; cocktail invitations and invites for tailgate parties; announcements for births and weddings and debutante *coming-out* balls—a phrase Kennedy would have snorted at, except she'd also heard it tossed around Blueheart Woods by some of her stuffier neighbors.

Etiquette was something her mother had tried to impart to both of them, but once Kennedy was giving advice on formal wording and matching napkins to the ink color of the invitations, she grasped better what her mom meant when she talked about privilege. Privilege was a thing that always belonged to other people. Never mind that Kennedy worked because she wanted to, because it was "good for you," because it would be a "growing experience."

For a second Kennedy thought she could apply for a job there again, but as a convicted felon handling money was out. What else was there? She couldn't get hired for most jobs in the financial, legal, medical, and education fields either. In her state she could not even be given an exotic dancer license. Parole at thirty-one had effectively sentenced her to being a sixteen-year-old girl again.

As she gazed up at the posters, she set aside that question and focused on the task she cared most about. What would she bring to her mother's grave? Flowers would be simple, but she had left prison with only a one-month bus pass and a check for her four years of teaching work at five cents an hour: $96.00. She would have to ask Gerry for money eventually, but she wanted to wait at least a day.

She decided she would bring the glass bulb from the garden.

IN THE MORNING, Kennedy got dressed in the same black dress from the day before. She couldn't fathom wasting another outfit. She walked down the hallway toward the stairs. If Gerry was the same, he had slept in the recliner until midnight, then showered and gone to his bedroom. Teen girls memorized the movements of parents through suburban panopticons like prisoners knew guard rounds.

At the front door Kennedy paused. Could it be that simple again? Opening a door and walking out? Before she could go out to the garden to retrieve the glass ornament she saw Gerry was standing in the foyer in his pajamas and robe, holding a cup of coffee.

"Escaping?" he joked. Over the years he had become as quiet as the house, it seemed. He was part of it. Like the carpeting. "I want to talk."

In the family room they sat beside each other in matching recliners. Gerry had a shimmering blue folder in hand that he passed to Kennedy. "That's for you."

Kennedy opened the folder. It was banking pamphlets and agreements.

"It's so you don't have to worry," he said.

"Worry about what?"

"Security."

Kennedy flicked through the pages and saw a balance sheet: $922,000.

"Where did you get this?"

"It's a couple of things. I did work for some guys starting a K Street firm and they paid me in stock. Company got sold this year. There's your mom's insurance too. The important thing is it's in an LLC. Numbered account. The Kimbersons are not going to steal this, okay?"

Kennedy didn't know what to say. For the last fifteen years money had had no meaning, and even as a teen she'd spent and stolen with no consequences. Like other girls at Liberty High, Kennedy perfected the art of shoplifting, shoving eyeliners, mascaras, and boxes of OB tampons in her waistband. Sometimes, even skirts were walked out of stores underneath longer velvet skirts. It was, they rationalized, just sticking it to "the man," but more often than not in privileged Blueheart Woods, their parents were the man.

"The country is different now," Gerry told her. "People don't mind being famous for horrible things. There's this woman from the Hilton family. She actually goes on the talk shows and promotes a tape of herself doing things. You know, with men. Anyone can say 'look at me' and then a camera spins around. It's a whole industry and I don't want you tempted by any of it. I want you to have a life again. A quiet life."

Kennedy looked up from the paperwork and realized that both $96 and $900,000 were amounts of money equally effective at limiting her ability to escape. Kennedy said thank you, and went upstairs and shoved the documents under her bed.

SHE WAITED HALF AN HOUR for the bus as the sky threatened her with rain. When it didn't come she started walking toward the cemetery, out along Smoke Line.

The woods stretched for fifteen hundred acres, between her house in Blueheart and Haley's in Longwood, and beyond. She had a sudden memory: it was this stretch of road Kennedy had walked that last long-ago night after she and Haley got separated. She remembered walking home alone along Smoke Line, the three miles of sparkling darkness—every time she passed below a streetlight, her shoes sliding on black trails of light. The hot orange crackle of fireworks far away, like an aching tickle in her ear, and having no sense of time. Why she'd been walking, she couldn't say.

That night had started with a phone call from their mother. "They won't let her leave," Carter had told Kennedy in her bedroom as they were getting ready to go out that night. Laine had driven herself to the hospital with leg pain and they wanted her to stay overnight.

"For leg pain?" Kennedy had been skeptical and thought her mother was looking for attention. Before she'd left, she'd said she didn't want to ruin their Fourth of July plans and not to worry about her—but her tone had a tremor in it, as if she were hoping one of the girls would disagree. Their dad was out golfing and having beers with other lawyers.

After Carter had hung up Kennedy asked her if she was feeling it yet.

"Feeling what?"

"The beginning. The acid."

The sisters, along with Haley and Berk, had dropped LSD and timed it to peak with the July Fourth fireworks show downtown. Two hours, they figured.

When Carter and Kennedy's mother had called they were sitting in Kennedy's room listening to My Bloody Valentine, as if the layered guitars and drifting voices could summon the effects of the drug quicker. Berk lay across Kennedy's lap on the bed and she played with his hair, silky. Twenty-one, Berk had chin-length gold hair and a scar in the middle of one of his thick eyebrows, some childhood game that turned to injury. Aside from the white stitch in his forehead, he had a rich boy's face: flawless and pale, with a broad cleft chin. He'd grown up in the West End, neighbor to most of the card shop customers Kennedy served, though he now had an apartment downtown. His feet lay across Haley's bare legs. He was only this physically open when high, and half the time Kennedy dropped or smoked it was only to see him like this.

He had talked often about the day he would be intimate

with her—*intimate*, that was his word for it—but it hadn't happened. He'd said he wanted it to be ideal, that they themselves would be *oneness*. But when the opportunity finally arose at his Memorial Day weekend party, it was anything but romantic. Kennedy hadn't taken him up on it. She was scared, though she told herself it was because she was celibate, like Morrissey claimed he was in interviews. She knew Berk and Haley had started talking on the phone even more after. Ever since, she'd harbored some resentment toward him and Haley both. She thought of Berk as her boyfriend, even though the possessiveness of the term seemed so preppy. Berk once said that they were meant to be, maybe in this life or the next—the fact that they'd been at the same Lollapalooza and had both seen *Bram Stoker's Dracula* in the same theater on opening night seemed like folded notes from the universe saying they'd been supposed to meet. Other times he said he only wanted to be an "influence" in her life, show her music and things she hadn't explored yet.

Carter was sitting on the floor, her knees pulled up. She looked tense and Kennedy knew she shouldn't have confided in her about Haley and Berk.

"I should go be with Mom. She sounded scared," Carter said.

"At the hospital?" Kennedy asked, the drug already making words sound rubbery.

"Yeah."

"You dropped acid. You don't want to be there. That's the worst place to trip."

"I only took half."

"Why?"

"Someone had to drive tonight."

Kennedy looked down at Berk. "Guess you're driving us downtown."

"If I have to drive I ain't going to the fireworks to listen to Garth fucking Brooks. That's twelve-year-old stuff, y'all know what I mean?"

Carter snapped, "Oh, is twelve too young for you?"

The dis flew over Berk's head, but Kennedy stared down at her. "Maybe you should go. Be with Mom."

Carter, who had never liked Berk, left the three of them there alone.

Berk looked over at Haley, who was stroking the hairs on his leg. Haley was a natural redhead; her skin was pebbled with freckles, but she wore her makeup thick to hide them. Sometimes Kennedy flattered her by telling her she looked like Tori Amos. She did a little. "What if we go trip in the woods?" Haley asked. "Be around nature."

Kennedy had walked a mile along the woods and come to the next bus stop. She paused to wait again, but her sister's Honda pulled up before there was any sign of a bus.

"Get in," Carter commanded, and Kennedy leaned down, shoving the glass orb from the garden that she'd brought with her into the backseat before climbing into the front. "Where are we going?" Carter asked.

"To see Mom's grave."

Carter nodded and accelerated. "Why are you wearing the same clothes as yesterday?"

Kennedy shrugged. She watched the woods fly by outside the windows. "I was just thinking about that night. The trip."

"Oh god, that fucking trip. I was sure Mom or Dad would know."

"I thought you only did half a tab."

"Yeah, but the hospital was a weird place to be. Just these bleached halls and doctors that looked ten feet tall to me, and the fluorescent lights were so bright. Thank god Dad waited in the car instead of being with us for most of it. I think he came in and spoke to the doctor for like two minutes."

Carter stopped talking. A dark look crossed her face and she glanced over at Kennedy, then didn't say anything more for a few minutes.

"I never come out here. It's too much," Carter muttered as they pulled onto a gravel area outside the cemetery. "It's in that back corner, I think."

Walking between the headstones, Kennedy carried the glass ball on its staff and was sure the look was somewhere between crazy and witchlike. She wore the tattered army jacket, too snug across the breasts to close. Carter was dressed more practically, even though she hadn't known their destination.

Kennedy and Carter paced up and down the aisles, the random names of the dead flashing past in thick engraved letters. *Bolton, Bunting, Byrd, Fortune, Hammond, Hunter, Moore, McRae, Tate, Wordsworth, Whiting.*

"That way," Carter said, pointing.

Laine Randall Wynn, 1952–1994. Kennedy drove the stick into the ground. The dirt was harder than she'd accounted for, even with the rain, and she twisted it and turned it, and said *shit* and *damn it* under her breath.

"Let me do it," Carter said.

"I got it!" Tears sprang to Kennedy's eyes. She repositioned the staff and its ornament closer to the headstone, where the dirt seemed softer. She jabbed at the ground, leaned her full weight against the stake. When it didn't go, she lifted it up and tried again.

"You're stabbing the ground. You're making a mess," Carter chastised her.

Kennedy looked down and saw that rust from the staff had come off on her hands, left a streak too on her dress. Divots now pocked the ground, like it was a tee box on a golf course.

"It doesn't matter," Kennedy said. "It's not like she's here."

"Did you know what you were going to do that night?!" Carter yelled, suddenly reaching out and grabbing the staff of the ornament away from Kennedy. "Is that why you didn't come with me to the hospital?"

"What?! No." Kennedy stared at her.

"You did," Carter said, her voice shaky.

Kennedy saw movement down the hill. A woman with short red hair was trudging along the pebbled path. She hunched, her hands buried in her coat pockets. It was Mrs. Kimberson.

"Jesus Christ, Kennedy! Answer me!"

"It's Mrs. Kim—" Kennedy whispered, but Carter had gone past listening.

Kennedy watched as her sister grasped the stick like a baseball bat and swung the glass ornament into the tombstone. The transparent ball shattered, tiny blue and yellow fragments raining down into the matted grass.

"No!" Kennedy yelled.

"You did it, didn't you?" Carter screeched.

"No!" Kennedy said again, emphatic. Kennedy dropped to a squat, as if she could hide behind her mother's gravestone. But the path came straight that way and Marly Kimberson would see her, whether she stood or sat. Not to mention her twin, who still stood, tears streaming down the sides of her face. To steady herself, Kennedy put one palm down, against the cold dirt.

She remembered she had called the Kimbersons the morning after. The little boy, Everett, was the one to answer the phone. He'd said he thought Haley was with her, hadn't she stayed over? Kennedy lied and said of course and not to tell his parents she'd called. Every time they were in prelim hearings, Mrs. Kimberson had stared daggers at her. Mr. Kimberson had just stared at the floor. The prosecution had their timelines and phone records and tried to say she'd phoned after she knew, after she'd done it. There was a ninety-minute gap in between the phone call to the Kimbersons and the 911 call Carter made. And during that time, from Kennedy's side, she had gone to look for Haley. Kennedy remembered those long afternoons in court more than she remembered the night. She wished she could say she didn't remember anything—that would have been easier—but she recalled a hundred different stories, the things the police tried to put into her mind as the truth, the things the others said in question-and-answer format, the stories of the photographs, of the newspapers.

"How do I make you believe me?" Kennedy said to Carter.

Kennedy blinked and realized Marly Kimberson was staring straight at them. Her mouth hung open, then scrunched, as if she would howl, but she didn't. She said nothing, though the cords in her neck rippled. Then she cut away from the path and walked in the other direction through the headstones. About a hundred yards away, she stopped and kneeled. Kennedy glanced back and could see the black stone read *Kimberson*.

"Oh great!" Carter said, finally seeing Mrs. Kimberson. She let go of the empty stick she'd been holding and it dropped onto the grass in front of Laine's grave.

Kennedy felt her throat grow tight. She stood up and strode away, and in a few seconds she heard Carter's quick footsteps close behind.

When they passed through the cemetery gate, they both slowed.

"Wait, I can't breathe," Carter panted. "My head's spinning. I feel like my throat is closing up."

"Don't be so fucking dramatic, Carter."

"We should have gone over there, expressed our remorse."

"Are you kidding?" Kennedy said. "That would not be a safe thing to do." She knew what she would do to herself if she were Marly Kimberson. A mother should not have to forgive a crime against her child. And there had been a crime, Kennedy knew, even if it had been committed out of love.

"You're right. Let's get out of here," Carter said, pulling a tissue from her coat pocket and rubbing her nose with it. "I'll drive you back to Gerry's."

"No, leave me with Mrs. Kimberson. It'll hurt less," Kennedy said, but as upset as she was, her hand was already on the passenger handle.

⫸ ⫸ ⫸

October 6, 2008

ASSIGNMENT 2:
Write about friends.

M Y HIGH SCHOOL practically made the day of my plea
change a holiday. The Kimberson family had campaigned for it. If this was going to be the only moment "Dead
Kennedy" was going to rise and speak, I guess her family wanted
Haley's friends in court as a sign of support for her. Ultimately
the school said no, but that they wouldn't punish any students
who took the morning off.

After months of preliminary hearings everyone, including
me, thought we'd be going to trial. It was my father's plan to
fight to the end. But that spring, after my mother went into
hospice, he changed. He looked ashen during meetings. He
started discussing plea deals with the lawyers. No one was hopeful. The prosecutor was in the news every week saying that
someone had to stand trial for Haley's death and he wasn't going to stop just because the accused lived in the same zip code
as him.

At my last appeal to throw out the charges my dad had
lurked in the very back of the courtroom: I thought he had finally grown ashamed of me. But as the proceedings began a

friend of my father's sat down and put his arm around him. The man was a federal judge from the fourth circuit. My own judge, the Honorable Cal Rafferty, glanced at the men in the back before asking my lawyers to the bench. Later, I learned that Rafferty made it known he would hold the lack of a plea discussion against both sides, should we go to trial. "The community needs healing, not grandstanding," he said.

An hour later, while I was alone in the holding cell, the prosecutor informed the court an agreement had been made. Judge Rafferty scheduled the new plea hearing for April 5, 1994.

I wondered what I could plea to, given I had no memory of the night.

"THIS IS SUCH BULLSHIT," I muttered at the defense table, glaring back at my former classmates. The court gallery looked like a gym assembly with bored teenagers but in formal clothing—ill suited to their nose rings and unwashed, stringy hair. *God, these were the nerds only a year ago*, I thought. *What happened to them?* Reese Blair had always thought Haley was trash and called me a Salome, a Jezebel, and a Delilah during a freestyle sermon in history class, but there she was now, with pink hair and an ACT UP pin on her dress. Caitlyn Coyle? I thought *we* were friends. Caitlyn's new look was an attempt at Lisa Loeb, but she came off more like Nana Mouskouri. Cole Plummer? Fuck him and his bootleg Fugazi T-shirt under his suit coat. Fugazi was too pure to do T-shirts. I remembered that Haley had known Cole since elementary school and he'd hated her ever since she told everyone that he used to jerk his dog off to impress people.

And these losers who had never cared about her before were all there to see me off to jail. I regret my anger that day, but I was still a teen. It mattered that Carter and I had made Haley cool. We'd transferred that rare element to her when no one else would give her the time of day. We'd taken her by the hand and brought her into the mosh pits of freedom, and that was going to be forgotten.

My lawyers were still explaining what an Alford plea was when I saw Charity Sauer run into the courtroom in a Sunday dress and Docs. "An Alford plea means you accept the charge without contest but assert innocence. It's limited, but it will give an opening upon appeal." The lawyer drew lines on his palm, as if he were laying out a football plan.

I ignored him and watched Charity whisper something to Cole, who then started weeping. I hadn't seen a boy cry since sixth grade. "You have to tell the judge that you believe you're innocent but that the state has a preponderance of evidence." My lawyer broke midsentence and looked back. All adult heads turned around as there was more whispering and more teenage crying that turned wet and ugly. The judge entered from chambers with a perturbed expression and all rose except the dozen crying teenagers.

Judge Rafferty shouted out that the gallery must contain their emotions or they would be removed. Mrs. Kimberson shed some tears herself, thinking the display was for her daughter. I wish it were—Haley deserved better than this group of death hags. Several of the lawyers from both sides went to the kids to calm them down.

When my lawyer returned, he tried to clarify the situation for the judge over the sound of their wails. "Your Honor, it's not the trial that's upsetting them. The teenagers are apparently torn up over the passing of a rock-and-roll singer."

"Who?" I whispered to my lawyer. He ignored me. My thoughts turned to heroin and likely candidates: Perry Farrell? Anthony Kiedis? Courtney Love? Just as quickly my concern turned to anger. The kids cared more about a celebrity than someone they'd walked past every day in the halls. I was still the dead girl's friend.

"In light of this disturbance we'd like a recess."

The prosecutor jumped up to help claim credit. "We absolutely agree, Your Honor."

"Court is in recess. We are closing the gallery today with access only to press and family."

In my holding cell, I was told by a guard that it was Kurt Cobain. I wept, just like my former friends. I wanted to go and hug them and be hugged by them, even if they were assholes. Later that afternoon I stood and accepted the charge of murder in the second degree in a quiet and cool courtroom. There were only the lawyers and the families as the judge spoke to me.

He leaned forward and looked down at me from the bench. "Though we may not be going to trial I know that the answer in our souls would be the same as it is today: This is a tragedy written and acted out by children. The victim will not become an adult. The accused, however, will become an adult, and the manner in which she does so is going to be affected greatly by my sentence. Under the charge of second-degree murder I have the guidelines of five to forty years to choose from. By choosing sixteen years, as I have, Kennedy Wynn will become an adult in the corrections system. But she will also have a life after, during which she can contemplate forever, as I know she will, the actions of children that night."

An editorial the next day said the judge used the word *children* so many times he made it sound as if the crime took place at a Montessori daycare. I myself wondered if my red eyes and trembling body helped my sentencing or made it worse. Were the emotions I felt for Cobain interpreted by the judge as guilt and remorse finally released? Once inside I stopped debating it when I learned that it didn't matter: sixteen, and hopefully out much earlier, was a gift for any murderer.

I didn't love Kurt Cobain more than I loved Haley Kimberson. The death of the 1990s for me is the image of her in the forest more than him in that greenhouse. But sometimes you cry because you've been given permission by something the world understands more.

—*Kennedy Wynn*
Heron Valley Correctional Facility

Chapter 8

GERRY GAVE THE TWINS TIME to start talking again, and hoped they would, but Carter didn't come out to the house. When the next weekend passed without a phone call, he began to worry. He'd been waiting a decade and a half to get his family back. Could they really split apart in the first days?

The week before Gerry had watched through the front window as Kennedy got out of her sister's car, slammed the door, and raced toward the house. Carter pulled out of the circle drive, her wheels leaving black marks even though normally she was a timid driver.

"Why didn't Carter come in?" he called after Kennedy as she threw off her shoes and flew up the stairs.

Gerry followed her up the stairs and stood in the doorway to her room, watching her body shake where she lay facedown on the bed. "I'm never not going to be Dead Kennedy. I'm going to live in this fucking room forever and this is never going away."

"What did she say?"

"Carter said I should take responsibility."

It was the central dogma of the Wynn family that Kennedy

was innocent, as surely as the host was the body of Christ for Catholics, or life was suffering for Buddhists. "She just needs time to adjust to you being out," he said to her.

It wasn't the first spat the girls had had over the years. That whole first year, when Laine was in chemo and he was working on Kennedy's defense, the girls had barely spoken.

He worried about Carter's being alone, without her family, or even Alex, to talk sense into her. She had always been more fragile than Kennedy. You could look at Carter sitting across the table and watch her fall into a deep place inside herself.

Gerry had picked up the phone to call her and broker a détente when the Wynn doorbell rang. He expected to see a neighbor, but instead a thirtysomething man in a blazer and a ball cap was standing there, bent and distorted through the peephole. Gerry stepped away without answering it. He wondered if Kennedy's release from prison the week before had been a little too quiet and this was the start of things again.

A few minutes later he went back to the foyer and opened the door to an empty porch. The man had left a business card tucked into the doorjamb, just like the so-called journalists had fifteen years ago. Gerry snagged it out.

JOSH WINTER, *Producer*
Fingerprint Productions

Gerry turned the card over. He flicked it against his palm. He reached back inside and grabbed his coat, then strode to his car. He was on the highway in a minute and downtown at

Carter's small apartment in twenty. Colonial pillars held up the covered porch, but once you were inside, the apartment was a dark hall and three rooms—living, bed, and tiny kitchen. The beauty of the place was still evident but it had been made affordable for student renters or couples early in their careers. He felt a pang of guilt for not having offered to cosign on a lease when she broke up with her boyfriend. He'd expected she would only be in the apartment a month or two before she and Alex renewed the relationship.

CARTER HANDED HIM what he thought was a coffee along with a look of reproach.

"You've got to talk to your sister," he pleaded with her. He took a drink and grimaced. It was some kind of herbal tea.

"The doctor doesn't want you to have coffee. And this isn't your concern, Gerry."

"She needs us. She needs a reason to get up in the morning. You've destroyed her when she needs to rebuild."

"You've destroyed her. Not me."

"You're using again, aren't you?" Gerry got up and grabbed a small ornamental box from a shelf. He lifted the lid and looked inside.

"Put that down, Gerry," Carter said. "What I meant was: you built this narrative of injustice. The Kennedy you want to exist doesn't. She is what she is and she did what she did."

Gerry continued stomping around the one-bedroom apartment, looking in spots where the pamphlets had told him to look: inside books and cups, under mattresses. Addicts can hide anything.

Gerry had never forgotten Carter's call in the middle of the night her first year at college, crying that she needed help. She had been thrown out of a motel in Tampa with nothing but sandals and her pink flip phone. *Why aren't you in Chapel Hill at school?* he asked. Carter confessed that she had dropped out weeks before and moved to Florida with some DJ. *You did that? For some clown who presses Play for a living?* Gerry thought but bit his lip. He booked a ticket for Carter at the airport, nonrefundable, to bring her home where he could take care of her.

Even if they didn't always like him, his daughters came to him for help. Middle-of-the-night-call taker was his job.

"This is controlling behavior. You don't get to come to my apartment and go through my things. They told you that. In therapy." Carter straightened books on the shelf he'd already checked. She said with resolve: "I'm not on drugs."

Gerry squinted at her. He wanted his daughter well, but he also wanted them all well—all together in this—and he knew that sometimes achieving what you wanted meant coming down hard. Daughters seemed to attract chaos. In the universe of women he'd wound up in, Gerry found it necessary to enforce rules.

Carter pulled out her iPhone and brought it over to him. He peered at the screen. "What does this mean?" *5 months, 20 days*, the screen read. *The price of anything is the amount of life you exchange for it.*

"That's how long I've been sober."

He handed the phone back to her. "This doesn't mean anything. It's just a number on a device. Doesn't tell me anything." He regretted slipping into lawyer mode, arguing nuances. He walked over toward the door and began rummaging through pockets on the coatrack.

"Dad, stop!" Carter yelled.

When he looked at the garment he was holding he saw it was a man's corduroy blazer.

"Whose is this?" He shook the coat at her.

"No one's," she said. The color had gone from her face. "It's probably Alex's and got mixed in my stuff."

He reached into the pocket of the sport coat, looking for hexagon-shaped pills or baggies of powder, he didn't know what. What he pulled out was worse. A card. Like the one that had been stuck in his door. A different name though.

DEE NASH, *Host and Executive Producer*
Fingerprint Productions

He tossed the card down between them on the coffee table. They both stared at it.

"It isn't mine," she said after a moment.

He grabbed her by the hands. "Don't, don't," he begged. "This is all of us, Carter. I know you're mad at her, but it's all of us—even your mother, god rest her. We can't let this happen."

She broke free of his grip and picked up the card and returned it to the pocket.

"You won't talk to them," he said. He had forgotten about the coat itself for the moment.

"No, but I can't stop it from happening," Carter said, turning her back on Gerry and taking her cup out to the kitchen sink.

He followed. They stood there for a second, close, like they'd once been, then Gerry said, "If none of us talk, it simply stops."

Carter replied, "We're not the only family that's part of this."

Chapter 9

THE FORMER HOMICIDE DETECTIVE was surprisingly warm in personality, her hair parted in the center and straightened around a broad, heart-shaped face. Upon arrival she'd hugged Everett firmly and told him with a laugh that the network was picking up the tab.

"How's your food?" Dee Nash asked Everett as he pushed a fork through and around his brisket. She was dressed more casually than on the ads. She'd put on a jean jacket over her expensive blouse—he suspected to make him more comfortable.

"Good. It's a little dry. Sunday's the better day for Extra Billy's."

"You used to come here with them, didn't you?" Dee leaned in. "Your mother? Haley?"

"Sometimes. My dad brought us. When there was money."

Earlier, when Everett and Dee had walked into the restaurant, he'd noticed all the women at the tables and on staff turn their heads, some mouthing her name. Dee saw it too and told Everett the women would all go home with a story of *You know who came into Billy's today?*

Everett looked up from his food. "How did you know about Billy's?"

"My grandparents lived in Norfolk during the war," she said.

"You're from here?"

"They followed the navy west. So mostly I grew up in Torrance, near LA."

"So you're really from California?"

"Sure, but you know, there's more that connects you and me than you to them."

"Who's 'them'?"

"I'm black. You're country. We both know the difference one street makes. How you can be safe on one block, then the next you feel like an alien in your own town. You do get that feeling from the rich folk, don't you? That tone underneath the niceness." Dee looked with some reluctance at her oversmothered Caesar salad, pushing the croutons to one side.

"Maybe." Everett nodded.

"I'm not the media, Everett. I'm not like the ones who took your sister's name and blamed her for her own murder. You know why the press did that? The defense attorneys. They told the papers whatever would make their case look stronger. Selective evidence. Lies even. The Wynns had the money to hire people like that. Your family? You had the DA. You had nothing."

"It's over. Years ago, you know. I don't want to be like Mom."

"Everett. When I was a cop, I specialized in domestic violence cases. My show is for the women I could never save back then."

"A girl killed my sister."

"Maybe not."

Everett set down his fork and looked ashen. "Please excuse me," he said as he started to get up. She might have been from TV, but Dee had started to sound like them: the People from the Internet, with their conspiracy theories and facts only they knew and if Everett could just please, please give them his phone number . . .

Dee changed her tone. "Wait," she said.

Everett sat back down cautiously.

"I'm not saying Kennedy Wynn is innocent. The evidence I have is new, but it is not exculpatory."

Everett winced at the last word and felt he was in the back of a classroom.

"It means that someone else may have been involved." She paused, as if waiting for a dramatic commercial break. "Take one hundred murdered women and ninety-nine of their killers are men. Look at the brutality of the wounds. Ribs broken. Little girl in a full-length velvet dress wielding a knife with that intensity? This case simply makes no sense as it has been told. The mistakes of that prosecutor—"

"Kennedy admitted it. I don't understand." Everett leaned forward, inclining his head as if he hadn't heard properly.

"No. She made an Alford plea, and that's different. The DA wanted to send a couple of rich kids to trial. They do that around election time. But they didn't have enough evidence to try both Berk Butler and Kennedy. So they put one against the other and saw who took the deal first. As well-off as the Wynns were, the Butlers had more: more money, more lawyers."

It was true that his mother still refused to buy anything from a Butler's store.

"What do you think of Carter?" Everett was surprised at his own question.

Sometimes he had read what the People from the Internet had written about the case, which felt like peering into someone else's hallucination: *It was a government LSD experiment; the military's Radio Quiet Zone is only an hour away; Vice President Al Gore and his wife, Tipper, wanted to delegitimize grunge and drive Cobain to suicide; it was Carter who did it.* He remembered thinking, *That's bullshit.* It was the first time he'd felt protective of Carter.

"What do you think of her?" Dee returned.

"She's a victim too. That's how I see it."

Everett felt embarrassed for even saying Carter's name.

"We're looking at a possible male accomplice or accomplices."

"Kennedy killed my sister." The fact defined Everett more than he could admit.

"Murder is an immense truth. All the little lies fall away from it. Except when they don't. Sometimes the truth threatens us more than the fictions that have been told."

He took a drink from his soda. "So what's this new evidence?"

"This." Dee reached into her bag and took out a manila envelope. It was wrinkled and sun lightened. She set it on the table but kept her hand on it, as if to say, *This is mine*, and for Everett to know what it was he would have to trust her.

Chapter 10

GERRY WAS NAPPING in his recliner in the family room—Kennedy wondered if it could still be called that when no one had lived there for years except him—and she walked through the house, running her hands over the objects she remembered and new ones that she didn't. She stepped into Gerry's office. The desk had a stack of paperwork on it, but to one side, as if he wasn't really working on it. Sitting atop a file cabinet was a mug with bubble lettering, a relic of the eighties. Laine had given it to him. *Pencil Me In*, it said.

Kennedy picked it up. An amber residue in the bottom. Carter had said he'd quit liquor when she did, but that obviously wasn't true: he simply didn't drink as much as he once had. Kennedy set it back down. She dropped into her father's chair and opened his desk drawer, which was full of office items barely in use anymore. She might have seen the folded one-inch note if a flicker of movement in the backyard outside hadn't distracted her.

Out there in the dark, someone was moving. Between the

gazebo and the Japanese pond. Her father had shown her the Japanese pond her first day after lunch—a new acquisition recommended by his cardiologist, though Kennedy couldn't believe a pond would actually calm him unless it was filled with Glenlivet.

The figure moved and Kennedy stood up quickly. She knew who it was, even though it was too dark to see his face. She knew his shoulders, his motion. She grabbed the letter opener from the drawer, then set it back down. It wouldn't defend her if she really needed it, she thought. She ran downstairs and pulled a knife from the block in the kitchen, slipped it up her sleeve, holding it with one hand. She looked out, hoping she was wrong. Then, after a moment, she slid open the back patio door in the kitchen. Nine wasn't late, but it was November-dark, late enough. She flipped on the outside light and he halted at the patio stairs without climbing them.

Berkeley Butler still had a football player's stance, as if he was ready to run, even though the years had added padding to him that wasn't part of the uniform. His blond hair was shaved short, and it took her a moment to realize it was because he was now balding. A white stone of scalp nudged up just slightly from his brush cut. He'd been twenty-one with floppy hair and a hemp necklace when she knew him, but he'd seemed so much older than her that she'd never thought of him that way: boy. Her father was the one who called him that. To her, Berk had been masculine, charming, and aloof, as broad chested and moneyed as the Wrong Boyfriend in a John Hughes movie. Now he was a man of thirty-seven in a work jacket with a logo patch on the chest that said *Butler's.* She'd gone into prison knowing only boys. She'd learned about men from the other women—enough to understand what Berk was then and what Berk was now, standing in front of her.

He stood there as ordinary as daytime. She stared. His eyebrow still had the distinctive split in the middle. She'd thought it sexy at the time. It was only later, during the investigation, when he agreed to testify against her, that she'd seen him as anything other than beautiful. She remembered how the patch of hair in the center of his chest always smelled like clove. How hard had she tried to make him love her? She tightened her grip on the knife under her sleeve.

"What do you want, Berk? I'm not going to talk to you." Kennedy raised her voice a bit more than she needed to, wondering if she could actually wake Gerry. He was far away though, the house too expansive. She'd had an imaginary conversation with Berk for years in her mind, and now suddenly he was in front of her and her mind was blank.

"I wanted to see the girl who wrecked my life all grown up now." Those thin, pale pink lips parted in a smile. "She looks fine."

He reached into his jacket pocket and then leaned forward and put something on the patio table. Kennedy heard the click of it, metal on metal, before he took his hand away and she saw it. It was a necklace. The size of a quarter and perfectly round: a yin-yang on a worn black cord. He smiled again crookedly. "Don't want to get caught with evidence right now."

Kennedy stepped closer, her bare feet on the cold stones of

the patio. The necklace belonged to Haley. Kennedy wanted to reach out and take it but she also didn't want to get any closer. She felt her shoulders tighten. She couldn't remember if Haley had been wearing it that last night. She stepped back.

"There's no more evidence. Everything is over and that necklace is just something you stole. Like my life," Kennedy said.

"I did two years."

"With stockbrokers. I did fourteen with murderers."

"I have to tell you, I kind of made a mistake. I talked to some TV people. Thought I could make some money, but I probably shouldn't have done that."

"Because you're a lying sack of shit?"

His chin tilted up. "Am I? That's not how I remember it. You were the last one with her." He gazed at the necklace on the table. "She gave this to me, by the way. Because she loved me."

Kennedy weighed the statement and decided it was the other way around: Berk had felt more for Haley than she had for him. Berk was a good talker, and she could imagine him convincing Haley to give it to him. Or his roommate Julian, who was never far away, winning it from her in some drinking-game bet. The past had to be stared at to reveal itself, and even then it was all interpretation.

"Journalists are your problem, Berk. Not mine. There's nothing more anyone can do to me," she said.

"I can think of some things." In the Wynn backyard, Berk smiled again and let his head loll to one side above his coat collar. "You still a virgin, hiding in the bathroom every time someone else wants to?"

Kennedy had gone out a foot onto the patio and now she stepped backward into the kitchen. She couldn't tell if he'd come there to seduce her or to hurt her, and she realized that may have always been the flickering doubt in Berk's eyes. Even now, he wasn't adult enough to consider she may have had a sexual life in the last fifteen years.

At the time he'd said he didn't want her lawyer father to get some lawyer friend to go after him on account of her age. Instead, they would slow-dance in his room. A teasing kiss. Even a make-out. His fingers trailing lightly over her breasts, her thighs. But never sex. Kennedy had almost decided to but had not quite become convinced. He said he wanted to experience love like Buddha said: "Love is a gift of one's soul so both can be whole." His persona was equal parts Charlie Starkweather and Allen Ginsberg, in spite of his pampered upbringing. Berk had attended Virginia Commonwealth University but spent most of his time in bars instead of classes. He and Julian had dropped acid every weekend, shared their pot with anyone with budding breasts. Julian wasn't as handsome, but he was tall and lean, with hair he wore in a long ponytail. She'd learned later that the apartment had been nicknamed Unplanned Parenthood by girls on campus. Carter had always said that all he wanted was to use her, and Kennedy had resisted that definition of the relationship. *Use*, what did it mean to *use* someone?

Berk stepped toward Kennedy. "Like it or not, we're in this together," he said, his hand going for her shoulder.

Kennedy flinched. She experienced a flicker of red, felt her veins throb, recalled the water around her ankles that morning in the woods when she touched her friend's slippery, cold skin. "Little threats. That's what it always was with you. If you're going to make a threat, make it a big one."

His eyes narrowed under his brow. It was the same Berk she had seen in the car the night of the acid trip. Ballistic Berk. His face warped. Kennedy felt light-headed. She felt the steak knife fall into her hand and held it where he could see it under the patio lantern.

"They say you know how to use that," he said as he stepped toward her. His voice had a rough edge and the put-on indifference of his earlier gestures was gone.

She swung the blade fast in front of his eyes, without touching him. "Stay away from me."

AFTER HE'D GONE, muttering, "Whatever, Dead Kennedy," and backing slowly into the dark, Kennedy returned to Gerry's home office. The adrenaline buckled her and she sank into the office chair. She opened Gerry's laptop.

She had never seen Facebook but knew you were supposed to be able to find people on it. She knew she would need an email address, and although Gerry's was right there in front of her, with no password on it, she wasn't about to use his. She sat there staring at the glowing screen. She was still shaking with anger though, and wasn't about to let her inexperience with this new medium stump her.

After a few minutes she managed to create a Yahoo! address for herself and opened a Facebook account without uploading any profile photo or revealing information, just her name. She searched *Berkeley Butler*. Because she had no friends yet, the search box didn't know which Berkeley Butler to reveal to her and half a dozen appeared. She scrolled through the tiny postage-stamp pictures. Her father's laptop was slick and weird, and she couldn't seem to make her finger move the way it was supposed to on the rectangular pad. Her vocational training in prison had been with a mouse and an ancient IBM clone. She fumbled the cursor again and again and clicked without meaning to. He was the last Berkeley: it had to be him. There was a photo of a pre-school girl in the profile picture. He was married, worked at one of the grocery stores his family owned.

He had come to the house at nine at night. After bedtime. Early enough to still get out, make some excuse of an errand, late enough that the child had been read her bedtime stories. Staring at the little girl's blond bob cut into Kennedy's heart. It was worse, knowing he'd come there to say those things to her when there were people at home waiting on him. It was too easy to imagine him coming after her, on top of her. She knew how fast he could move once. She knew the weight of his body even if he'd never been inside her. Kennedy clicked Log Out.

He'd never loved her, she realized. Something about seeing that he had built a life, made a commitment, put the word *married* right there in print on his profile—along with the things he'd said, his cold tone just half an hour before—solidified that understanding for her. As a teenager she would have gone any-where with him, made her life about him, with him, but it was a blind love. Carter had tried to tell her at the time, but she hadn't listened. The appellate attorney had also said it. Berk had treated her as a stepping-stone to get to the next girl; the prettier girl; the less guarded, less careful one. All of the above. Haley. Kennedy turned in the swivel chair, looking around Gerry's office for the box of Kleenex that Laine had always stationed in every room. But the maid service didn't seem to make tissues as much of a priority, and as Kennedy sobbed, she found her sleeve would have to do.

She took a shaky breath before she picked up the phone and called Carter. She didn't say hello. "If I go to a website, is that part of the computer forever?"

She wanted to tell her about Berk, but something in Carter's brittle voice as she explained to Kennedy how to erase her history told her there was a part of their own past that needed to be erased. Already Carter didn't trust her, and now, when she was just barely out, Berk was back in their lives again.

In the morning, when Kennedy went out onto the stone patio, she saw the necklace was still there on the table. Berk had used Haley and she hated the way he was still using her. She picked the pendant up and turned it over between her fingers. It was cold and dewy. Kennedy was sure he had held on to it all those years to hurt her one more time.

Chapter 11

As Everett pulled up the long gravel path to his father's house, he saw he was dyeing his hair deep black too, like Judy's. Ted Kimberson now looked like a politician campaigning—country style—as he waved, standing inside the barn door in his fleece vest with a thumb hooked into new jeans.

The barn wasn't a barn. It was more like a private hangar, larger than the actual house on the property in the middle of the Cumberland Woods. Everett had invited himself out that weekend under the pretext of pulling out that tree stump whose roots were still growing into the weeping tile. The last two times he had come out to do that, he and his father had ended up sitting on lawn chairs inside the barn, Everett drinking beer, his father Diet Cokes, until it was late and the mosquitoes came for them and Judy said it was dinnertime in that voice.

Everett was on his second Coors and the tree stump still secure in the ground when he said, "Kennedy Wynn got released."

"You know the state sent me that letter too." His father shrugged.

"Still got those boxes from the lawsuit?" Everett had already scanned the shelves in the barn, looking for that stack of banker's boxes propped up next to the duck and swan decoys.

"I'm not your mother," his father answered without missing the opportunity for a dig.

"Be nice, now."

"I'm not the one who made an altar to pain, if you know what I mean."

"What d'you mean?"

"I mean that woman can go anywhere in the world and she still lives practically next door to Wynn. What's she waiting for? A sequel? I think about Haley every goddamn day, but not the way Marly does."

Dee Nash had asked Everett if he had any access to documents from the civil lawsuit. It might be a way of getting at police files: there's always crossover, she said, and things that shouldn't be in civilian hands but often are. When she asked him to look he realized he wanted to see the reports too, for the same reason he needed to see Carter.

"What do you want 'em for anyway?" his father asked.

"I don't know. I never knew Haley."

"Funny way to learn." Ted ran his hands over his jean knees, as if smoothing something away.

THE LAST TIME Everett had seen his sister was the funeral, held only four days after Haley was found, autopsied, and released to her parents with a shakily drawn signature. That week was a

twilight between truths for Everett: after his mother's screaming, but before Kennedy and Berk Butler were arrested. Strangers began collecting funeral money, and that soon grew into
donated flower displays and funeral homes competing for the
booking. The bank wouldn't give the Kimbersons a credit card
before Haley's murder, but after they set up a scholarship fund
in her name. The day of the service, crowds gathered outside the
church, and seats were strictly assigned to family and Haley's
fellow students, though that didn't stop rubberneckers from trying to get in. Kennedy and Carter did not attend, so they never
saw Haley as Everett did, snug in a compact magenta casket—
her favorite color. Her face was painted and sculpted unnatu-
rally; she looked to Everett like a doll that might be sold on TV
and noted for its heirloom quality. Whatever Haley had been—
a girl with eyes that trusted everyone, a sister who still read to
him as her Pantene-scented hair brushed his face—was gone.

After Aunt Kathy walked Everett back to his seat, a detective set a strong hand on his shoulder. "Let us all know if anyone acts funny, *Deputy Everett*," he leaned over and told the
nine-year-old. "That goes for strangers or even someone you
know real well, like your daddy."

Everett had been at home with Marly on July 5, already
bored of the summer, when that same detective had shown up
and asked her when was the last time she had seen her daughter,
not telling them what was wrong. He asked where Ted had
been the night before and Everett overheard his mother say
some woman's name. When the subject came up a couple of
years later and Everett asked where he was that night, Marly

said he was with his "alibabe" and left it at that. Everett figured
that was why his father could move on past Haley's death. Even
when he was part of their family, he wasn't. When Ted got sober he apologized to his son and said that his cheating was com-
pulsive. "Hell, I don't even remember half of them, I was so
soused." Everett accepted the apology but remembered thinking, *Best of luck, Judy.*

NOW EVERETT SIPPED his beer to empty and saw that his
father was crying. He felt bad for the times he hadn't trusted
him, just like that detective.

"You've been hanging around Marly too much." Ted snif-
fled. "Why don't you move out here? I can get you in at the
shop. A job would be good for you."

Everett couldn't tell him he needed to stay in the city, near
Carter. Before he could think of a way to avoid the question
they heard the sound coming in long and sharp from the house:
"Teddy!"

His father shrugged and tossed his empty soda can into a
blue bin. "Time to face the judge. Set me up another one of
those Cokes for when I get back."

After Ted let the barn door shut, Everett sprang out of his
lawn chair so fast it fell over. He righted it and walked around
the dark corners of the barn, looking for the boxes. He lifted a
dusty bundle of camouflage netting and found one: water
stained and heavy. He didn't see the others and didn't think
he'd have time to get more than one without Ted knowing.

Everett hauled the box outside the barn and into his car. He grabbed his jacket out of the back so that if his father heard the car trunk, he'd just assume Everett had gotten cold. But his father didn't come back right away, and Everett sat again in the barn waiting, feeling like he should make it easy on his father and leave. Let him get on with a life that made no room for ghosts.

Chapter 12

Every morning, as week two slid into week three, Kennedy exited the house and walked toward the Macaulay estate at the end of the curve. She knew it was a mile from their house to the end of Silver Creek Lane because her mother and father used to walk it together to stay in shape. Her father's firm had often taken work from Macaulay. Their offices were near each other's. Here was the Hall house, there the Schofields and the Wilsons. Mrs. Wilson's claim to fame was that she owned a dress that had been worn by Lady Di. The Johnsons were supposedly descended from some Confederate general, and Kennedy wouldn't doubt it. The Cains were the only black family in Blueheart Woods, though the mom was white with blond hair. Kennedy's walk turned into a jog. One crescent over, around Stonemeadow, and soon she'd gone two full miles. She felt fiery with exhilaration.

She watched her shoes—a pair of puffy white Nikes she'd worn when she was competing in tennis back in 1991—the shape they made in front of her. *I'm not the monster everyone thinks I am. I'm a human,* she told herself. *I can change, and heal. I still have this crazily beating heart at my center. Those are my feet, my legs. This is my body going forward. I'm just going to keep putting one foot in front of the other.*

Having her twin doubt her made it hard to believe it.

A *For Sale* sign swung in front of the Farrells'. She had no idea how many of these families remained anyway. The Farrells had a daughter three years younger than her and Carter, whom they'd liked to pick on. The Chamberses had a son four years older they'd both coveted—Daniel, who wore his shirts inside out so the brand wouldn't show, even though everyone knew his clothes were expensive. For god's sake, he drove a Lexus. Still, she'd thought it was sexy at the time, his taking a stand against consumerism. Things his mother wanted him to be pressed against his chest all day long: backward, inside out. His father wanted him to join the family business, but instead he worked summers at the employment office and helped students get jobs.

When she was sixteen and he twenty—before Laine had landed her the job at the stationery store—he'd shown her how to fill out the forms to apply for part-time work. She'd hoped he knew how to get work in the city: a music store, a record store, Guitar Center, the Byrd Theatre, MAC Cosmetics. But being able to stare at him across the desk and list her accomplishments was good enough. She got calls back from the nearby hotel and a lawn care service, nothing remotely interesting or cool, and she wondered how she'd presented herself, to both Daniel and future employers.

She'd fantasized about Daniel Chambers at least two dozen

times in the decade since then. She could fall into his dark hair, his dark eyes. Where was he now? How stupid, fantasizing about a boy when she was now a woman. It was stupider even than thinking of a film star or celebrity. Maybe she had done it to avoid the image of Berk Butler. It was Daniel who'd introduced her to Berk and Julian one night when her band played in the city. A long, narrow café/bar called End of the Trip. Carter said it was a cell phone store now. At the time they'd been stoner college guys who knew every new indie band. Even in her mind, the name *Berk Butler* felt like the first few strums on her guitar, an exhilarated hum she'd never gotten past.

She and Carter had sung three or four times in the bar. She'd told Carter that they would be like the Deal sisters— Kim Deal, who was in the Pixies and later the Breeders, and her twin, Kelley. The band was Kennedy on guitar, Carter on bass, and a paralegal named Kevin from their dad's office who still wanted to play drums even though he had a wife and baby. His old band had opened up for the Replacements in '88 at the University of Virginia. The other member was a nineteen-year-old guy, Robin, from their church. He played keyboards, and the twins couldn't tell if he was gay or just Christian. They hoped gay because that might make the band cooler. Both guys in the band tucked their shirts into pleated pants and favored folky stuff and pop covers. Kennedy had to convince them to let her do the Pixies' "Wave of Mutilation." Carter had wanted to call the group the Ophelias, and Kennedy had suggested Head Like a Hole. The drummer said they couldn't have a folk-industrial band and should just call themselves A Bloody Mess,

which was pretty accurate in terms of how they played. It stuck
for a few gigs—as long as they lasted.

Daniel had been friends with Berk, but later he'd told her
not to be stupid about him. She could remember exactly what
he'd said, there in his driveway when she'd asked for Berk's
number a couple days after meeting him: "No, don't. Guys like
that . . ." He'd shaken his head. She got the picture, but she also
got the number. Not from Daniel. It was in the directory. She
wondered now if all of it had been her way of trying to get her
neighbor's attention in the first place. But that wasn't true. In
retrospect, he was the first person to try to look out for her.
And she'd gone and sexualized his nobility over the years. He'd
been completely right about Berk.

At the bar the first night she and Carter played, Berk had
ticked a finger back and forth between them and asked, "Y'all
want a beer?" nodding at the bartender. Kennedy and Carter
had looked at each other and laughed. Carter then held up her
wristband and Daniel explained they were still in high school.
Robin, the keyboard player, had already loaded his Korg into
his dad's van and left.

"We're almost seventeen," Kennedy had put in, a slight ex-
aggeration, leaning one elbow on the bar, as though she belonged there. *We.* The questions and answers always with
the pronoun *we.* We *go to Liberty High.* We *learned to play when*
we *were twelve.* We *live in Blueheart Woods. It totally sucks.* We
might take a beer, if we *weren't here. Do you know somewhere*
we *can go?*

"Cute," Berk said as the night went on, clucking into his beer bottle, his cheeks pinkening as he drank more. He threw his floppy golden hair back with a flick of his head. "I can just imagine you skipping through your little suburb holding hands."

Now she felt her face burn thinking about what Berk had said to her in the backyard. How presumptuous of him to come there. How predatory. He had been charming once, but he never had been fair. He'd always told her to bring Carter with her to his place. But Carter had never liked him, so she'd taken Haley instead. She'd put Haley's necklace in between two sweaters in her dresser drawer, like it was something that needed to be hidden.

HER JOG TURNED into a sprint and she left the concrete cul-de-sacs behind. As she picked up speed, Kennedy felt the insistent earworm of an old song, and she longed for a Walkman or MP3 player to accompany her. Gerry still had CDs, but Carter would know about that kind of thing. She talked about juggling rent and bills and yet she had all the gadgets.

Kennedy jogged, rounding the final curve that separated the subdivision from the actual Blueheart Woods for which it had been named. She took in the brown tufts of the trees, a string of yellow leaves hanging here or there like forgotten birthday streamers.

Kennedy stopped running for a moment. She could feel the backs of her thighs already aching. She should have stretched more. She stepped off the shoulder and into the grass. She put her shoe up against a tree and leaned into the pain.

She gulped in agony, not realizing how tender everything was. She stared at the leaves underfoot: little curls of red-brown.

She tried not to see the body, the face. But Haley was there in her memory looking up, as if she'd fallen over backward for no reason but to stare up into the sky, compare cloud shapes. She was white and still. It was Haley but not Haley.

She would open her eyes, Kennedy had thought. It had to be a game, an act, the kind of play they would have put on at school—her and Carter—or the scene in *Anne of Green Gables* where Anne performed "The Lady of Shalott."

This wasn't where she'd found Haley though. It was farther, deep in the woods. She'd tramped into them early that morning, thinking that Haley and Berk must have gone in, toward that little clearing. Kennedy could see it all now so plainly, and as she gazed toward that direction, she thought she saw a smear of marigold fabric—the see-through blouse Haley had on—floating, weaving between the trees.

It was nothing, she told herself, squeezing her eyes shut, then opening them again, leaves flying around.

There was a little glade where kids from Liberty High School went to smoke up, drink, make out. Toward the back of the woods. A place you could even pull into with a car if you knew how. Then she remembered: they'd fought. Berk was upset with her when she'd thrown up in his Jeep. His taillights. She remembered how they looked—angry red stars—as they pulled away from the closed Mobil. She and Haley high in the gas station parking lot, hugging each other and giggling into each other's faces. That was all she could remember until she woke up the next day.

Now Kennedy found herself drawn by the woods. She walked in, stepping over the old trails. She was a mile in when she came to the place.

Haley had been lying half in and half out of the creek. From a distance, she'd looked like nothing more than a log, a patch of moss in her yellow blouse and her suede-brown miniskirt.

Later, it was Kennedy's boot print detectives lifted from the crime scene, though the sisters were the same size and shared a wardrobe, so no one could say for sure whether it was hers or Carter's. That was something police pointed out, threatened Kennedy with, taking her sister in.

"Haley was cold," Kennedy shouted that morning when she told Carter, but Carter insisted it was from sleeping outside all night.

Kennedy had held her own dirty, bloodied hands up to her sister as she dialed. In the background of the call—a moment she would later hear replayed in echoing Pine-Sol–scented rooms in the courthouse—she yelled, "Don't! They'll arrest Berk."

Kennedy knew that when her sister phoned 911 she had no idea what had been set in motion, no idea that suspicion would turn to Kennedy. Or that Carter herself would soon suspect her own twin was responsible.

It was the novel the police had found the hair lying in, like some sad tassel bookmark. Kennedy managed to hold on to the little piece of Haley for a day before police got the search warrant and went through the house on Silver Creek, claiming everything.

She told herself it was love, a girl's love. A romantic desire to protect her friend and keep some part of her safe, apart from what had been done to her. In front of her now, the creek murmured cheerfully. She supposed it was the kind of spot where teens still came to hike, kiss on the tiny wooden bridge just over that way. Unaware of what had happened here.

Kennedy felt chills up and down her arms and hugged her body as she walked to the bridge, wishing she'd put on more than a sweatshirt for her jog. She put her shoe up on the rotting wood structure, sucked in a breath, and leaned again into the sharp pain.

I wrote you a note, she heard a voice say, almost as if someone were standing beside her. But she knew it was only Haley's voice in her memory. Something she had said that night.

Quickly Kennedy straightened, and breathed out, and ran back out of the woods, over the cracking twigs, muttering the lyrics to an old Cure song, as if it could ward off spirits.

OUT ON THE ROAD, she turned a corner to head back toward the Blueheart Woods enclave. A vehicle was driving up the street. The driver was an older man, maybe fifty, and beside him in the passenger seat was a younger guy, closer to her age. She didn't recognize either of them but as they approached her they slowed. Jogging, parallel with them, she glanced over when the window went down. A half-full water bottle hit her in the side, lobbed at full force.

"Dead Kennedy!" the younger man yelled out the window.

The older man leaned forward so he could see her, the vehicle braking. Why were they braking? What else did they intend to do? She raised her hand to the tender spot along her ribs. She didn't hear what the old guy said because she knew she should run now, really run.

Chapter 13

CARTER WAS HANDED a perfect Americano when she walked in, an invitation to sit down and be normal. She knew Everett must have spent days mastering the machine, watching videos online and researching beans and grinds, and would talk about it with the same passion as he had the arcane differences between sports quads and utility four-by-fours. Glancing around the condo, she saw he'd hung up Christmas lights along one wall. The door to his bedroom was open and she could see he'd painted the walls a sienna color since the last time she'd been there. It looked inviting.

"This is hard for me," Carter said. "I feel embarrassed of, you know—the last time."

"You said that you felt embarrassed then, that you were afraid to be naked with me."

It caught her off guard.

"Don't you remember? I assumed it was because you were about to see her. I mean, you never have been shy."

"The morning before she came home?" Carter shook her head. She blushed. She felt more self-conscious. She didn't remember anything shy about the last time. She remembered only the sweaty crescendo. "It was hot, wasn't it?" she said.

Then he said yeah, of course it was. Not just the last time either; it always was.

She registered that he said *was* instead of *is*, but she dismissed it as she sat down and unwound her scarf. "I feel out of control. I broke . . . this thing—it meant a lot to Kennedy." Carter stopped short of telling him about seeing his mother at the graveyard, wondering if Marly might have already mentioned it. "And I feel all this panic I can't breathe through."

"Did you see Dr. Brathwaite?"

She nodded.

"What about yoga?"

"I went twice this week."

He set down a plate of cookies in front of her. "You know, there's something we should talk about."

Carter had expected they would have coffee and talk a bit, then eventually they'd let themselves into his bedroom, pretend they weren't going to, then wind up falling on top of each other. But it was clear from his tone that wasn't what was on his mind. She hoped it wasn't the card Gerry had found in Everett's left-behind blazer. She braced herself.

"You know it's a competition between her and me."

"Who?"

"Your sister. And I can't win. I know that. I've always known. That's why we have to break up."

She hadn't expected this and she bit her lip. She'd thought

he might discuss his doubts with her, his anger. His saying the words *break up* suddenly made everything between them more serious, and Carter wished he would take it back. She fingered the sugar bowl's ceramic lid before removing it. She grasped the small spoon and added a tiny amount to her cup.

He stared at her until she thought it might actually hurt her.

For a second she had the crazy adolescent thought that if she didn't acknowledge what he'd said, it would go away. She stared at the sugar bowl instead of him. She wasn't even sure she owned a sugar bowl. What she and Alex had used for years was really just a jam jar, now that she thought about it. They were so punk it had never occurred to her to buy china. They'd gotten sober together and he'd eventually left his band, but their normality had still never made it all the way to normal.

She and Everett sipped their drinks in silence, and the sunlight fell between them. She reached out and took his hand suddenly. "Please don't. I can't explain what we're doing, but it's important to me. I don't know if I can do this without you."

"Do what? Imagine me and your father in a room!" he said, standing up.

She was right. She shouldn't have said anything. Maybe they would have gotten through the moment and it would have passed.

Me and your father. Her father would start by correcting his manner of speech. Carter laughed, but nothing was funny. It felt like a bubble popping, something delicate disappearing. She thought of Kennedy, how if Everett were in the same room as her, he might become unhinged, capable of male violence. She had seen his expression change whenever she said her twin's name. Carter felt her eyes narrow and then fill.

"Haven't you planned the ending," he asked, "rehearsed it? We both knew it would come. We've known from the start."

"No, I haven't," she said. Carter watched him, his face. The lines of his eyebrow hairs all leaned in the same direction; the lines on his lips were pale and dry. His ears stuck out just enough to make his otherwise handsome face seem as if there might be humor in there somewhere. But not today—his eyes were serious and dark. She wished he were joking. She sat there on the uncomfortable plastic chair. She wanted to hurt him. She thought about that awful glimpse of his mother at the cemetery, how it felt like her stomach was falling. "Maybe you only sleep with me as a way to get closer to Haley."

"You're as fucked up as Kennedy," Everett erupted, his voice louder now than it needed to be, his chin tense. "You Wynns, you think you can do whatever you want, take whatever you want. You sleep with me to prove you can."

He grabbed their empty cups and charged around the small kitchen area, dropping them into the sink and running water in them. She'd never heard him like this before. Watching him from behind, she saw the space between his shoulder blades where she always liked to put her hand. But she didn't get up to touch him. She'd pushed it. She knew the words were too dangerous spoken out loud.

When Everett turned around, he fixed her with a long gaze, and Carter studied him. It wasn't just his soft features that she

loved, or his toned biceps and athletic build; it was that his
sister's death had left a boyhood tattooed forever on his face:
his distant eyes and gaping mouth.

"That's not why I'm with you," she said. "I'm with you because you're the only one who understands what it's like."

"What is it like?"

"We're both broken."

"Whose sister did the breaking?" Everett asked. He didn't
come back to the table and she felt the distance between them
growing longer.

"I don't—" Carter faltered. Her shoulders stiffened.

"Go on."

"I don't disagree with you." She had thought verbalizing it
would place Everett and her on the same side, but he shrank
back against the sink again.

He asked the obvious: Had Kennedy finally come out and
said it?

"No," Carter said on a hard exhalation. "I don't think she
would ever admit it."

Neither of them spoke for a long time.

"Well, she isn't hiding. She's on Facebook," Everett said,
wiping his hands on a dish towel with a picture of a fish on it.
"Everyone needs a life, I guess. I saw she friended a couple people from Liberty High and she put a photo up. She doesn't look
as much like you as she used to." He tossed the towel down and
put one hand against the edge of the sink.

There was something clouded in his expression and then he
said, "I had a meeting with a television producer last week, the

host of a crime show. Dee Nash. She used to be a real detective. They want to look at Haley's story."

"I found the card. It was in your pocket at my place. But, you won't. You won't let them," Carter said, getting to her feet. She hadn't mentioned it, she realized, because she wanted to believe in him.

"It just needs to be done. Maybe it will even help you too." His tone was matter-of-fact, even if his eyes flickered. He said the writing team had already begun to research the murder. They would be going through all the public files from the investigation and any he could help them with from the civil case. It occurred to Carter that he must have had some idea of this already and held it back, that the card in his pocket wasn't just an offer, an idea: the wheels were in motion the last time she'd been there, when he'd held her wrists and climbed on her, when she'd panted that directive at him to stay inside, as if— *what?* As if she'd wanted to make a baby, make a solid thing inside her body that spoke of him, make something that no one could deny existed.

She didn't know what she said in reply because the next thing she knew, she was lying flat on her back on his couch with her eyes streaming. She was gasping for air. She felt like her head might explode: a vise was being screwed tighter and tighter around her eardrums and all the while she was being held underwater. He had betrayed her. She could hear a voice telling her to calm down, and then he brought her something, said he wasn't doing it to hurt her. He held out a pink pill and some water and she took it without asking what it was. He held her for a few minutes, one hand rubbing her back, and she stopped crying and drew a breath, feeling the air like a long ribbon moving across her tongue.

He told her he didn't think she should drive, and called a cab for her and walked her out to it even though her car was parked in his space. He kissed her forehead and said goodbye, but she barely heard him.

"I'm sorry. I just . . . have to," he said, his final explanation. Why was his face so pretty and his logic so simple? He shut the cab door and the driver turned and looked at her, in need of directions.

October 13, 2008

ASSIGNMENT 3:
Write about something that wasn't what it seemed.

ALL STORIES ARE like things told in translation. For instance, I could easily find words for the little memories: the feeling of a joint rolling forward into my hand from a cassette case, where the lyrics sheet had been hiding it. The tiny ecstasy of that sensation. How, when I was high, it seemed like the sun was shining on me even when there was no sunshine. How, though, do I get at the bigger things? The simple fact of a person I knew, cared about, instantly gone.

THE THREE OF US piled into the boy's Jeep and headed to the woods. The acid had more of an effect than I had ever seen in Berk before. That was the danger of the drug. Sometimes it was just speedy and made us grind our teeth. Sometimes the stuccoed ceiling of a suburban living room became the white protoplasm of the universe.

In his Jeep, he pushed a cassette into the player and sampled guitars rang out: Trent Reznor singing with Ministry on a cover of Black Sabbath's "Supernaut." The song was heavy burnout music I would have made fun of a few years before, when I won an award in eighth grade for Best "Just Say No" Stage Play, but I was now, technically, a burnout too. When I was with him, we smoked or tripped and the world levitated for a few hours. I didn't think about my parents' problems, or the LAPD trial on TV, or Bosnian rape victims, or Waco flames. I didn't even think about what had happened a few weeks before between Haley and Berk. Our trio bobbed heads in unison as the vehicle drove into the country and the streetlights ended.

He then took his hands off the wheel. "How long do you think we can live?" he shouted over the music. "The drum solo?"

"Fuck off!" I shouted.

"Stop it," she agreed, leaning forward from the back.

And he laughed that laugh of his that ended in a slight whistle. "Calm down." He put his hands back on the wheel. He then took them off again.

He could have killed us then, I suppose, innocently. Was it all a joke to him?

"Stop! Let me out," Haley shouted.

In the front seat I had trouble focusing on the road ahead. The median lines danced, bent, and shimmered. The music throbbed and became my heartbeat. The dashboard lights cast him in demon green, and for a moment his tongue flicked out, forked like a lizard's. I felt a wave of vertigo. "I'm going to be sick."

"Oh man! Not in my Jeep."

All I remembered after that was she and I standing outside a closed gas station on Smoke Line, alone in the beautiful night, listening as cricket sounds turned into electronic rhythms in my mind.

But what about him? That's the fiction I can't get at: what he did. Berk said he drove an hour to the coast to sit alone after the crowds had gone and simply trip on the repetition of the waves. He was alibi-less. What if I believe that story and use my breath to mimic those waves, pulling in and out? Imagine there's only that rising and falling water, and no blood.

DURING AN APPEAL MEETING after my conviction, when I had protested that Berk could never have been the one responsible for Haley, my lawyer let me read his deposition. I remember more of that transcript than I want to.

COMMONWEALTH ATTORNEY: So Kennedy's your girl that spring?

BERK BUTLER: No. It wasn't like that. Kennedy [pause]. You don't touch something like that.

CA: Like what?

BB: I could do better than that, you know what I mean?

CA: Of course you could. Haley was more attractive. That's what you're saying? She was the one you were after.

BB: Yeah, you could say that.

CA: The better teenage girl? Hotter. Pure, right?

BB: Don't. Don't do that. I'm cooperating.

CA: But Kennedy is jealous.

BB: Yeah. Absolutely. You got it. She hated the fact her friend liked me. After that party—

CA: The party at your apartment?

BB: Yeah, that didn't go so well. Kennedy left me a message, said she'd do anything for me. Other stuff too—she called my mom and dad's place crying.

(That was true. I did.)

BB: I actually only hung around after that because I was afraid of what she might do.

CA: Like what?

BB: Kill herself, maybe. Guess she turned that feeling on someone else instead.

CA: You don't sound like you believe that.

BB: I was trying to smooth things over, that's why we were all together for the Fourth. Something low-key, friendly-like.

He had told me that there were girls "meant for that," and I wasn't one of them, as if it were a compliment that he wouldn't touch me. My appellate attorney said he was just using me to groom her. She stressed that he was a predator and even that prosecutor knew it in his line of questioning. She asked me if I had been molested as a child. I said no and my lawyer almost seemed disappointed. My appeal never made it past the court parking lot. It didn't help that Berk still had a phone message of my yelling at him the morning after the party where he had hooked up with my best friend.

Berk never came to court for the preliminary trial, or the

day I made my plea. For the first year in prison I wished he would come visit: a thousand things I could say to him. But by the end of that year, when I closed my eyes at night, I didn't see his face anymore, only hers—frozen in time, her eyes dim and her mouth open.

—Kennedy Wynn
Heron Valley Correctional Facility

Chapter 14

KENNEDY OPENED HER EYES AGAIN. Every morning when she woke it took her a few seconds to acclimatize. Remember where she was, when. The room was that of a sixteen-year-old but her body didn't feel sixteen. She went into the bathroom and washed her face. She felt older, too, than thirty-one. As a teenager, she'd spent more time looking at her sister than she had into a mirror. Both their faces had changed, yet Carter's still felt more familiar than hers. She stared at the new hair she had had to get for her job search. She still wasn't sure it suited her. Her scraggly haircut had been turned into a variant of a pageboy. It felt very typical, nice. Girl-next-door. The $96 from her prison work was almost gone, but she would have her very own paycheck soon. As it turned out there was a telemarketing program that hired only ex-cons. It may not have been the first thing she'd have put on her to-do list in a new life, but it was something.

She didn't want to touch the Gerry money, but Kennedy had no idea what to do with the early hours of each day. For the past two weeks, she had been taking jogs through the subdivision every morning, but she felt self-conscious, as though above every immaculate lawn there was a window and someone behind it standing in a bathrobe, looking out and saying, "The Wynn girl. Where do you think she's heading?"

Even with the new haircut, even with the new clothes Carter had bought her, Kennedy was aware she was still a criminal—would always be, as long as she stayed here. And right now she had neither the means nor the method to be anywhere else. Neighborhoods like this were tight-lipped and judgmental, unforgetting. No matter how many divorces had passed, how many secret DUIs, daytime hustler visits, or relatively old-fashioned affairs and abortions. She reached into the closet and took out her old tennis shoes. She found a sweatshirt. In Carter's old bedroom, which was now a guest room, there was a pair of yoga pants left in a dresser drawer.

She paused for a second, glancing at the bed. She remembered long ago she and Carter had had a system: they would leave each other secret messages under the mattress or inside the seams of the comforters. Places to meet. Who would be there. Or sometimes just little reminders, jokes like: *Don't steal my best lipstick, bitch.* Texts, essentially, before there were such things. But the bed wasn't the same bed it had been. And that was long ago. Kennedy walked over and sat down on it. She felt under the mattress. There was nothing there. The comforter wasn't like hers: it was expensive and didn't unzip. She looked up at the blank ivory walls and wondered if she should start sleeping in here instead. It was a better mattress, and less dusty, that was for sure.

Kennedy went back to her room, reached under her own mattress. She pulled the duvet from the bed and unzipped it, turned it inside out. She had a nagging feeling there might have been a message there. But the white comforter fell out of the purple linen, nothing with it, so she stuffed the whole thing back together. Probably it was nothing but paranoia.

Kennedy looked at the messed-up bed. She took in the posters above. River Phoenix had overdosed during the investigation. Beside him on the poster, Keanu Reeves. They barely kissed in *My Own Private Idaho*, she remembered, yet it had been groundbreaking, a thing no one could stop discussing. She wondered now why it had been such a big deal. Then she jumped up on the bed and pulled down the movie poster. It made a satisfying sluicing sound as the paper collapsed. She folded it neatly and laid it on the desk. She plucked the tacks out of the Cure, Nirvana, Jane's Addiction. At some point, she stopped folding them. Many were ephemera—left up but her passion for them over even before she'd gone. They cascaded to the bed and the floor and then she became less careful. She jumped as she took down the others. Johnny Depp's face ripped in two as Edward Scissorhands came down, his somber expression torn so distinctly his own blade hand could have accidentally done it.

Looking at the blank wall, the paint bright in rectangles where it had been covered all those years, she felt a rush of relief.

Chapter 15

CARTER STARED AT THE QUESTION on her phone for half an hour—*Why are you going through with the show?*—before she hit Send to "Rochester." He didn't return her text. She felt so tired she couldn't think. She lay down and went back to sleep. What Everett had given her to help her breathe: it must have been Benadryl.

When she woke up she phoned the Wynn house and got Kennedy. When she heard Kennedy's voice, for a second it did lift her mood. Carter didn't say why she was calling and didn't mention the fight they'd had at the cemetery. They slipped into the ordinary routine of sisters and Kennedy made it easy on her.

"I found a job in telemarketing." Kennedy sounded happy, detailing her news like anyone would. "The entire room will be ex-cons who need a job within one month of parole."

Carter wondered if she should tell her about the TV show: *Crime After Crime.* She'd looked it up. But how could she tell Kennedy without telling her about Everett? She couldn't. She could *not.* Carter could hear something playing in the back-

ground. Sinéad O'Connor, *I Do Not Want What I Haven't Got.*
It was her tape and Kennedy must have found it there, squir-
relled away in some drawer of track and field ribbons. Carter
had listened to it a thousand times in her youth, fallen in and
out of love a hundred times to the songs "Nothing Compares
2 U" and "The Last Day of Our Acquaintance." When Sinéad
sang about loss, Carter believed her. Until that point, Carter
hadn't known any. The songs were about real relationships, the
type of thing she could only imagine. She'd thought of no one
special really: Boys who sat ahead of her and had eyes like jade
or onyx—why had she always compared them to gems? Boys
with skater bobs or their hair spiked to look like Morrissey.
Boys whose names she could hardly remember. She had seldom
spoken to them, only snickered or whispered behind her hand
with Kennedy. Kennedy was the one who had made things
happen. Kennedy had moved away from Sinéad though,
toward grunge, then goth. Carter had followed her toward
Kurt Cobain but stopped just short of Nine Inch Nails, opting
for primal female voices like Tori Amos, Björk, and Sarah
McLachlan. Later, Kennedy would talk to her passionately
about Erykah Badu and Jurassic 5, sending Carter to the record store after their visits. Even in prison, Kennedy was still a
tastemaker.

SHE REMEMBERED AT ONE OF THEIR GIGS Kennedy sang
the Pixies high and sweet, and not a whole lot like the original
version. Their mom had videoed one of the gigs—the second

maybe—and Carter wondered if the VHS had disintegrated or was still around somewhere.

Kennedy had wanted her and Carter to form their own band—*just ours, ditch these lame-os*—though it was the guys in their band who'd gotten them the gig. The bar staff always tagged the girls with wristbands, a reminder that they were underage. Carter had said no to striking out alone, even though Kennedy pointed out they could bring Haley in. Three singers didn't make a band, Carter had said. Kennedy was the only musician, Carter was so-so on bass, and Haley didn't play anything. Kennedy sulked, then quit.

Carter had never understood boys. Not the way her sister and Haley had. Haley had had her red hair that said *look at me*, soft thighs with faded pen hearts and boys' names written on skin and showing through frayed jeans. She'd had full breasts she'd been unable to hide. Ryan Whittles and Ty Anderson had both dated Haley briefly—which meant walking through the hallway together at Liberty High, holding hands. Haley had said she gave her virginity to Ryan Whittles only for practice. *"Why him?"* Carter had said, repulsed.

"Because he's slept with everyone anyway so it almost doesn't count, and besides," Haley hissed with a rationale that was almost reasonable, "by the time I get to college I want to know what I'm doing."

Haley went to church every Sunday, but she said she could believe in God and still believe in pleasure. If she'd been a boy, Carter supposed, no one would have held arguments like that against Haley. But many things were held against her. Carter's own father learned to sling mud of that sort in the aftermath, and the press didn't shy away from the personal details.

By springtime in eleventh grade, Carter began to feel in a club all her own, the Virgo Intacta club, or some other less polite name, so she pierced her nose at a kiosk in the mall and made out on the quad after school with Isaac Richmond, who wore plaid pants and eyeliner, though he never brushed his hair. Even Kennedy hadn't made out with a boy who wore eyeliner yet. Isaac had cutouts from Nation of Ulysses zines pasted up in his locker. Carter hadn't known what a zine was until she talked to her and then she mispronounced it. She knew he was far too cool for her and had only deigned to speak to her because she and Kennedy had a band and had played an actual gig. He tasted like Gitanes and tongued her so aggressively she couldn't decide if she liked it, and when they parted ways she knew he'd never kiss her or talk to her again. Her stomach felt funny—half excitement and half nausea.

"Holy god, Isaac Richmond!" Haley screeched at Carter, grabbing her hands, but Kennedy rolled her eyes.

"He's a snob. *You can do better.*"

The second comment stung because it was something she herself had said to Kennedy only a couple weeks before when she'd met Berk.

She remembered how she and Kennedy used to sit in the hallway at school and judge the girls who walked past: guessing whether they were on the pill by the size of their boobs and their butts—as if they themselves were above everyone else somehow because they'd found ankh necklaces, applied questionable hair dye, and divined the deeper meaning of the Stone Roses.

When Kennedy picked out a large silver skull ring at the mall, Carter bought a heavy ring that featured theater masks, sad and happy. They had better jewelry at home: given to them by their mother, or aunts at Christmas. But they didn't want good jewelry. They wanted to distinguish themselves. It didn't seem to matter: people couldn't tell them apart anyway. With Haley, it was as if they'd found a triplet—a bright streak between them as the three sauntered down the halls of Liberty High. When they whispered their secrets now it was into Haley's ear, and a game of telephone began where the twins' communications could be mangled. But not completely understanding one another made sense in a way. It was as if the two of them had been too intense before Haley—a circuit that was always burning out.

Funny, Carter thought now, that such little things could divide them: whether they had sex, tried drugs, shoplifted, smoked cigarettes. Only a couple of years later, everyone, Carter especially, would do these things at college. But by the time school let out for summer, Carter was spending very little time with her sister and Haley.

CARTER REALIZED THEY'D STOPPED TALKING. They were both listening to the cassette.

"Do you want me to play it again?" Kennedy asked, and Carter laughed and said no.

Kennedy surprised her. "Dad is definitely drinking again."

"Is he okay for driving you around?" Carter asked. "You're going to need rides to work now."

There was a pause on the other end of the line. "I could take the bus. Or maybe you could pick me up sometime."

Carter felt a hard knot of dread in her stomach but wasn't sure if it was the idea of talking with Dead Kennedy, or because she was using the conversation as a way to avoid Everett: the desire to call him, the desire to go back there. She would have to go back for her Honda—tomorrow, probably. She couldn't push it longer than that.

When Carter didn't respond to the request for a ride, Kennedy gasped.

"What is that? That sound you're making?" Carter sat up on the bed, alarmed. She knew what it was: it was crying. "Stop it, Kennedy."

Kennedy sniffed. "I don't get it," she said into Carter's ear, sniffing back. "You don't come see me for half a year and then you accuse me—" She stopped talking. "And then you call me, but you don't want to be around me?"

Carter walked over to her dresser, where she stared down at a framed photo of Mayan ruins. A younger version of herself, sun pinkened, not quite smiling, in front of it. She and her roommate from the single year of college she had managed to complete had gone to Belize. It was just after Laine died and her friend had said it would be good for her. She stared at the photo. Carter remembered sitting every day on a beach and trying not to cry. At school that year, two hundred miles away from home, girls in the dorm asked about her parents; it was a regular small-talk question. She wasn't just Dead Kennedy's sister there, like she'd been in Blueheart, but no one could really fathom what it meant to watch a parent die at that young age, to hold the jaundiced hand or hear the last whispers. After the trip Carter began using: one pill popped in her mouth at an all-night dance party that showed her a world without death, or Wynns, which by then meant the same for Carter.

"I should have moved away," she said, aware she wasn't answering Kennedy's question. "Gone to a big city like New York, or overseas or something."

"Why didn't you?" Kennedy asked. "I told you hundreds of times that it would be better."

"It's hard to take the advice of someone in prison. I mean— Sorry."

She didn't have any photos of Everett. Now it was probably too late. Why hadn't she thought to take any? She should tell her sister. She should tell her about the relationship. About Gerry's finding the card in Everett's pocket. About all the pain that would be coming. She pulled at her hair until it hurt, then swooped it up into a makeshift bun.

When Kennedy spoke next Carter heard the hard edge creeping in. "You know, you're nice, but then you pull away. You don't get to punish me like this just because I'm your sister. You think I wanted to be the one to find her? You think I wanted to go to jail?"

"Of course not." She wanted to make Kennedy say it. She could hear the words on the tip of her tongue: *Say you didn't do it.* But she couldn't bring herself to ask a second time.

After Carter hung up the phone, she hurled the picture of her nineteen-year-old self at the wall. It hit and the glass scattered. Another thing to clean up.

The morning Kennedy had found Haley was the same morning they'd first learned about Laine's cancer. Kennedy had walked into Carter's room and found her crying, and later she said that she thought for a second Carter already knew about Haley.

Looking back, her dying mother and Haley were now entangled in her mind: her mother wrapping a crimson scarf around her thinning hair to sit through the preliminary hearing, and the photographs of dark red wounds, Haley's own hair brushed out by Kennedy's hand.

She looked at her cell phone for messages from Everett. No voicemail. No texts. She clicked open the sober app and saw the counter. Almost six months. The app provided a quote: *Nothing is so painful to the human mind as a great and sudden change.* She set down the phone and went to get the broom.

Chapter 16

T HE GAME WENT TO COMMERCIAL and Berk muted the volume. "Lions are playing like a bunch of ballerinas," he said, sipping his beer. The Lions weren't his team and it was more an attempt at small talk with his father than an expression of genuine despair. His father, Oz Butler, sat across from him in a matching recliner and said nothing in return, only nodded.

Oswald Butler had been a local celebrity in the years before Berk was arrested. Oz appeared in commercials for his own stores: a voluble figure describing weekly specials on honey hams and pecan pies, even enacting sketches where he was being committed or arrested for his crazy prices. Berk's arrest changed Oz, brought on the gravity of old age decades before it should have, and the commercials stopped. Berk remembered his father picking him up at the courthouse with three lawyers, one of them a former commonwealth attorney, and the swell of WASP hope making him burst into tears: Daddy was here. He'd make it all go away. But in the car on the way home there were no hugs or pep talks. Berk started to tell his father what he remembered of the night. Oz stopped him cold. "You don't remember a damn thing," his father commanded him.

That tone between them had stuck since, and Berk long ago had figured out why. Even after the murder charges were dropped, and his two-year possession sentence expunged, a part of his father still believed he did it. It was one of the reasons Berk had briefly considered going on the crime show—that and the hope of a payout. But since his meeting with Dee Nash, Serenity had convinced him that none of it would benefit him. Even though he'd kept many of the details from her, she was right: he'd only be exposed all over again. When the producer from *Crime After Crime* had called again he had slammed the phone down.

"Have you thought any more about the house?" Berk asked Oz. Outside Berk's house a *For Sale* sign had been swaying in the wind for months. The mortgage he'd taken for the three-thousand-square-foot monster was crippling, given his manager salary and empty trust fund, but it was the same size as his brother Wyatt's house, and that mattered.

Oz chortled. "Warned you. No such thing as a sweetheart deal. A bank don't send chocolates after the first year. They send the sheriff with a new lock."

As real estate brokers had turned Berk down—the McMansion was dead, they said—he'd turned to his family, offering to sell it for what he'd paid, just to get the hell out of the mortgage. He lived in the subdivision of Bittercress; he'd thought it was like Blueheart but apparently no potential buyers thought so.

"You helped Wyatt out this year," Berk whined. The game was back on but he left the volume off.

"Wyatt can afford his house."

After his sentence at Morgantown had ended, Berk had left his home city, like Kerouac, he thought, but for real and not like some poseur. Berk had been in prison after all. Club Fed, it was called, but it was still a prison. He promised his parents he would finish college but wanted to disappear for a year and wait for the Kennedy business to die down into forgetful politeness. His family agreed, but the one year turned into ten: tree planting in Washington (which he was fired from for being too high); teaching English in Taiwan (where he lied about his degree and was caught); card dealer school in Nevada (which turned out to be a scam). Each turn in his life made more of a mess of his résumé. Each new city was farther away from Haley, but he never stopped thinking about her: her smell, her body, his anger at the girls that night, and how stupid absolutely everything was in retrospect.

During that time Wyatt had taken over the family business, looked at the competition from Walmart, and made moves: he'd added pharmacies to the stores and ended racist hiring practices. Each Butler's location would serve its community, he pledged. Wyatt inherited the keys to the city. Berk got complaints about the okra.

"Where's Shiloh at?" Oz asked. Berk had been tasked with watching his daughter while Serenity went to the Butler's nearby for more Thanksgiving supplies. Oz doted on the girl and Berk knew he could always swing the family Thanksgiving to his place because of it.

"Probably in the doll room." Berk sighed as he stood up out of his recliner.

"*Probably* ain't the same as *sure*, so find her." Berk felt the absence of trust behind every word his family said to him.

Berk walked up the carpeted steps from the family room to the main entrance. "Shiloh," he said. There was no response. He went up another flight of stairs toward the bedrooms and Shiloh's playroom.

He had never connected his desire for this house with his memory of the summer of 1993, but the layout was a mirror of the Wynns' house, and made by the same developer.

He glanced into the doll room, which creeped him out on the best of days. The figures looked back at him. There were Bratz dolls, with their long hair and stiletto boots. There were at least forty Barbies of different vintages and baby dolls in tiny strollers. On a shelf across from the door, two Cabbage Patch dolls from the eighties caught his eye, their round plastic heads with loops of yarn hair, colorless smiles on doughy bodies. Serenity could sit on eBay like a tiger in the night. Berk vaguely remembered a doll like these at Kennedy's place the one or two times he'd been in her room. He'd teased her for still having kid stuff like that.

A large pink house with hinges stood in the middle of the playroom. When he walked behind it, expecting to find Shiloh crouched and moving small pieces of furniture around, there was no one there except an American Girl that looked uncannily like his daughter. The blond doll lay on its back staring up at him, her arms up over her head, her small jean skirt peeled back over her belly, exposing her. Shiloh wasn't in the room.

Berk took off as he went down again, toward the kitchen, shouting Shiloh's name.

Through the patio doors he saw Shiloh at the far end of the yard, the part that ran against the back of Blueheart Woods. She was talking with a red-haired woman and then, briefly, they held hands. A few people had stopped to look at the house since he'd put the sign up, but Thanksgiving Day was a bit rich for a browse, and why was she touching his kid?

He ran into the backyard in bare feet. "Can I help you?" he barked, sounding like the grocery store manager he was. She didn't look up when he called out. As he got closer he saw that the woman was only a girl. He realized she was in a yellow blouse.

"Haley?" he said as he stopped. The girl let go of Shiloh's hands, turned, and walked into the trees. He reached his daughter, crouched, and examined her.

"Who were you talking to? What did she say?" he yelled.

"I was just singing," Shiloh said, and then began to cry. He looked down and realized he had dug his thumbs hard into her shoulders in his panic.

Without thinking he picked Shiloh up and ran back to the house. As he brought her in, she was still howling.

"Everything all right up there?" Oz shouted from the sunken basement where the big screen was.

"We're okay," Berk shouted, but he didn't feel okay. His breath was still coming fast. He set her down on the kitchen counter. He lifted her chin with his finger, forced her to look him in the eye. "Tell me what really happened," he whispered. "I swear Daddy won't get mad."

She stared at him, still sniffling.

He quieted his voice. "Did that girl do anything to you?"

His daughter shook her head.

Berk grabbed a tea towel off the counter and mopped it along his hairline where he'd begun to sweat. "Don't tell anyone." He squeezed her against him until he heard Serenity come back in.

When his wife asked what was going on, Berk said that Shiloh had gone in the backyard by herself, given him a scare. Serenity glared at him like he was an idiot, but it was better than Oz's telling her.

Later, after the relatives had left and his wife was asleep, Berk went into the spare bedroom, opened the closet, and rummaged around. He pulled out what he called his "evidence." Proof, in his mind, of who Kennedy Wynn really was. Proof of what Haley looked like when his memory failed to revive her.

He looked at the pictures and compared her face with the face of the girl in the backyard. It couldn't be a ghost, he thought. Must have been some sick joke of Kennedy's. She'd probably paid some high school kid to dress up and come by. Someone who looked exactly like Haley the last night of her life.

Chapter 17

CARTER CALLED IN to the pharmaceutical advertising office where she temped and asked for a half day off. No text had come from Everett. She called and he didn't pick up. She tried to go get her car that morning, but when she came within view of the condo tower she began to tremble. She felt sick to her stomach. She went and stood at a bus stop, using her scarf to wipe her tears. *Just go get it*, she said to herself. But her body wouldn't move. An old man beside her offered her a handkerchief without speaking. It looked dirty and she didn't take it.

It wasn't just Everett or heartbreak she was afraid of—it was everything coming back. When the bus finally pulled up, she got on and rode, looking out the window, wiping her nose on a very old Kleenex that she'd scrounged from the bottom of her purse. The bus rattled past a florist shop, rows of glass, a sign that said *Vases on Sale*.

Carter had a flash, an image of Haley in her mind, a garage sale table in front of her strewn with knickknacks. Florist's vases. A macramé lampshade. A decorative bowl made from a coconut. Somebody's basement had clearly been rid of its lingering seventies and eighties paraphernalia. A box of games: Operation, Speak & Spell, a Donkey Kong board game, Bargain Hunter, Trivial Pursuit, Sorry!. A few Atari cartridges but no console. A ThighMaster. A wok. An old tape recorder. Kennedy had grabbed the recorder. Behind it was a wood-handled jackknife in a box, a four-inch blade. Haley picked it up, and Kennedy peered at it, said it was cool. Carter interjected that carrying a weapon was more dangerous than not having one. Haley said that she'd take it camping and bought it for five bucks. At the time, it bothered Carter that Haley seemed as though she'd do anything Kennedy said was cool.

She'd been Carter's friend first. Earlier that year, just after Carter got her license, they'd driven around in Laine's Taurus listening to the *Phantom of the Opera* soundtrack. Kennedy and Carter had seen it with their parents in New York at Christmastime the year before, and although Haley had never seen it, she'd learned all the words. She sang "Think of Me," changing the lyrics to "Think of me *fondling* . . . ," belting it at the top of her lungs with the windows open, making a diddling motion with her hand, one pinky out, but never losing the key through the other girls' giggles. Silly things like that.

Now, when Carter thought about the knife, she felt ill. She wondered if the universe had sent her a premonition, if she'd known something that day, when she told Haley not to buy it. She thought again of Kennedy stabbing the ground at the graveyard with the ornament stick.

———

WHEN SHE RETURNED TO WORK at noon everyone in the office was cold to her—although they were never warm. The real receptionist was on family leave and would be back in four more weeks. She heard another girl gossiping that if Carter was going to take mornings off, they could just pay *her* more and she'd gladly be the one to do the phones. She didn't know why they were being so grumpy about it. She had taken only a single sick day since she began. It was the first day back after Thanksgiving and everyone was gearing up for the December holiday parties and gearing down on work, anyway.

She worried their attitudes were because of the article that had appeared in the *Richmond Times-Dispatch* about Kennedy's release. Carter had seen it two weeks before, below the fold, her sister's Department of Corrections photo, their faces the same except for nature-versus-nurture differences: Kennedy's age-darkened hair and ghostly jail skin. Carter had stared at it, as if the words were foreign, before walking to the kitchen to get the Windex. She'd used the same newspaper to clean the bathroom mirror and every window in her apartment, rubbing until the black ink of her twin's sulky face smeared and beaded and surfaces came clean.

No one in the office had asked her directly whether she was related. Carter answered the phones, and sometimes she helped proofread name tags for medical conferences against a list, making sure the names of the doctors who'd registered to attend were correct. The foyer was filled with posters of drug company names floating on images of blue sky and clouds, or birds beside water—as if their products would put a person closer to nature somehow, lift them up. She needed medication. The irony of her present occupation wasn't lost on Carter.

She tried to work, but her thoughts were stuck on Everett, like a CD skipping. If Everett was intent on going on the show, doing this thing that he knew would hurt her family, why had he held her and rubbed her back like that? Why kiss her as he put her in the cab? Was that the ending—the last kiss, not even on the lips? It wasn't fair.

Carter left a message asking her therapist, Dr. Brathwaite, if she could have an emergency appointment after work that day. Was she in crisis? he asked when he phoned back.

"Yes," Carter breathed quietly into the phone. "But I mean, I'll be okay."

"I don't understand. Tell me what that means," Dr. Brathwaite said.

Carter sighed. She glanced around the foyer but half the staff was in a meeting and the others were cloistered in their offices on their own phones. "Well, I think I've been in crisis the whole time I've been seeing you. All fall at least."

She heard a long pause, then he said tentatively, "Okay," and she wondered how tightly controlled she'd kept herself. When they'd first started the sessions she'd told him she wanted to talk about the breakup with Alex and her sister's release, some depression. She had never mentioned Everett except in the past tense. Had she really not let him see how vulnerable she was?

PERSEVERANCE. Carter stared at the word on the poster in her therapist's office.

"I think I had a series of panic attacks," she told Dr. Brathwaite, not looking at him out of shame. "I left my car in a parking lot. I honestly don't know when I can make myself go and get it." Not to mention everyone at work was treating her weird—so far it was just the one article about her sister's release, and it was small. Would there be more? she worried. She took a breath, looked down at her lap, her hands, which she'd scrunched up in knots around each other. "I think I need medication for anxiety."

Dr. Brathwaite leaned forward and said, "Let's break this down. Where is the car and what happened just before?"

Carter's heart pounded and she thought she might be sick as she stared at the large area rug that covered most of the room. It was patterned with lime-green and gray diamonds. "I'm sleeping with someone."

"This is an ongoing relationship?" Dr. Brathwaite's voice was steady even though this was obviously something Carter had omitted in their sessions.

Carter wouldn't look at him. She explained it had been maybe serious, maybe not, for a while—and how the day before he'd told her about his intent to see the investigation reopened.

Dr. Brathwaite didn't dwell on the particulars but got right to the important thing. "This person . . ."

Carter dug her fingernails into her palms until there were crescent-moon marks left on her skin as she unfolded them. "The brother. Haley Kimberson's brother."

Dr. Brathwaite didn't speak for several moments. She thought he might be silently going through the stages of therapist disbelief, first thinking, *What the hell just came out of this fucked-up girl's mouth?* before arriving at something speakable to a patient. He made a slight humming noise in his throat. "It's possible you went to him for forgiveness."

"But why? I only knew him when he was eight or nine, a kid. And mostly his sister spent time at our house. It was one of those fast, intense friendships with Haley. I got to know her in history class, and then Kennedy had to be friends with her too, she had to see what I saw in her, if you know what I mean? Haley was smart, funny, serious, and wild. They had eleventh-grade English together. Kennedy made the teacher move their desks next to each other. That was how the whole *Jane Eyre* thing started."

Dr. Brathwaite didn't ask what Carter meant by "the *Jane Eyre* thing" so she assumed that like everyone, he'd read about the crime—that it wasn't just the two of them in the room, as he'd always said. The media was there too, even if silently.

"I ran into Everett when I was out for dinner with Alex. Even before I knew I was going to break up with Alex. He took me to Heritage, of all places."

It seemed odd to Carter that anyone could name a restaurant that, but Alex had made the reservations. The Wynns had come from Ohio originally, and even though Kennedy and

Carter had been born in Virginia, they were still treated like outsiders. *Heritage*: it was a word the South used to divide the *us*es from the *them*s. The Wynns were well-off, but they weren't among the generations-deep white families of the city. She remembered that a strange number of the newspaper articles surrounding Kennedy's arrest contained the detail that the Wynns were from Ohio, as if to say "not us."

Heritage hadn't exactly delivered a romantic evening. Alex complained about the prices, and by the time the mains came he proposed that they should move in with Gerry to save money until he got work again. He had a big empty house, Alex pointed out, more than anyone needed.

"Some houses are empty for a reason," Carter told him. She excused herself to the bathroom, but when she got up she went directly to the bar.

Carter didn't recognize Everett until they'd already started a conversation. She remembered his face that night—before she realized who he was. She saw a man in a well-fitting gingham shirt, laughing with his friends. His head was tipped back. He looked beautiful. Later she'd learn they were celebrating his move into his new condo.

He glanced over, once or twice. During a lull in his conversation with friends he walked to her end of the bar. "Can I buy you a drink? You look like you need one."

"Yes, I do," she said. She didn't wait for him to introduce himself. She remembered the singing of the glass as the bartender took it down from the shelf. One. She'd allow herself that. Gin, lime, tonic. She clinked against his beer. She put her lips on the rim and swallowed.

"You should know, this drink's extra forbidden for me," Carter said, and when he asked why that was, she set her glass down, already half-empty. "It's been two years, but I think it's going to be worth it."

He smiled and spread his hand over the glass to pull it away. He reached over the bar and dumped it down the sink. "I wouldn't be a gentleman if I was the one responsible for that."

Carter looked at him. The man was younger than her. She felt foolish.

"Some people in my family are in the program," he said.

"You're right. I should probably go." She glanced over at the table where she had left Alex. He was still sitting with his back to her. He was staring into his iPhone. He hadn't even noticed how long she'd been gone.

"You didn't do nothing wrong, Carter."

He knew her name, but she hadn't said it. Carter's body sank away from his. She nodded, began to turn, and accepted it was her yearly public shaming as a Wynn. He placed a hand on her shoulder. Carter paused and he said, "I knew who you were when I came over. And you know who I am. No reason to let that ruin a good talk though."

She looked again. She hadn't seen him in years. He had gone from being a child, four feet tall and shrill voiced, to a man: handsome, tall, well built, leaning on the bar.

Carter finally saw Haley's green eyes, although she realized a part of her had sensed his familiarity, the same way she knew what Kennedy was thinking before she said it. It wasn't a psychic connection, as people liked to think, so much as the patterns of human thought, behavior. There were things you could feel in a person, not unlike when you stepped outside and could tell it would turn colder, or rain, by feeling the moisture in the air or looking at the sky.

Everett leaned in. How gently he grazed her lips with his, both their eyes open, like he was asking permission. He put his hand on her jaw but didn't deepen it, just held Carter there, their two breaths meeting. She was the one who grabbed him and put her tongue in his mouth as if she'd been waiting for this. They kissed for about a minute and then he pulled away.

"How's that for forbidden?" he asked.

Chapter 18

GERRY DROVE DOWNTOWN because he liked the old cobblestone streets of Shockoe Bottom. Sometimes he went to see a movie or a show. Sometimes he had lunch, or a beer. He would pressure old colleagues to meet; a few times, he'd managed to convince his decorator, Laura, though he knew she only humored him in the hope of future business—anyone he could use as an excuse to go there.

Today he and Kennedy went to the Civil War Museum. She hadn't wanted to come—she was to start her first shift that night at the call center. But he'd convinced her she had time. He paid for them, as if she were still a child. Then she walked off and didn't stay near him. So what? He could stand in the cool, dark silence, spend an hour staring at the worn and wrinkled boots of dead soldiers, their feet almost child sized, some of the shoes no bigger than his hand; they'd only been boys. How had they died? Their boots were still black with polish, and their kraft-brown uniforms were ripped where they must have been penetrated by bullet or bayonet, the chests of the mannequins only ten or twelve inches across.

No one knew him here, and even though he'd lived in the city or just outside it for thirty years, he would never run into anyone he knew. Only tourists, with their chattering, their surprised hush as they came to exhibits they didn't expect. Gerry and Laine had moved to the South from Cleveland and never quite understood this place's obsession with saying there were two sides to the story, with reliving the battles.

He'd watched the reenactments in the park when he was younger, but the girls were never interested. Even Carter, though she had excelled at history, had been happier to go to the tours that included shops or candle dipping, or old-fashioned homemade ice cream. War seemed less important than silk ribbons or basket weaving. This was the life of a father of girls, he told himself. And now, fifty-seven and alone, he had no one to please. He could read every plaque, stand before pictures of Gatling guns and warships, linger as he liked. He supposed Kennedy would come find him when she was ready.

He dawdled in front of a display of revolvers, looking at their rounded wood handles. These had killed people. Here was one: a weapon that was both pistol and blade—a smooth, frightening transition to a thick, flat knife similar to the kind a hunter would use. Could it be considered a bowie knife? Gerry wondered. Gerry stared at it until he could imagine the blood on it, and a shiver ran through his whole body. He seldom thought about violence.

Kennedy found him. "They're rewriting history," she said sheepishly, her smile pale.

He'd noticed she never wore makeup now even though

Carter had bought it for her and stocked the bathroom. When she was young her lips had always been painted, from thirteen on. He still thought she was beautiful, in a way, but prison had taken the girl out of her. Now she was beautiful like a statue was. He felt a pang of regret, as he often did, for who she might have become.

"They're not mourning lives. They're mourning a way of life built around slavery," she insisted.

"Yeah, well, the boots got to me," Gerry said. "Can we agree on the boots?"

After, they emerged into the afternoon, and Gerry stood for a minute, letting his eyes adjust to the daylight. It was overcast but seemed bright, comparatively, after being indoors. He clipped a pair of shades onto his glasses and said, "Let's walk a bit. A lot has changed. I'll show you." As they hiked up cobble-stone streets, he said there was no point in living somewhere this physically beautiful if you didn't get out to see it.

But physical beauty perplexed him more and more with each day. Filling out his green polo sweater, he panted. Looking down, he thought his gut had become more rotund. That must have been why his heart raced. Why he sweated from the hairline, from his armpits beneath the London Fog jacket that Carter had dutifully given him last Christmas. He could smell himself, even in the cool November air, and still he strode forward.

The condo tower was located between expressways and along the river. You couldn't get there by accident. At the same time, you couldn't ignore it. It was taller than the other buildings and its surface shone, all glass and steel. It was like an ostentatious gem on the finger of a recently engaged woman.

"You see this? Only been here a few years," he said, pointing. He stopped and Kennedy did too. She didn't look very interested as she glanced up at the condo tower. It was just a condo tower to her. "I own one of these units."

"You do?" Kennedy looked confused. She stared up at the building and he could see her puzzling over why her father would have a second place.

He grinned lopsidedly. "Sure. That Kimberson lives there."

Gerry didn't know which unit belonged to Kimberson. Half the time he couldn't remember the boy's first name. What he saw when he looked at the building was money, his money, and lost opportunity. When he looked up at it—it was almost indigo the way it mirrored the sky—he experienced a pain like running one's finger over a violent bruise.

He'd meant it as a joke but there was an edge in Kennedy's voice when she said, "Why do you know that?" She was already turning around to go back the way they'd come.

Since Kennedy had come home, he'd remembered more of that time—the way he would enter the kitchen slowly on those long-ago mornings and breathe easier when he saw Carter or Kennedy, not Laine, standing at the kitchen counter. His gaze had always flitted to their hair before he spoke, uncertain even after years beside them which daughter was in front of him. It didn't matter because he hadn't known what to say to either of them. Kennedy would rail about current events in an insubstantial and idealistic way, and he didn't have the strength to disagree, knowing it usually led to his being called a planet killer, a racist, or *the patriarchy itself.* He'd felt distant and un-moored and ultimately useless that year.

It had only been a few weeks now, but each day felt extraor-dinarily long and the hours between them filled with small talk and silence. He hadn't realized how silent prison would make Kennedy—sometimes he thought it was her manner, other times that she had nothing to say quite simply because life had not begun for her yet. He was intensely proud of her, the way she'd held up through the years, but he couldn't express it—and he could see she didn't want him to. The girl held herself with reserve. She'd always been harder than Carter, more likely to put her emotions into a physical outlet, like running, which she had started to do every day. Meanwhile, he knew he had a tendency to ramble, but even he couldn't fill up every meal.

Gerry didn't follow her. Kennedy walked along the canal and sat down on a bench, peering at the water as if there might be fish. It was a perfectly reasonable place to bring his daughter for a walk. She could see that; that was why she'd sat down. He put his hands in his pockets. He tried whistling but it only made him self-conscious. A woman with a little girl passed him. They looked at him like he was a kind old man. The wife had an expression of gentle pity. Women looked at him like this more and more now, he'd noticed. It was the stupid raincoat, he was sure. The comfort shoes. When he'd had his own law firm, he'd had the best business suits, and women were helpless then. They'd practically swooned before him. Flirting at work had been as common then as turning on a light switch.

Perhaps he and Laine should have separated in the early eighties, when many of their generation started to split up, when they would have still been young enough to go on. It was just a marriage that had become like a long sigh. In the aftermath, it was easy to forget that they were faithful to each other for sixteen or more years. It was only that spring they both began to wake up infuriated, the first breath of morning sucked in with ire. If it hadn't been for the cancer, there would have been a divorce. But she'd spared him the mess and the money and died instead. He had mourned her, in his way. Certainly he had missed her over the years.

Gerry glanced at Kennedy and saw she'd taken out a cigarette and was smoking, one hand dangling between her knees. Although she was only five foot four, she sat like a basketball player on the bench. Her moods worried him constantly, even if he pasted on a smile. Carter tolerated him but would never forgive him. After the separation she'd gone to live with Laine in an apartment for a few months—as if they could afford to rent another place on top of everything else—had heard all the stories of the marital discord over tea late at night in what he imagined must have been a tiny, dark kitchen. All the while, Laine growing frail, her eyes yellowing and her hands iridescent as a spider's web. There was no way Carter could see Gerry as sympathetic after that. He knew that. She had become Laine's, and Kennedy was his, even if she rebelled against the fact. That was why he had to focus on Kennedy, keep himself in her favor.

He stared up at the glassy building.

"We had something once, I'm sure of it," he said aloud, knowing she heard even if she didn't respond. "Now Kimberson has it—he and his mother. That poor woman, listening to every ambulance chaser."

Gerry had hired the best appellate lawyers. He'd never given up the fight for Kennedy. He put a private investigator on that monster Berkeley Butler every couple of years to see if he messed up. A part of him felt for the Kimbersons. He did. They'd lost a daughter but they'd also been seduced. A poor family looking for money, seizing upon it, as if the crime weren't already being paid for in years, as if their ship had finally come in. It wasn't even about money; it was about pride, or the lack of it.

Gerry turned and walked back to Kennedy. He could see by her face she had heard him. She gave him an owlish glare and he was surprised to realize she'd thinned and become more muscular even in the short period of time she'd been home. She stood and they began walking back toward the car.

"You don't have to be angry with them on my behalf, Dad."

"Sure, sure," he acknowledged. "When did you start smoking?" He attempted a tone of light concern rather than badgering dad.

"I try not to," she said, crushing the cigarette butt between her fingers and putting the stub in her coat pocket. The move confused Gerry until he remembered. His beautiful girl had spent her youth in prison.

Gerry drove around several blocks, pointing out other landmarks to Kennedy as though she were a tourist, then wound down by the condo again. He couldn't help himself; a part of him wasn't done. He felt his heart speed up again, erratically, he might have said, but perhaps that was just his driving as he braked for speed bumps. He knew Kimberson's Mustang was usually parked in spot C7. But as he approached he saw today a different vehicle, similar to Carter's. A blue Honda Fit, backed into the spot facing outward. He was already past it by the time he thought to slow.

"I don't think you can go this way, Dad. It's a dead end," Kennedy said.

"Goddamn." *And goddamn Kimberson, probably running out and buying it to try to look like us,* he told himself as he pulled into a tight parking space to use for turning around. *These Longwood people. If they don't know what taste is, they watch someone else, then mimic.*

Gerry backed out again and drove through the lot. As he approached the Fit he let his own vehicle come to a crawl. There, in a green rectangle of sticker on the front bumper: *100% Vegetarian.*

He stopped and let his car idle in front of Carter's. She wasn't in it. He looked up through his windshield at the building. It was a Monday at one o'clock, a time she ought to have been at work. It was a large building. Perhaps she had another friend who lived here. After all, she and Alex used to live close enough to there, and her apartment now wasn't that far away; it wasn't unreasonable to think she might. Another car pulled up behind him and honked. Gerry accelerated out of the lot. No, he realized, she was in C7, Kimberson's spot. It was no coincidence.

He felt the hair rise on his neck. The business card he'd mined from that blazer pocket at Carter's—it was Kimberson's.

He glanced over at Kennedy but her face was blank. After they'd left the downtown and gotten onto the expressway Gerry finally spoke, almost to himself: "She wouldn't lie to me. Not about this."

"About what?" Kennedy asked.

"Nothing." He accelerated.

Chapter 19

G RAB ANY FREE DESK," Kennedy's supervisor told her, gesturing to the row of cubicles where her coworkers sat, side by side and back-to-back, wearing headsets. The small room hummed with voices reciting scripts, the dull rhythm of the words like the throb of an ocean.

Kennedy thanked him and walked down the row. She started to sit down between a black woman in a tight blouse and a white guy in glasses.

She felt a tug on her jacket and turned.

"Sit there if you like, but I should tell ya that Giselle likes that spot empty and Jon there's a registered sex offender."

Kennedy looked at the sex offender, who stared at her without any emotion, as if he hadn't heard what had been said about him, though clearly he had.

The dark-haired guy who'd tugged her coat nodded to a free seat beside himself. "I'll give you no problem—if you don't own an ABC store or a Butler's we should be all right. I'm Nathan Doyle."

Kennedy decided to sit down at the offered carrel beside him, and he stuck out a hand to shake.

Kennedy looked at the large knuckles. His hoodie sleeves were pushed up and there was a Calvin and Hobbes tattoo on his forearm. Judging by his age, he couldn't have had it more than ten years, though the ink had settled into his skin as if it had been birthed there, not placed there. He had the kind of carved musculature one only got from working out for hours on the yard, but his clothes were oversized, as if he didn't care enough to show it off. His dark hair was shaggy and he looked like he hadn't shaved that week. Below thick eyebrows, his brown eyes were unblinking. In a breath, she got the impression he'd looked at every awful thing life could throw at him and found it as tame as a kitten.

"Got a name?" Nathan asked. He shook the hood back onto his shoulders.

Kennedy smiled. She put her phone script in front of her and turned on her computer. She didn't want to let Nathan know he'd made her speechless just by looking at her. The last time a man had looked at her that way she hadn't even been of age. Now that she was, she could see how dangerous it could be, what it could lead to. As the screen flickered to life, he made a call.

"Hello, I'm phoning today to ask if y'all might be interested in donating to the policeman's ball? Yes, ma'am, I understand, but just so you know: your gift directly supports the families of law enforcement officers who have made the ultimate sacrifice."

Nathan leaned back in the chair as he spoke, keeping his tone warm and low. He winked at Kennedy as he said *ultimate sacrifice*.

While he worked the woman on the line toward a donation she clearly didn't want to give, Kennedy glanced at his black cargo pants beneath the table, a pair of black Nikes.

"Pop quiz," she said as he clicked off. "Who was our thirty-fifth president?"

He tipped his head back, stared at the ceiling. "I don't know, Roosevelt? Later? Nixon? Don't really matter when neither of us can vote."

She smiled. "Kennedy. That's me."

"Whatcha doin' here, Kennedy?"

Behind them, Giselle grumbled, "That's all right. Keep talking."

Kennedy glanced at Giselle, then scrolled through a list of phone numbers on the screen. She dropped her voice to a whisper. "Why don't you let me make my first call before you start asking the intimate questions?" When he raised an eyebrow, she explained, "It's kind of like asking, 'Where did your whole life go wrong?'"

"I guess. But only if you think one direction is better than another." Below a nose that looked like it'd been broken at least once, he had a wide smile full of sharp canines.

Suddenly she wanted to feel his teeth against her skin. Her lips felt as though they were stinging. She itched all over. She felt parched and thirsty. A feeling pooled low in her abdomen, as though she were carrying something heavy there, a desire she'd been lugging around for years. She wanted to get out of there, and they had five hours before the shift would end, and then her father was coming to pick her up and drive her back to that awful house. How could she sit here in a packed room and make calls to strangers, keep her voice steady and read the lines?

She knew that whenever she and Nathan Doyle had the opportunity to get out of there, he would do what she said, take her wherever she asked, and allow her requests.

NATHAN HAD A GUN on his hip. Black ink. The handle showing above the waistband of his jeans. She ran one finger over it where they lay on his bed. His hipbone was a scallop under the surface. He twitched as if Kennedy had tickled him and grabbed her wrist. He looked at her, let it go.

When they'd first come into his place, he'd put a CD on, something metal with guitars and drums so fast it became a wash of sound and air, like being under a waterfall. He'd moved faster than she expected, snatching at her clothes as if they were bothering him, tossing them aside. She almost hadn't minded. His hands were callused and rough—a man's hands. A decade and a half ago, the last time a male had touched her, it had been with warm, smooth boy fingers. Sitting next to Nathan Doyle for three evening shifts in a row had been the foreplay; fourteen years of incarceration had been the foreplay, she'd told herself. What she couldn't have guessed was the rush she'd get from clinging to his muscled frame, his smoky scent, his movements, his scruffy mouth on hers. She'd always thought she would want to be adored, and instead she felt her fingertips flicking over his shoulders, neck, adoring him.

Kennedy looked around now for something to put on and threw on the hoodie he'd worn earlier. She zipped it up. Her legs were shaky, and she felt raw inside, strangely triumphant, like she'd left Berk Butler behind at last. Nathan told her to go ahead if she wanted to get herself cleaned up. He was twenty-nine, a man who came and went but obviously mostly went. The maltreated apartment above Extreme Pizza showed it. As Kennedy walked through the main room, she realized she'd never been in a dwelling that had absolutely no reading material before. In high school, even the Kimberson house had been strewn with celebrity magazines and romance novels—the kinds of things Laine and Gerry Wynn didn't allow.

When she returned to the bedroom, Nathan was smoking, sitting on the edge of the mattress, his naked back to the room, the window cracked for her benefit. She gestured with her hand and he passed her the cigarette. She took a drag and gave it back.

"Did you really pull a job on a Butler's?" She lay down on the bed behind him.

"Wasn't so hard. Hard part was surveillance footage. They picked me up two days later."

She almost said she had known a Butler when she was a kid. A *kid*. It surprised her that that was the word that came to her mind. But she hesitated to reveal that she'd known Berk. To admit that one fact was to admit everything. "That family's fucked up," she said instead.

Their name appeared in the paper regularly and everyone knew at least something about the Butlers.

"True that." Nathan stubbed the cigarette into an ashtray and inched down onto the bed next to her. She leaned her head against his shoulder. There was a blurry clock with no hands on it, a prison tat, on his biceps. But an expertly done tattoo-parlor rose unfolded black petals over his heart. His body was a visible mesh of hard and good times. "You come from nice people," he said gently.

"What? No," she scoffed, nosing against his chest. He put a hand on her hair.

"I can tell. You come from someplace. You're tough, but you have grace." He turned his face and looked at her with those intense dark eyes. He took her by the chin with one thumb and finger and kissed her. She felt embarrassed by her emotions. When he'd been inside her she'd felt as if she'd burst from both happiness and shame.

He said she must have been young when she went in, and she said yes but not to be mistaken, she hadn't been that inexperienced.

"Lotta time," he pressed. "What'd you do, kill someone?"

Kennedy could see by his face he was kidding. Still she pulled away from him, unzipped his sweatshirt, and found her own clothes on the floor. She didn't say anything and pulled on her pants.

"I tell ya though: from the outside that Butler's store sure shone. White-gold in the dark. And I wanted it, I had to have it, you know what I mean?"

Kennedy nodded her head, wondering which location he'd robbed and whether Berk had been working there. She put on her shoes, combed her hair with one hand. "I was high. I've never known what I did," she said.

"Honest to god?"

She smirked and asked if he believed in God.

He leaned forward and pointed to his back, where Gothic lettering spelled out *Apostate* across his shoulder blades. "Used to be an altar boy, until I got caught hocking the chalices."

"I was near the place it happened. I found her. I moved her. And I didn't tell, not when I should have. I was scared."

"That ain't good. But killing someone? I've known some who have. Seems to me you ain't likely to forget it."

Kennedy considered it. "Haley had a few boyfriends. It could have been one of them, but that whole night—it's like trying to remember what happened in a dream from fifteen years ago. One of them is stalking me. I don't know if he wants me to talk or not talk. He was always an idiot."

"Who is he?"

She brushed her hair with her fingers, then slid her arms into her jacket. "You'd know the name."

Nathan sat up and pulled Kennedy to him by her army jacket collar. He put his tongue in her mouth, his beard bristles on her lips. Even though she needed to call a cab, she lingered. "You're sweet, Kennedy. I don't see it."

She picked up her purse and said she hoped he was right.

Chapter 20

GERRY POURED HIMSELF a scotch and carried it up to his office. He'd set a daily limit and stuck to it most of the time. It was part of the agreement he'd made with himself after his first coronary episode a few years back. Nonetheless, he loved the first few sips: that unfolding flavor of woody caramel with a hint of floor wax. He wanted to be ready to pick Kennedy up if she called after work. She kept insisting on taking the bus, saying she wanted to live a "normal life," whatever that was—but usually he would push and she would eventually accept his ride. In those moments, he felt a quiet triumph. He enjoyed the peaceful rides, her looking out the window. He enjoyed the feeling he could do something for her.

When she was a teenager too, giving the girls rides had meant winning their loyalty. He could recall picking Kennedy, Carter, and Haley up from the school. Kennedy had been in the front seat, and she was the one to ask him to find a job for Haley—it was clear they'd hatched a plan before he came, and worked up to their ambush. He'd said he had no room at his firm for an intern. He'd called up Doug Macaulay. Doug had said he could find room in his office, and the school was thrilled. They'd never placed a student alongside a paralegal. A couple weeks later he'd stopped in at Macaulay's to drop off contracts and it turned out to be her first day: Haley begged him not to tell the twins how she dressed "at work." He'd looked at her plain navy slacks and white blouse, exactly right for the law office. Her orange hair was plaited into one twisting rope down her back. "You look like a young Hillary Clinton," he said, and she blushed. She'd go far, he remembered thinking. He'd wished his daughters had the same drive.

He shook the memory away. He was glad Kennedy was working, even if he had some concerns about what type of people she'd meet at the call center. She was his responsibility, like Haley had been when he put her into that adult environment, he thought, swirling the scotch, watching how the alcohol whispered its shape to the glass.

As he'd thought many times, Kennedy was his; Carter was lost to him—especially if her car's being parked in Kimberson's spot meant what he thought it did. Gerry began to feel his temperature rise and he took another swig of his drink. It melted the anger.

He could probably have two drinks, he reasoned, since Kennedy's shift went all the way until ten. He sipped the scotch, savoring it, telling himself to make it last, just in case he needed to drive later. He opened the top drawer of his desk and felt around under some CDs for the note. It wasn't there.

That was right; he had moved it. He went to the closet. Inside, behind the vacuum cleaner and some old suits, was a panel. The bathroom was adjacent. The closet panel led into the water heater for the shower, and the only reason to ever open it was to make repairs. He flicked the latch and pulled the plywood off. His fingers found the book and he yanked it out, already feeling warm. The note was inside the cover where he'd put it. He replaced the panel, flicked the latch closed again, and carried the book and note over to his desk.

The one-inch-by-one-inch note was written on ordinary notepaper in the rotund flourishes of a teenage girl's hand-writing.

Gerry opened it and reread it. He ran his hand over the page. When he'd finished, he refolded it carefully—he only struggled a little, but the folds had been there for years and that made it easier to feel which way the paper should go.

If investigators had found it at the time, it might have exonerated his daughter. He wondered if Kennedy had seen it and forgotten in the chaos that came. More likely it had been placed there and never found. But what was done was done. It did her little good now and therefore he had no intention of showing her. It was better for both of them to keep the past in the past. She was doing well, he told himself. Slowly she was moving into a life.

He put aside the note. The book cover was silver and embossed with a single word: *Sex*. He flipped it open to one of his favorite pages. *I'll teach you how to fuck,* it said in large letters. The opposite page showed the blonde in leather, sitting on a stool, her legs spread slightly, one hand between them over the body armor that covered her. Her nipples peeked through holes in the bustier. Below a black silk mask that mostly hid her eyes, she sucked defiantly on her middle finger.

He would bet his life on the fact that neither daughter remembered his confiscating the Madonna book from them. Not considering everything that had happened since. Laine had been furious to discover the twins had it—*It portrays gangbangs, and skinheads*, she'd whispered, though she'd been afraid to take it from them because she didn't want them to know she had snooped, had read something about the breaking of trust between parents and children. Nonetheless, she worried they must have forged IDs to get it. Gerry had waved his hand; ridiculous, he said. He knew how kids operated. They'd probably convinced someone else, some boy, to buy it for them. Laine wanted them to find a way to ask the girls without a terrible confrontation, but Gerry just walked into Kennedy's bedroom and demanded it flatly. The girls provided the explanation. An older boy they knew who was gay had lent it to them. Robin, Gerry suspected, the one from church who hung around and played the keyboards with them. But the girls wouldn't say, they only pleaded for him to give it back. Otherwise they would owe the boy fifty dollars.

"Who do you owe fifty dollars?" Gerry asked, wanting them to sputter out the boy's name so he could feel he'd won, but the girls wouldn't tell.

"What are you going to do with it?" Carter asked, practically in tears.

Gerry had flipped it open in front of them and leafed through the pages. Pin-up shots of the pop star in a bra, naked

on the beach, in garters, examining herself while kneeling with
a mirror. That was the tame stuff. Then the skinheads. So
many skinheads. A muscular man on a leash licking her fish-
nets. Photographs of her tied to a chair, tonguing other women
who were pierced, tattooed.

"No, Dad!" Kennedy pleaded.

"Don't look!" Carter screamed.

"This is just trash. Tell your friend it was destroyed," Gerry
said, and left the room. Later, he'd asked Laine if this was what
was in women's minds.

"Not mine," she said, though he'd suspected as much.

What had the girls felt when looking at it? Horror, revul-
sion, or secret intrigue, the hot rush of excitement? Gerry wondered if it had been passed among other hands, imagined a
whole group of teenagers with the material, giggling. But no,
Gerry had thought, there were some things that Kennedy and
Carter kept to themselves. As much as they drew the world in,
the bond between them also kept it out.

When his wife had asked later what happened to the book,
he'd coughed and said that he threw it in the garbage.

But something about the book had captivated him. Everything was in black and white, as if it were art. He couldn't
shake the idea that thousands of kids had bought the book,
hidden it from their parents—that he and Laine and their
whole generation had missed out on something. Something
wild and dangerous. The boomers had invented rock and roll,
and yet what had they ever really tried? He had ridden on a
motorcycle once—one time—but he had never tied his wife to

the bed and spanked her. He wondered now if it would have made any difference. The cover was starting to come off the spiral binding and he had to turn the pages slowly. He stared at a picture of Madonna surrounded by men who were outfitted in women's nylons and heels. It did nothing for him. He flipped to ones of her in the leather bustier. She looked afraid, enraptured, angry. She looked like no one in Blueheart Woods. He stared at her breasts threatening to pop from the thin, slick fabric.

He remembered breasts under his hands, all sorts of breasts he had known, of different sizes and calibers, their nipples dark brown or pale pink or even hovering reddish, poking from cotton, polyester, knits, sheer blouses—it didn't matter. Each was as lovely as the moon in the moment. He reached down below the desk, felt himself over the top of his pants.

The light stopped him. For a second, it seemed as if the hallway grew brighter, his office darker. She passed by the open doorway.

He sprang to his feet.

At first he thought it was Kennedy, that she must be there, but he knew that wasn't true. She was at work. And the hair— the hair was red. It was a young girl, he saw that clearly. She walked at an ordinary pace and was past the doorframe in a second. Gerry called out, "Kennedy? Kennedy?!"

He stood listening, his heart racing. He couldn't hear anything.

The light in the hall looked normal now. Perhaps it was just a blink, a stutter of the light. Some kind of surge. He'd set the alarm downstairs, he recalled, when he'd come back in from dropping his daughter at the call center. It was something he'd been doing in the evenings since Kennedy got out—a bit afraid that having her here might bring them unwanted attention. He downed the rest of his scotch and grabbed a design magazine his decorator had gifted him, *Coveted*, depicting a large, immaculate bed and a pair of club chairs in pale tones. He threw it on top of *Sex* to hide it. No one could come upstairs without walking past his office first, he reasoned. Even though she knew the alarm code, Kennedy couldn't have come in. He would have seen her. It was as if the girl had been in his bedroom all along and walked from there past the office and guest bedroom, which were across the hall from each other.

"You must be drunk," Gerry told himself as he edged around the desk toward the hall to assess the situation. It was possible his tolerance for alcohol had gone down since he'd cut back. He placed a hand on the doorframe and leaned out. There was nothing, no one. In stocking feet, he stepped from the carpeted office onto the hardwood and started down the hall to look into Kennedy's room. He tried the knob, then pushed the door back hard. It hit the wall with a *thunk*. She'd left a light on, but the room was empty. He felt something cold and looked down. His sock was wet. He leaned one hip against the wall, pulled his leg up, knee out, peeled off the wet sock. Had he sloshed his drink on the way up earlier? It hadn't been that full, he told himself. He turned his head. Farther down the hallway were droplets, a streak of brown, dirty water, like something tracked in from outside.

There was a loud clatter that seemed to come from the kitchen and Gerry straightened. He stepped back into his office and grabbed the first thing that looked like a weapon. It was a large glass decanter. It was a fifteenth-wedding-anniversary present, given right before the marriage began to shatter. He and Laine had never believed in guns, though now suddenly he wished he had one. He took a breath and forced himself back out into the hallway and down the stairs to the main floor, holding the decanter up, ready to swing and crack it across a face should anyone emerge.

"I've called 911," he shouted, though his voice was not loud enough to carry through the whole downstairs. He could hear his own terror, scratchy in his throat. He *should* have called the police, he realized as soon as he said it, if he really did believe there was an intruder.

By the time Gerry had made his way through the dining room, he could see there was no one in the kitchen. A wooden block of knives that normally sat on the marble island had been knocked over, and they shone all over the floor. He stood still, staring at them, Wüsthof, the black handles, long blades like mirrors. His gaze went to the patio doors that led out to the Japanese garden, but they were shut and locked. He ought to have sensor lights installed, he realized. It would be easy for someone to come through the back of the property.

Setting the decanter down, Gerry stooped, armed himself with the largest of the knives, and circled through the other rooms. In spite of the disturbance he didn't really believe there was anyone in the house but him. He knew what he'd seen in the blink of an eye but didn't want to admit it: it was Haley. She'd been wearing the outfit she died in, mud-smeared garments they'd all seen in the crime photos.

Gerry picked up the knives in the kitchen. When he had put them all back in the block, there was one missing. He couldn't think why. He checked the sink and the dishwasher. Perhaps Kennedy had taken it. There was nothing really there to say he'd seen a ghost. The house could have shifted. Kennedy could have left the knife block askew on the counter. Or maybe he had moved it himself when he took the scotch out of the cupboard, he reasoned. Since he tried to ration himself on the hard stuff, he didn't like keeping it within easy reach. The water in the upstairs hall could have been tracked in earlier, or just a spill from his drink, like he'd already told himself. He sat down at one of the island stools.

A ghost of a girl. What was he, fourteen years old? It was just his guilt manifesting from looking at that dirty book. Anyway, he hadn't thought of Haley Kimberson in years. He thought of his own girls, the impact it had all had on them. He thought of Marly and Ted Kimberson and the boy and how they behaved afterward.

The telephone rang, and Gerry startled. His arm shot out and knocked his drink, but he grabbed it again and it didn't spill or topple. He picked up. It was Kennedy.

"Some people here are going for pizza after shift. I'll get a cab. Be there in a bit."

"Okay, darling. Hurry home," he said, feeling a genuine need to see her, to have someone else there with him.

"You sound— Are you okay?" she said, and he realized he was out of breath.

"I was worried."

"Don't be."

Gerry went upstairs to squirrel away the Madonna book. As he trudged back through the hall where he'd seen the ghost, if that was indeed what it was, he felt cold and his fingers trembled again.

He stood staring at the hall light, as if it might glint bright again, wondering if it really had. He put the book away and then hurried into his bedroom at the far end of the hall. He looked into every corner and the closet before shutting the door firmly, telling himself that he always closed his door at night, it wasn't because he feared the ghost would come back for him.

Chapter 21

K ENNEDY CALLED SOFTLY, "Dad—you awake?"

As she went up the stairs she felt as startled as he looked. Vulnerable. She knew why she felt that way after being with Nathan Doyle but didn't recall her father's looking vulnerable ever. Could he tell? "What is it?" she said to him.

"I thought someone was in the house earlier."

"Someone? How do you know?" Kennedy felt her hands and then every part of her body go cold. *Someone is stalking me,* she'd said to Doyle, but she'd thought she was exaggerating.

"There's a knife missing from the block downstairs. Did you take it?" He clasped her hand, where they stood, he at the top of the stairs and she two steps down from the top.

"There wasn't one missing before?"

"No." He eyed her, scrutinized her face. For a second he looked afraid of her, and she wondered if—after years of hiring lawyers and declaring her innocence—he might actually believe she had committed the crime.

"Well, I didn't take it. I've been at work this whole time."

She wriggled out of his grasp as she removed her coat, then turned to pad back downstairs.

"You always take your shoes off at the door?" Gerry asked. He pointed to her shoes across the front hall. She was in her stocking feet.

"Of course. Why?"

He gestured to the floorboards. "It's just . . . there was dirty water all through here."

Kennedy went into the kitchen to check the patio door. He followed. It was shut tight and locked. She felt along the edge for any place in the rubber that a crowbar or screwdriver could have been shoved through it, but it was intact. She moved to the counter, examined the knife block.

She was just about to write his concern off as paranoia— when she saw it. She kneeled and swiped at something with her thumb.

She brought it over to him. In her palm was a yellow leaf, egg shaped, about three inches long.

They both stared down at it. He sucked in a breath. He asked when she'd last gone out in the back garden, and she shrugged. Not since she'd gotten the job at the call center—she hadn't run in a couple days. Her thoughts turned to Berk Butler, the way he had come through the dark. The necklace he'd placed on the patio table. The way he'd advanced on her even after seeing the steak knife in her hand, like he had no fear. Her legs felt weak, and she reached for one of the kitchen stools and sank onto it.

"Should we call the police?" Kennedy was certain her face had turned pallid.

"It's just a leaf," Gerry said, trying to joke it away.

But a knife was missing, and they both knew what damage a blade could do.

Chapter 22

I N THE PASSENGER SEAT beside Everett, Dee Nash held a thin file folder in her lap. He could guess there were forms, police reports, witness statements, other things, similar to what was in the box he'd taken from his dad. She still hadn't told him what was in that manila envelope she'd brought to the first meeting. He knew she must have seen photos of the wounds. Probably worse than he could imagine: hideous smile shapes blackened with blood, dull and deep. The skin had been punctured easily as paper. It was why he hadn't gone through the box yet.

"I remember feelings. Moods," he told Dee. "Not so much, you know, facts."

"Children always hear more than parents think they do," she said, lifting one side of her mouth but not both.

He remembered his parents' forgetting he was nearby as they discussed the details of the case with lawyers on the phone, or sometimes over barely eaten dinners. He peered out the windshield. Outside the parked vehicle, Dee's producer, Josh Winter, was walking back and forth filming the school's empty quad. A wired young guy in a blazer and ball cap, he paced, smoothly shooting exteriors of Everett's old high school on a digital camcorder. Everett wasn't sure he trusted him as much as Dee. He seemed to keep forgetting his sister wasn't just a story. Riding in Everett's Mustang, they'd already circled once around Longwood with Everett driving and pointing out locations to them: his mother's house, the playground where they hung around when Haley was younger, the convenience store where they bought chips and Cokes. He held back the detail that once he'd watched her shoplift an extra candy bar.

Josh had been in the front seat, shooting footage out the window, saying, "This is great, this is great."

But now Dee had climbed into the front, where she could see him and converse with him.

"We'll do the on-the-record interview later. Don't worry about today. We're just talking," she reassured him. "I saw your Facebook profile. You have the same birthday as my son, André."

It surprised Everett that she was old enough to have a son his age, but more so that she'd gone and looked at his profile. He thought of the photo he'd put up and how Carter's hair was visible in the background even if her face wasn't.

"You have a girlfriend?" Dee asked.

"Sort of. Not really."

"That's normal enough. You're young. She know about your past? Or Haley?"

He cringed into the steering wheel but when he realized he was doing it, he made it look like he was stretching. "It's too soon in the relationship."

Dee nodded. "Tell me about Haley's boyfriends from that time. Any that you remember besides Berk Butler?"

"Ty Anderson. He was from our subdivision. My pa didn't like him . . ."

"How come?" She was interested now.

Everett put his tongue against his lip, thinking how to phrase it. People had always said Ty looked like Lenny Kravitz. But Haley said he didn't, that it was just a white way of saying he was black in a school that was mostly not. "Ted Kimberson wasn't the most open-minded."

Dee made a sound in the back of her throat.

"Ryan Whittles—I remember hearing his name. They seemed to hang out . . . a month maybe? There were other boys she liked, I think, but she didn't really have a boyfriend, like someone who called at the house." Everett thought his parents had not been prepared for a child who moved at daughter speed. One day it was Jem and the Holograms. Next she'd been caught stealing lip balm at the Body Shop. In contrast, Marly still treated Everett like a little boy. He worried whether he would betray himself in the interview with Dee, let out all these stories he was still holding back.

Dee nodded her head. "I know these names from the files. So I know they were checked at the time; the question is always how closely."

"How closely," Everett echoed.

Dee faced him. "I know it's tough. It's your family, but this violence tells us that this was someone who was very intense in their feelings. Personal. Probably happened quickly."

Dee nodded to the man outside the car and he gestured that he was going to circle the campus.

Everett thumbed the key chain in the ignition. A Butler's discount card hung from it. "So you should look at Berk Butler again. I remember him picking her up that night. He stood at the door, looking in, but not too much. He hovered. Didn't take his sunglasses off. I went back to the Nintendo and Haley ran out, told me to tell Mom that Kennedy picked her up. Probably because he was older and all. We're talking thirty seconds."

Everett closed his eyes and tried to picture Berk's vehicle. He couldn't even recall what kind it was. He reckoned he must have told all this to the officers at the time, but now it was a fog.

Dee opened the file and looked at his face. "That was the last time you saw your sister?"

He felt his breath hitch.

She touched his shoulder. "You were a child, Everett."

"I don't know if she got in the front or back seat. If anyone else was there."

She looked at the file. "At the time, your mother told the investigators Haley's black bra was new. Most of them were white. Do you remember that?"

It was about him and his mother, this file, he realized, glancing over. That's why it was thin. It was notes on what he and Marly and Ted had said the day Haley was found. There weren't going to be photographs. Everett felt himself relax a little as he shook his head.

"Josh's thought was that a black bra was her trying to be . . .

more mature. Do you think maybe she had someone older she wanted to impress?" Dee asked.

In no way did Everett want to think about Haley's bras, even if he did remember the strangeness of the black one that year, dripping dry on the shower bar amid the usual white and taupe ones. He shrugged.

Josh came back and opened Dee's door, waited for Dee to get out and pull her seat forward so he could squeeze into the back. Everett had volunteered to drive because he knew the area, but he hadn't thought about how impractical the Mustang was for multiple passengers.

Josh spoke while still looking at his footage. "She bought a knife at a yard sale with Kennedy and Carter. Do you remember anything about that?"

"Her teacher, Mr. Harding, caught her with it at school. She got detention and was real upset about that. Haley liked Mr. Harding. Ma said he was the one who set her up with an internship."

Everett watched as Dee threw Josh a reprimanding glance.

"We don't know that's the weapon," Dee said firmly.

"Four and a half inches, not serrated," Josh answered. He knew Haley's murder like Everett's father knew baseball stats.

Dee raised an eyebrow at him. With two of them there, it began to feel a lot more to Everett like those conversations with police officers.

"My pa was always saying he would take us camping, but he never did. That's why she had it." He grabbed the key chain, started up the car, checked his rearview mirror, and headed out of the lot. "He wasn't great about following through on things. He's recovered now, but—"

"Did they get along?" Josh asked from the back.

Everett took a corner too sharply, realized he should slow down. "He wasn't in a great mood with anyone, I'd say." Everett remembered the clink of beer bottle caps hitting the recycling bin within a minute of his father's coming home from work. He'd always tried to steer clear of drunk Ted. The only time his father seemed relaxed was when he was watching baseball, a sport Everett had played and watched mostly to gain a few hours of peace with him.

Josh said he had the footage he needed, if Everett wanted to drop him off at the coffee shop lot where they'd met.

"Your father hasn't returned our call," Dee said, and asked if Everett had discussed the show with him. Everett pulled the car into the lot and parked beside Josh's car.

After Josh disappeared into his car, Dee suggested Everett drive around and talk a little more. As he cruised up and down the streets of Longwood, Everett said he'd gone out to see Ted and Judy and come home with a box from the civil trial. Dee turned quickly in her seat, the softness she usually employed gone.

"Have you found anything in it you think we should see?"

"I haven't really looked."

Everett was driving along the east side of the woods. In his peripheral vision, the trees were brown and yellow shadows dancing. He and Haley had hiked there. She'd taken him to fish in the creek, though he doubted there were ever fish there.

It was probably just an older-sister game of make-believe, to keep him busy when their parents had to work late. She'd taken him to some of her favorite spots, and he remembered how they lay on their backs, staring upward at the branches, the peaty smell of damp earth. She'd carved her initials in one of the trees, he remembered her telling him. He may have responded with something like, *Don't tell Captain Planet! Trees are living things.*

Everett peered ahead at the road as the sign for the Mobil gas station flew past. In the trunk where he'd stashed it, he knew the box smelled mossy, damp, like the earth he'd lain on with his sister. He had peeked in and seen what looked like police files alongside a family album and some old VHS cassettes labeled by year, names of vacation destinations he could barely remember. He'd put the lid back on and left it in there.

"Why don't you bring me the files at the office?" Dee suggested. "I don't mind helping go through them."

"I couldn't take them out. They're still in the trunk," Everett said.

"The trunk of the car?" Dee's voice rose. She looked over her shoulder as if she had X-ray vision and could scan them from where she sat. She directed him to do a U-turn and go back to the Mobil lot. They could have a quick flip through them there.

DEE COMBED THROUGH MUCH of the box quickly, wearing a pair of reading glasses, sorting manila envelopes into piles she twisted around and placed behind her on the backseat. Almost all of it was transcripts of depositions. Sitting in the front seat, Everett tried to read them, remembering some things but confused by others. The box was wedged between Dee's feet on the passenger-side floor. She was more efficient and confident than he was, or maybe she retained every bit of information with a glance—Everett wasn't sure.

"The thing about this case is it's rich kid against rich kid. Butlers vs. Wynns," Dee said, looking up from a transcript. "And when you get that many lawyers in a room, oh my, the victim disappears. No one knows what the truth is anymore."

"I don't even know what I'm looking at." Everett smoothed his hands over his jeans to try to get the sweat off them. He wondered how all this typing—the *um*s and the *uh*s left in, the wandering questions and answers—could add up to horror, remembered how twisted his dreams were throughout his childhood, how he'd be almost swimming rather than running from someone or something unknown through the black woods, how he'd see his sister trapped somewhere and not be able to get there.

"This is good." Dee tapped a file folder against her chin, then set it back in the box. She glanced at the station. "We need some coffee," she said excitedly.

After she'd gone, stepping out from the car, careful not to upset the box, pushing her glasses case back into her purse, Everett watched her walk across the lot. He had no idea who half the people in the transcripts were. Experts in the effects of LSD, child psychologists, and even knife-wound specialists who argued—using words like *plunge lines*, *spines*, and *ricassos*—that "a young girl simply could not inflict those wounds." That statement struck him and echoed what Dee had told him at their first meeting.

Everett dug his hand down in the box, feeling around, and found an envelope unlike the rest of the things in it. It had the Longwood Baptist Church logo in the left-hand corner and his father's name where the addressee should go. Everett picked it up and opened it. There was something heavy in the bottom of the envelope but he pulled out the sheet of paper first. It showed a simple female body diagram with many dots marked on it, mostly on the torso, one on the right hand, and over her pelvis a large pen circle. *Gestational Age: 6 wks* was written on the side.

Everett looked back at the envelope. In the return address was "Dr. Carpenter." He was a deacon at their church. Everett remembered his slicked-back silver hair and cough-drop smell. Grady, his dad called him. As a kid, Everett had assumed he was a medical doctor. Now he realized the old man was a coroner. But Everett didn't remember ever hearing his parents or anyone else talking about Haley's being pregnant.

He peered inside the large envelope and pulled out a small baggie, which contained something clunky and white. He held it up. There was a small speck on it, like a bug trapped in wax.

Written in black marker on the other side of the bag:

Fetal tissue, Kimberson, July 6, 1993.

He glanced up from the bag to see Dee struggling to open the door of the gas station store, balancing two coffees and a handful of creamers.

Ted knew this, Everett thought. And this, a piece of Haley, had sat in his garage all these years with his decoy ducks and swans.

Dee placed the coffee cups on top of the car roof and shook her hand as if the heat of the cups had burned it. Everett stared dumbly at her through the window, knowing he was supposed to open the door for her. He felt paralyzed and didn't move. Her gaze went to the baggie, and unlike him, it was clear she registered what it was without reading the label.

‖ ‖ ‖

ASSIGNMENT 4:
Write about the place you grew up.

MY MOM AND DAD argued a lot in the first years in the "new house," despite their insistence that problems were for other people—people who couldn't hold on to their jobs, who couldn't maintain their relationships, who looked a mess. They weren't for people like us—ones who color-coordinated which Fair Isle sweaters they would wear in their Christmas card photo. (Blue for Gerry and me; white and gray for Laine and Carter.)

The space was big, just big enough to hold the rise of voices. You could pretend not to hear. Carter's room was farther from the living and dining rooms than mine was, and it may have been why we spent more time in there. Also hers was cleaner.

The day I got my period we'd been in Blueheart for a year. I was twelve. I stared down at the long scrape of brown on my underwear and for a second stupidly thought I'd somehow pooped. Then I realized it was blood. Crusty, dry, disgusting. I felt nothing like the heroines in the Judy Blume paperbacks Carter and I had whispered about and traded as currency with the girls at Liberty Junior. I edged downstairs to tell my mom, hoping that the moment might blossom into something better. I walked in on her crying. Her shoulders shook silently, and it took me a moment to understand, with her standing where she was with one fist on the kitchen counter, that she was sobbing. I looked around but no one else was there. I wondered if she cried because she secretly knew what my body was doing. Then I wondered if Carter might have gotten her period too at that same moment, locked herself in a school bathroom stall. But neither was the case, of course.

Carter was at French Club, and I didn't take French. I lay on my bed upstairs, waiting for her, listening to my mother cry— my walls at that time freshly painted and clean except for a picture of the Olympic figure skater Brian Boitano, arms out, gold leaf on his velvet jacket. In retrospect, I wonder if my love for velvet began that year, lying there under the figure-skating icon.

It wasn't long after that Laine began to blame Gerry's long hours, saying he wasn't "present" when he was with us. When I heard them argue she said the house in Richmond had finally been exactly how she'd wanted it and he'd picked us up and moved us to the suburbs to curry favor with Doug Macaulay and try to climb up a little more in social status. She'd had to start all over again, decorating, joining committees, building friendships. She said the women were snotty, shallow, and their politics were *maddening*. She felt she couldn't leave the house without spending an hour on her hair, lest she be judged. She made us watch *The Stepford Wives* on cable one night, Carter and I falling asleep and her nudging us awake, saying, "Wait for it."

My dad did seem to have a shorter fuse after we moved, to treat Mom as simply the person who handed him his dinner plate. As much as he lectured my sister and me about how we could become doctors or lawyers, he didn't always respect us. Once, one of our black cassettes fell under the gas pedal in the car and he was so perturbed it was in his way that he picked it up and threw it out the window as he drove us home from tennis. It was Debbie Gibson, *Electric Youth*. Years later he got confused between her album and another band we liked, Sonic Youth, which made us collapse in hysterical howls. But at the time, we were devastated by the loss of the tape. "Go back for it," we pleaded. He refused to apologize and told us, "You have to learn to behave like guests in my car."

We were only half an hour from where we used to live, but it was another world. Most of the time Carter and I exulted in the freedom—people who didn't know us yet as nose-pickers or nerds. There were new friends and we were allowed to roam in a way we never had been in the city, to stay out until ten at night. But I remember my mother staring out the window a lot in those years. Lonely, like the women I would later wind up waiting on in the card shop downtown.

I didn't think it was fair of her to blame Blueheart Woods for everything, but then again, I never asked her what made her cry.

—*Kennedy Wynn*
Heron Valley Correctional Facility

Chapter 23

G ERRY STEPPED ACROSS the placed stones in his Japanese garden, assessing the land behind the house. There was a low wooden fence all around the property, the kind of thing he realized now could be easily hopped. With the exception of what happened with Haley Rae Kimberson, Blueheart Woods had so little crime, it had never been an issue. The alarm on the house had always seemed enough to him.

Although it was December the pump in the decorative pond was still going, and he could hear it softly fizzing as he wandered throughout the garden, touching the various plants. The only yellow plants in the yard were the hostas and the Japanese forest grass, but the hostas had leaves as large as his hand. And the grass was long and wispy. Both were drastically different from the leaf Kennedy had found in the kitchen.

"Maybe she's wrong." Gerry tossed aside the strand of grass in his hand. "Or maybe she's lying." Perhaps Kennedy had run that morning or the day before, winding through the subdivision or to the woods. She could have tracked in anything. It was much more probable than a ghost, or an intruder. But just in case, he wanted to know where the yellow leaves in the neighborhood might be, from which direction the person would have come.

Gerry placed his hands firmly on the fence as if testing it, then vaulted himself over, landing uncertainly and putting his arms out, the inside of his thigh only stinging a little where he'd scraped it. He strode across the grass that divided his place from the house where the Halls lived, knowing they were never home during the day. Anyway, it was one in the afternoon and if anyone spotted him, they would know him. The Halls' place had no fence at all; they had opted for large junipers to line the property, reminding him somewhat of a golf course. If that was what it was, then Gerry was in the rough. He found he could walk all the way around their property with ease, as well as the Wilsons'. The Cains had a heavy-throated boxer that barked at him from behind their tall backyard fence, but if one wasn't intimidated there was still space to walk between their property and the garage belonging to the Johnsons. Then there was a large gap: a field almost, with the Macaulay mansion at the top of it.

From across the grounds, Gerry eyeballed the enormous stained-glass arch above the door, the multiple rounded rooms with windows everywhere, the turret where he recalled Doug had had his library office on the second floor. It was something in between a manor and a church in terms of its design. Ostentatious, Gerry saw now.

Doug Macaulay didn't live there anymore. His second wife had been from Maryland and he'd moved there after he retired.

He had struggled with cancer, Gerry heard, but didn't know or care if he'd survived it. Rather hoped he hadn't, if he was perfectly honest with himself. Jim Stone, Gerry's onetime partner, would have known, but Gerry never spoke to him anymore. Someone else in the Macaulay family had taken up residence in the house and everyone still called it the Macaulay Castle. Gerry had always wanted to impress Macaulay, and maybe that showed weakness. The man had paid him back in the worst of ways.

Gerry remembered the Christmas parties he'd been invited to there, earlier, when they were still friends and peers. The children of lawyers all cloistered themselves away in the game room while the adults slurped bourbon milk punch and old-fashioneds until they could barely stand. Only Laine ever stayed sober. The crackers and caviar, calamari, spinach dip in a pumpernickel bowl, salads with strawberry-poppyseed dressing that the girls went bananas for, and pesto crostini, a new thing that left everyone feeling continental but trying to humbly check their teeth for green flecks. "It's great stuff, but I look like I went down on a mermaid," Macaulay joked loudly. He could get away with saying anything. Gerry recalled his saying, "Hey, look, the barely legals are here!" when two of the female paralegals arrived together.

Macaulay had everything once promised by 1970s subscriptions to *Playboy*: money and brains, hi-fi equipment and character, a wife and a mistress, and one of the mistresses eventually became his wife. He was the kind of guy people both remembered and resented. If one wanted to hate somebody, Macaulay made a good target.

Especially for Gerry. And yet, Gerry had never thrown a punch.

HE MIGHT NOT HAVE BELIEVED it if he hadn't seen it himself: Laine walking down the cul-de-sac that led up to Macaulay's house. It was a gray February afternoon and she held her arms around herself as though she was cold, and she may have been, dressed as she was, in a blouse and a thin sweater, as if she had thrown it on and run across the fields. Gerry had stood watching her, hand on top of his Cadillac Seville, her own vehicle still parked there in the driveway. It was four o'clock, so who knew where the girls were—it was Laine's job to keep track. He'd planned to work through the evening but had come home to get a floppy disk with some files—the phone having rung and rung through the house and no Laine picking up. He saw the guilt on her face before she'd reached their driveway. She could have come up with a lie, and he wished she would.

"Let's go inside," she said, and walked past him quickly into the house.

Neither of them said anything. Laine turned to face him and perhaps there would have been an apology if he hadn't reached out and slapped her. He hadn't known he was going to; it happened before he could stop himself. He'd never lifted his hand to her before. But the slap was more than a slap—it was a cuff, and she went down and then held her hands over her

head to defend herself. The anger didn't subside and Gerry
kicked over the ornamental umbrella stand instead of hurting
her. It hit the wall with a clang and Laine flinched and began
to sob.

"Him? Anyone else out here but him. This is my business,
my life."

"I'm your life." She lifted her chin. "And you never listened
when I said 'I hate it out here. I don't know you anymore. I
want a divorce'?" Her lip quivered on the last word, and he
could see the pain and fear in her eyes. Her cheek had reddened
along one side where he'd struck her.

A half hour later they were sitting at the dining room table,
as civilized as possible, him with a whiskey and her with coffee,
when she told him everything. It was worse than he'd thought.
She protested that she hadn't slept with Doug, only fooled
around. That indicated to Gerry it was not a onetime mistake
but something that was ongoing, a thing she'd considered, kept
hidden, returned to off and on. She had thought about Macaulay while showering in their house, thought about Macaulay
while serving Gerry supper, thought about Macaulay when
Gerry attempted sex and she rejected him. It filled his mind
with the worst of images.

Laine clutched the ice pack against her face, weathering his
outbursts but still spilling more details than he wanted, the
kinds of things she ought to have told a girlfriend rather than a
two-timed husband.

"I gave you everything," Gerry said hoarsely, "and you destroy me. My business. My social life. I can't show my face at the club after this. I just phoned Doug yesterday, and I'm talking to him and you're up there in that house, you can look out the window and practically see our place from there."

"I wasn't in a position to look out the window," Laine replied.

"There's mistakes and then there's being a whore."

"You got a tax schedule for that formula? Have you filled it out yourself?"

"Fuck you, Laine."

Laine's face blanched, but it wasn't the word. Her gaze was fixed on something over Gerry's shoulder. When he turned, he saw one of the girls standing in the doorway.

"Don't gawk," he said, standing up, taking the drink he'd poured with him. "All couples fight. One day you'll see."

When the din of their conversation had turned down, Gerry heard other voices in the foyer.

It was Carter who'd walked in on them, it turned out, and he apologized after. Laine made him. Apologies and shuffling seemed the way to deal with the biggest pains in a family. Laine had wronged him, yet Gerry was the one who had to say something. "I didn't mean what I said," he'd uttered, ducking his flaming face in, then out of her room, where the girls were curled on the bed flipping through music magazines.

Later, he'd edged past Haley in the upstairs hallway on her way to the bathroom.

"I'm sorry. I'll pray for you and Mrs. Wynn," she'd said softly, and he'd wondered if the apology was about more than just having walked in on a bad moment. If she meant she was sorry he was disregarded, sorry he was vulnerable. But of course she didn't. She didn't know anything.

NOW GERRY SHOOK AWAY the question and pulled a holly leaf from a shrub. He twirled it between his forefinger and thumb. So far he hadn't passed any yellow foliage except two high autumn-turned oaks, which swayed and rattled. Their leaves were the wrong shape.

He had hoped to make it as far as the woods, go in, see what was there. But his chest felt like it was on fire, and he'd only walked a mile and a half. Once he'd been able to walk the golf course all day. It was silly, anyway, he told himself, to hunt a leaf as if it could reveal something to him. And that missing knife? Gerry wondered. *Knives go missing every day. Just like socks in the laundry. Or daughters at fourteen.*

He turned around and trod back the way he'd come.

Chapter 24

Berk taped the laser printout to the pharmacy counter: *Butler's Does Not Sell Plan B.*

"Like you could knock anyone up," the shithead stock boy Liam said as he was walking by.

Berk swore at him, mumbled something about having a kid, then turned to look at the sign again. He reached out and pulled it down, added another piece of tape to the back, and smoothed it back up on the wall.

When he'd picked Haley up the night of the Fourth before Kennedy's place, they'd driven around talking. She was wearing that transparent blouse as if it would distract him from what she had to tell him.

"How late?" he asked, putting on his signal and pulling over to the side of Smoke Line. Cars passed them. Once in high school a girl had almost said the same words to him, but having heard the whispers, he'd avoided her, and eventually she'd stopped even making that pleading eye contact with him in the hall and he knew she'd managed on her own, as easily as hitting the Backspace button on a typewriter and going over the mistake. Berk didn't know if Haley would make the same decision, and he felt a heavy feeling in his guts.

Haley shrugged. "A month, maybe more."

Berk put the Jeep in park. His hands dropped off the wheel into his lap. He turned and met her eyes. His father had told him that if a man looked at a girl, really looked at her, she would almost always do what he wanted. "Are you going to take care of it?"

Haley broke his gaze and looked down. "I can't do that."

"Is it mine?" He had worn a condom, the free kind, generic and raspberry red, passed out on campus.

"Right now it's all mine, isn't it?"

It wasn't the answer he'd expected. They were supposed to drop later—Kennedy had told him to *bring something*. Maybe if Haley did, she'd realize it wasn't the right thing, keeping it.

"Do you want to try pennyroyal tea?"

"Like in the song? That could kill me."

"No. It could just help you, you know, have your period. Lots of hippie girls on campus take it for cramps."

"I'm not having cramps." She flipped down the visor and applied her lip gloss angrily, dipping her finger into the tiny canister and smearing it across her bottom lip. She ground her lips in toward each other, dragging the stuff across them both.

"Would you try it? Maybe you're just late."

She pouted and said she didn't even know where to get it.

"They have it at health food stores in the city. I'll get it for you."

She said okay, and he said really it wasn't the same, because he could see what she was thinking. She shook her head, her eyes shiny. "No," she said.

He pulled back out onto the road before she could cry.

As they turned onto Silver Creek, he rambled, "I'm not saying it's mine. Because maybe it's not. But I have plans, you know. I'm not like these trash boys you got out here. My dad is going to give me the stores to run and I'm going to run a record label too. I'll start with Kennedy's band. They'll be the next Breeders. Do you want to fuck that up for her?"

He brought the vehicle to a hard stop before they came into sight of the Wynn house.

Her head snapped forward, the seat belt catching her. She looked over, alarmed. "Calm down."

He didn't say anything but continued to grip the wheel.

Haley reached up and unfastened her necklace, handed it to him. "A little bit of balance," she said. "Don't be afraid of the good in you. Or me."

He looked down at the yin-yang necklace, then tucked it into the pocket of his baggy beige clamdiggers. He leaned over and kissed her. She tasted like strawberry lip gloss.

"Maybe it should just be us tonight?" he offered.

"She's my friend. I can't do that to her."

—————

BERK WALKED OUT of the grocery store pharmacy and onto the loading dock. He grabbed some bare skids and tossed them around the parking bay, listening to them clatter and not caring if knife-sized splinters dug into his hands.

His dad had said he had to go to Haley's funeral—if he didn't, people would say he had done it. *Just be present, it's your best defense.* Haley was five-six—the top of her head, he knew, came just under his chin—but the quietness of death made her seem so tiny. One hand folded over the other, hiding what the police called defensive wounds when they shoved the photo in his face. But in the casket, you'd never know to look at her what had happened to her.

Chapter 25

CARTER NEVER WENT to a Butler's store if she could help it. But tonight, she needed the pharmacy. She stared at the selection of pregnancy tests, wondering why anyone bought packs of two or three sticks. Women who were trying, she supposed. Was the $12.99 test more accurate than the $9.99 one? She picked up the single-use kit for ten bucks.

Her period had been due three days before, and perhaps it was just paranoia, but she was a meticulous charter and knew she was seldom late at this age. She imagined her abdomen was swollen, though it was probably only PMS. Were her breasts more tender than usual? Her hair stringy? She'd peered at her reflection in the bathroom mirror at work and thought, *Everyone knows.* She imagined the fetus under her skin, two inches below her belly button, not even pea sized yet, just a cosmos swirl of Kimberson DNA.

Do I want a reason to phone him? she asked herself as she walked past the contact lens solution and back through the grocery aisles. She'd put off going out to buy the test until after dinner, telling herself it was shame turned worry, the fact that she'd begged him to stay inside her that very last time.

She'd watched the *Crime After Crime* show, wanting to see what it was all about. The detective had tried to shine new light on a case from California in 1989: a real estate developer who was murdered after he and his wife joined a swingers' club. Carter felt sick to her stomach as she imagined her own photo, or Kennedy's photo, splashed up there on the screen. She'd clicked Off on the remote and walked out of her apartment with ten minutes left in the show, not caring if she found out if there was new evidence. She passed Ellwood Thompson's organic grocery, not wanting to be seen by anyone she knew. Nauseated and sweating, she parked at the Butler's and ran inside, clutching her purse, beelining for the pharmacy area before the store could make its announcements and shut down for the night.

Carter was passing by the deli counter when she came to a dead stop. Berk Butler, wearing a short-sleeved polo shirt, was scowling at the employee behind the counter.

"That blade ain't been cleaned the entire shift. It's dirtier than my dog's ass," he berated the meat cutter, who was not much older than a high school kid.

Carter remembered in a split second how she'd always felt Berk would stay stuck in a high school mind-set for life, even though Kennedy hadn't been able to see it. The way he'd bragged constantly about his football career, his ability to cut class without reprimand. Then again, maybe those were his topics because high school was the only thing he'd had in common with her sister and her.

The young man in the apron looked off across the store like he'd rather have been anywhere else. He'd been cleaning up and stowing things away for the evening. Carter saw there were silver trays being emptied of premade salads and entrees, which were being packed into Tupperware. The lunch-meat slicer, however, was still dusted with the confetti of meat. The deli worker caught Carter's eye and she looked away. But it was too late—Berk turned to see what had distracted him.

Berk leaned back on the glass counter as she passed, and she could feel his gaze on her. She clutched the pregnancy test on the other side of her body, behind her purse, and wished she'd picked up a shopping basket to hide it in, or a magazine or some other product to cover it up. She'd made it to the cheese display when he let out a low whistle. "Do you still sleep on your stomach?"

Carter felt an involuntary shiver, and it wasn't just the icy breath from the milk section. She was shocked he could still tell them apart at a glance.

Behind her, she could hear him as he tapped his wedding ring against the glass counter and laughed. "Tell your sister hi!" he called out as if they were old friends.

AFTER PLAYING THE GIG that first time, Carter had felt flush with excitement. Like Kennedy, Carter had been curious about the attention they were getting from the older boys at the bar. Daniel Chambers had come to see them play, which made them feel like they were halfway signed to Geffen. While Kennedy stared at Berk Butler, Carter retreated somewhat behind her, sipping her Coke through the straw. He was good-looking, Carter thought; that was how he made everything sound sexy instead of crude. But the things he said weren't so different from what boys at high school said.

Berk had a few beads on a cord around his neck, and a small silver disc with a symbol on it. Carter watched as Kennedy reached up and touched it, asking, "What's this? It looks like a sixty-nine."

The guy choked, laughed. Asked what she knew about that. Kennedy just smiled. He said it meant Cancer, his zodiac sign. He reached out and plucked at the ankh between Kennedy's breasts. "How about this?" he asked, but before Kennedy could answer, he was peering over her shoulder at Carter. He wanted to know about her charms too, he said. He reached over and stroked the sun-and-moon-kissing pendant that lay several inches under Carter's collarbone.

"So you're into dualities? That's so Zen," Berk said. He pulled up his sleeve to show a tattoo of an old-fashioned wheel. "That's the dharma wheel. It means the universe will never stop turning."

Beneath her skirt, Carter felt wet. She couldn't tell if the sluicing feeling was excitement at the sight of the tattoo on his solid arm, or if she was wobbly and sweaty from standing half the night and being up on the stage. She had chosen a scoop-neck velvet bodysuit and thick leggings under a transparent broomstick skirt. The layers now felt hot and stifling.

He was stupid and beautiful. Carter didn't say anything to warn Kennedy off, but his friend did.

"Don't go listening to Berk, now. He likes to quote from Intro to Philosophy, but he's really failing out of Business and Marketing," Daniel said before moving to the far end of the bar with his beer.

"Mom's picking us up soon," Carter said in Kennedy's ear a short while later. The bar had gotten busier than when they'd played. Kennedy had managed to secure a rum and Coke and was drinking it seated on Berk's lap—because there were no seats, of course.

"I can make room for you too," Berk said, but Carter shook her head and blushed hard in the dark as Kennedy passed the drink up to her and Carter took a small gulp. It was only later, when Carter saw him with Haley, that she saw how dangerous Berk was, that he wanted all of them.

IT WAS THE DAY she bought the theater mask ring, and Kennedy the skull ring—one of those April days that had turned warm, almost hot, and the girls stripped off their jackets and stood bare armed in the sun.

Haley had been supposed to call her dad for a ride, but when she called the Kimberson house, the phone just rang and rang. Kennedy and Carter were smoking on the curb in front of the pay phone, Kennedy waving her newly adorned ring finger with each drag on the cigarette.

"This happens sometimes," Haley said as she joined them. They all knew her father had a problem.

"We understand," Carter said.

"Our dad's, like, borderline alcoholic." Kennedy might have said more but stopped at the glance Carter threw her. Carter didn't like Kennedy's talking about their own father's unreliability. She wanted to keep it secret, even from Haley. "Aren't they all?" Kennedy said, their radio working perfectly.

Haley didn't look comforted.

"I know who I can call," Kennedy said, and she passed her cigarette to Haley to finish and jumped up to grab the phone directory.

While Kennedy was at the phone, Haley looked at her boot toes. Carter reached out and hooked her arm around Haley's head and pulled her down onto her shoulder. She could feel Haley's tears running onto her neck. Haley's smoke was going in Carter's face, but she didn't say anything. Finally, Haley flicked the cigarette away and they watched it roll toward the sewer.

"Thanks," she said, straightening. "I don't know why I'm still embarrassed of it."

"It's okay. I get it."

Then Haley sat up straight and began singing Whitney Houston's "So Emotional." It was the sort of goofy thing she did—seizing on a thing that wasn't in at all and making it fun again. Carter joined in at first, surprised how many words she knew, but then Haley stood up and finished the entire song.

She had a beautiful voice and Carter's own voice fell away. Haley belted it loud enough that shoppers coming out were looking at her.

Kennedy came over and plunked down again. She pulled a lipstick out of her army jacket pocket and darkened her mouth, using her round sunglasses as a mirror before sticking them back on her head. "Guess who's coming to get us. Berk Butler."

"The hot guy from the show you played? Who took you to that movie?" Haley reached into her purse and yanked out a tissue. She wiped her nose with it, and then took out her compact and rubbed more foundation on her cheeks and forehead. "Do my freckles show?"

"I like your freckles," Carter said.

When Berk pulled up in a Jeep, Kennedy ran to him and he grasped her in a hug as if they were lovers who had been separated by war. Carter was stunned. He'd taken Kennedy and her to a movie, *The Crying Game*, at the rep cinema and halfway through he'd reached over and grasped Kennedy's hand. Carter had seen it but said nothing. After, at home, as Carter tried to dissect the film with her, Kennedy had told her that she couldn't concentrate on the plot. She said she felt like her whole life had changed the minute he held her hand. But Carter had expected it would dissipate, like the crushes she had on the boys from Liberty. After all, he'd only held her palm in his.

Now he came over and gave the same lopsided smile he had before and tossed his hair back off his face, sticking out his chin. He was wearing army shorts and a hooded poncho that showed a creamy patch of chest hair.

He tapped his nose, indicating the nose ring Carter had gotten since he'd last seen her. "Nice one. Now I can tell you apart."

"This is Haley," Kennedy said, hopping nervously on and off the curb.

"Hi there, Jennifer Jason Leigh."

Haley beamed at his compliment.

The thing about him Carter noticed was that when he looked at a person he really looked at them. It was that habit that had made Kennedy feel special at the bar, and her too, if only for a minute.

Berk stuck out his index finger and touched the medallion on a cord that lay along Haley's clavicle. She had purchased it a half hour before inside the mall. "Good and evil. Eros and Thanatos. Looks like you're starting to figure it out," he said softly. "You're almost ready for *On the Road*. I'll bring it next time I see you."

Carter tried to radio Kennedy, *Who is this clown?*, but her sister looked away.

Kennedy yelled, "Shotgun," and skittered around the other side of Berk's Jeep, climbing into the front passenger seat, where she would ride beside him.

‖ ‖ ‖

Chapter 26

A WOMAN WAS RUBBING Everett's cheek with a sponge and covering the growing bruise. He winced and asked how it was looking and she said not too bad. She told him he had nice skin. Not a smoker, she observed, and he confirmed.

"You won't do too much?" he asked as she picked up a brown pencil.

"They don't usually interview people with, you know, injuries. Not the ones that show up on camera."

THE NIGHT BEFORE, Everett had woken up in his condo and realized he had to talk to his father before being interviewed on camera. There was no way he couldn't. Before dawn he drove the forty miles out to Ted's place, parked as the sun came up, and sat in the barn, waiting.

Everett got up from his lawn chair, pacing every few minutes, looking at the time on his phone, knowing Ted had to wake up and come out with food for the dogs. He wondered if there were more boxes in this place and he got angry that what he did know about Haley's death was whatever his parents thought he should. It felt like an hour but it was probably only twenty minutes before Ted walked into the barn, annoyed. "Judy saw your car and said you must be here."

"Haley was pregnant. Who else knows that?" Everett's voice was raised in spite of the early hour.

The annoyance on Ted's face hardened. "You went looking. I told you—"

"I'm not the only one looking," Everett said, quieter.

Ted ran a hand back over his dark hair. "Your mother doesn't know. It would have killed her to know Haley left us . . . like that. It would kill Marly now, so don't tell her. Grady gave me those pages so it wouldn't go to the police, and then everyone else."

"They got tests now. DNA. They can find things out— who's the father."

"Jesus Christ almighty. Who are you talking to, Ev?"

"People who want to find out who killed her!" Everett yelled.

Ted's voice remained calm, cold. "They don't care about you. They don't care about Haley."

"They care more than you ever did."

Ted struck Everett across the face. "You come to my home with that garbage?"

Everett touched his cheek. His father's hand had been half open, half closed, and the sting was much more than the slaps he'd been given as a boy.

Ted raised his hand again, but Everett grabbed it, held his wrist in a hard grip. He was stronger than Ted now.

"Did you do things to her?"

Everett's father fell silent. He glared at Everett but said nothing. At that moment, Everett knew.

"You did. You did. You sonofabitch."

"Get out and leave us alone." Ted's voice wavered.

Blood rushed to Everett's face as the sting faded to numbness. He wanted to hit back but couldn't. He turned around and kicked the shelf of decoys, sending the plastic birds scattering onto the concrete floor. "How many times?"

Ted tilted his head back, his eyes closed. "Once. It was only once." Ted was beginning to sob now. "I came in drunk and Marly left me sitting on the bathroom floor, like an idiot, half undressed. I passed out and then Haley, she came in and must've tried to help me up, but she couldn't. I fell down and she came down with me. I looked at her and I grabbed her and I kissed her."

"Shut up!" Everett yelled. Neither heard the door of the barn opening.

"I stopped, but Haley stared at me like I had broken everything inside her at that moment. I never touched her again. I never did."

The sound of the door swinging closed caught both the men's attention. They looked, and through the window Everett could see Judy running back to the house, and probably away from Ted forever.

THEY WERE SHOOTING the interview in a hotel room on Broad Street. It was called the Heavenly Suite. They used the bedroom as the greenroom. The makeup artist had Everett seated at the desk, the king-sized bed behind him. The sitting room would become the studio, with a sofa and coffee tables that would pass for someone's immaculate apartment.

"A bit of definition. I promise you won't notice a difference." The makeup artist winked.

Everett knew there were other guys who would have asked for her number, made some flirtatious conversation back. But he didn't. Women had always liked him, in part because he talked to them like regular people, in part because he didn't hurt their eyes. But when every woman flirted with you, it didn't get your attention anymore. Not much had ever really held his attention, until Carter. As much as she'd talked about feeling out of control, he realized, she had grounded him. She was a listener. She would know, he supposed, about that horrible touch between his sister and his father. If Haley had ever told anyone, it would have been her.

THE INTERVIEWER WAS DEE NASH, but she didn't look like she normally did. Her hair and makeup were done, and she was wearing an emerald-colored dress. The guy, Josh, still wore his usual khakis and cap, and stood beside the cameraperson. As he pointed to the chair next to Dee, he told Everett to relax, the interview would be the same stuff he and Dee had talked about before, no biggie.

Everett nodded. "Do I look at the camera or at you?" he asked Dee.

"Look at me. Don't edit yourself. That's Josh's job." Dee smiled.

"Sometimes those random things that just come into your head are the best bits," Josh put in from where he stood off to the side. "Ready?"

Everett glanced down at the mic clip on his jacket and said he was. *Best bits.* Everett tried not to turtle into himself at the language of a guy with a clipboard. He straightened his shoulders, let his neck elongate.

"Tell me what happened that day," Dee started.

The first question was basic but not, as Everett realized he'd never really told anyone his part of the story. Suddenly he didn't feel like a twenty-four-year-old man in a tie and coat but a puny kid.

"I had this information and I didn't tell my parents," Everett said, his voice weaker than he meant for it to be. He cleared his throat.

"Let's start at the beginning," Dee said, as if he needed directions.

"This is the beginning. She called that morning. Kennedy Wynn—" Everett adjusted his stance in the chair they'd seated him in and followed Josh's rolling hand telling him to keep going. He wanted to do a good job and he'd thought he would be better at this. "Kennedy Wynn phoned that morning and asked where my sister was. She sounded weird. We didn't know Haley was missing then. Kennedy asked me not to say anything and I didn't—all day. My parents must have already found out from the police that she was . . ."

He stopped. He realized his eyes were getting shiny. Already. He had thought he'd get further in before that happened. He'd rehearsed various versions of answers at his condo in front of the bathroom mirror, but they'd been about what happened after, information told to him during the investigation, nothing as basic as *start at the beginning*. Nothing as obvious as his own role.

"I'm sorry," he said to Dee, who nodded. Over by the camera, Josh rolled his hand again, although this time with a look of sympathy on his face. "They'd already found her body before I told anyone about the call. I remember I didn't even know that she was, uh, gone. I mean, I sort of did, but . . . My mom was crying and then— They—my parents, I mean— pushed me into a car with a neighbor and the neighbor drove me to my grandparents' place."

Dee interrupted. "Let's go back. Let's talk about that call. What did Kennedy say?"

"She asked to talk to Haley. And I said, 'I thought she was sleeping over at your house.' And she said, 'Yeah, she is. Never mind. Forget I called. Don't mention it to your parents.' 'Don't mention it to your parents'—that was exactly it. Not 'Don't mention it to Haley.' Because she knew. She knew Haley wasn't alive anymore." Everett paused. He said it because it was what he'd thought for years, but he didn't think it anymore.

"So you think she was making an alibi for herself?"

"I did." Everett realized from the tilt of Dee's head she wanted more. "At the time I thought she was trying to make an alibi, but now I'm not so sure. She was an easy choice for them: Kennedy was the last one with her and the first one there."

Dee had a slight smile on her face. It was clear she liked the answer. "The easy choice?" she echoed.

Everett sighed. He wasn't sure how much he was supposed to reveal. The tissue he'd shown to Dee would be tested. He'd agreed to it that morning before the interview.

"What if Kennedy wasn't the last one with her?" Everett said simply. He looked down at his lap, feeling like he'd just betrayed his mother, by doubting what the Kimbersons had called truth for years.

Dee let the moment linger and didn't press him. He could hear the buzz of the spotlights they'd set up. After another half minute she said, "They kept asking about boyfriends, didn't they?"

"Sure. They took dogs and they sent a search team into the woods. They found her pretty quick. I don't know if they looked at the right people though." He shifted in the chair.

"Let's pause here," Dee said to Josh and the camera guy. She leaned over. "We can't point fingers at anyone for legal reasons. You're doing great, Everett. Do you think you can talk generally about Haley at that time? Give people an impression?"

He said he could and they were rolling again.

"She was a typical teenager. She loved music, dancing. I would hear her talking on the phone, giggling with Kennedy or Carter—" Everett felt himself visibly flinch as he said her name. It was another Carter in his mind than the one he'd spent time with. This Carter was bigger than him, with eyeliner, a nose ring, a beaded necklace, and hair that had been dyed dark and flat-ironed. Beneath her black baby-doll shirts lived a mystery. She wore loose jeans or peasant skirts, the crinkling folds a universe of color.

The Mole-Richardson lights were hot, aimed almost directly into his eyes. He smiled suddenly, in spite of himself. Why was he smiling?

"When you're a kid, you sort of read people differently than adults do. You see things simply. You sense things."

"What did you sense?"

"Carter was soft. Kennedy was hard. They were like these bookends, my sister in the middle, these opposite forces."

Dee nodded for him to keep talking.

"Kennedy could pressure a person, make Haley feel like she had to compete or something. I remember Haley getting mad one time, saying something like, 'I'm more *experienced* than either of them understand.' Stressing that word."

Everett felt his brow crease. He'd assumed she meant it about Berk Butler, but now he wondered if it had to do with other things. "You know, I don't want to talk about this. I'm realizing it makes my sister sound bad. She was just a kid."

Dee nodded and said of course, but when Everett glanced in the direction of the camera he noticed a sneaky look on Josh's face and worried the show would use the footage anyway. Maybe Marly had been right. The one thing he wanted was to make things better for Haley, do right by her. What if he'd done the opposite?

October 27, 2008

ASSIGNMENT 5:
Write about a moment you shared with a friend.

HALEY AND I WERE THE FIRST to show up at Berk's Memorial Day party. We had only been to high school parties before, where parents were going away and the rituals of exclusions, food, and sourcing alcohol were planned over days, as if by generals preparing for war. It was still daylight when we showed up at Berk's crumbling apartment building. He wasn't even home and we sat in the shade on a thin grassy strip. "I'm seeing someone," Haley blurted out while looking up at the sky. "I don't know if it can be called that actually."

"Are we talking about Berk?"

Haley laughed and shook her head, but I wasn't sure it meant no. I knew they'd been talking on the phone as much as or more than he and I did.

I looked at my friend, who only a year before had spent her time dancing to Billy Ray Cyrus and volunteering at her church. Something had turned on inside of Haley. Haley needed boys and men, their approval and attention. It was her sunlight. I wanted Berk, but I didn't _hunger_ for adoration from the world. If anything, my heavy eyeliner and dark lipstick, obsessively applied and reapplied, were meant to repel as much as they were to attract.

I knew Haley was about to tell me more about this new guy when Berk's Jeep pulled up. He opened the rear flap and began stacking twelve-packs of Budweiser. "No problem. You two just enjoy the day," he called to us, flipping his hair back with a head toss. We stood, shaking the grass off our legs. We carried one pack each up the stairs with our girl arms as thin as spaghetti.

People came in and out of the party that night, never more than nine or ten people there at a time. There were lots of parties held by students who lived near campus after classes had ended: older students who ran campus radio, or taught, or worked at the cafés and bars. Students who actually talked about books. At the beginning of the night, before he got drunk, Berk snapped a Polaroid of everyone who showed up, placing the washed-out images on the dusty fridge in the kitchen and securing each with one of the many magnets he'd collected from head shops, bars, and sporting events.

Haley and I sat in a corner by ourselves on a forlorn futon— in awe of this new world and annoyed that it made us feel like girls, inexperienced and uncertain how to act. The music got worse the drunker Berk got. He was playing the Jesus Lizard, loud, and talking with a group of men on the couch about how last month at the Flood Zone the singer had dived from the stage and his boots had caught Berk in the head. He was proud of strange things.

Haley wasn't having it. She made an ugh sound and started digging in her purse. She brought out a cassette and went to the stereo. The swirling, high-pitched guitar noise ended with sudden silence. Haley pressed Play on Madonna's "Erotica." When the go-go beat started she danced over and pulled me up from the futon by my hands. Haley swayed back and forth against me. I couldn't dance as naturally as Haley, so I flicked my hair around, back and forth, and made dramatic arm moves in the air, things that would show I didn't care what I looked like when, in fact, I desperately did. The men of the room whooped and the two women at the party stared in shock, noticing Haley and me for the first time.

"I just read that essay about Madonna by bell hooks," one of the women said to the other.

"How old are they?" the other cut in.

Berk took his camera and started flashing photos of us as we danced with each other.

Haley ran her tongue up my neck. Her lips stopped at my ear. "I'm so fucked up," she said, a little too loudly. The statement cut through the alcohol and music filling my head. My swaying stuttered.

I saw one of the women, wearing a ski hat in spring for some reason, get up and begin arguing with Berk's roommate Julian. "How old are they?"

Haley kept dancing when I yelled back in her ear, "We should go. I'll get us a ride."

Haley's eyes widened and she started laughing until she couldn't dance anymore.

—*Kennedy Wynn*
Heron Valley Correctional Facility

Chapter 27

THEY WERE CALLING FOR SNOW. Virginia never got snow. Sitting in the restaurant waiting for her family, Carter scrolled through the news feed on her phone. It must have been why traffic had been crazy—people ran out to Butler's and Food Lion, buying the stores out of milk and bread, stocking their shelves with pantry goods as if the apocalypse would come because there was a layer of frost on the ground. At home Carter had some cans of soup, dry pasta but no sauce, four half jars of jam of dubious ages, and a bin of wilted greens. Perhaps she ought to have been more concerned.

She pulled up her sobriety app, which told her: *Focus on a dream.* Carter sat there staring at the four words. She'd really never had a dream—unless disappearing counted. She'd disappeared from her life in a swirl of addiction, then she'd climbed out and disappeared into Alex. Then, if she were honest with herself, she'd disappeared into Everett, into the thrill of a secret. The only time a man could be considered a dream, she thought, was when Austen and Brontë were writing. But even their characters were given jobs and struggles.

She should go back to school, she knew. She needed a career, a direction. She'd always thought she would become an actress, move to New York, but she was too old to start something like that. An English teacher, she thought. It was something she'd considered when she was in high school, but it hadn't seemed like a grand enough ambition, coming from where she did. At that time, Gerry and Laine had expected the girls to break records, compete for the Ivy League, become stars or leaders. Carter set down her phone and stared out the window: she'd make a great a teacher, if she could stand to go back, begin again.

The pregnancy test had come up negative. A slim minus line. She didn't know if she should consider herself lucky. It had never occurred to her to want a baby before—which she knew made her different from other women. And Carter didn't know if she wanted one now, but now the idea was there, in her thoughts as a possibility where it never had been before.

She looked up before Kennedy came in, as if her shadow had a familiar shape outside the glass. Her sister was underdressed for the restaurant, in an oversized shirt, low-slung jeans, and a black knit cap, but she had on the mid-calf boots that Carter had picked for her. She shrugged off an anorak and fell into the chair across from Carter.

"He's circling for parking," Kennedy said, meaning Gerry, and accepted the menu Carter slid at her.

"Hey, I'm sorry if I fucked up," Carter said. Since she had started on the medication from Dr. Braithwaite, an SSRI called Lumalex, she found it easier to say what she really felt.

"It's okay. It's all fucked up. Like every day, I'm trying to navigate living with a whale without any water. If you're on edge, he's *really* on edge."

"Gerry? Gerry just does Gerry. You'll be okay. He suffers from anxiety, like me. It's hereditary."

A few minutes passed in silence.

"Is that a new jacket?"

Kennedy said yes, she'd gotten her first paycheck. She hunched at the table in a way that Carter guessed was a prison habit. She scratched up under her hat but didn't take it off.

Kennedy glanced at the door but there was no sign of their father. "I have a boyfriend now. Sort of anyway. I don't want Dad to know."

Carter leaned in. She hadn't considered that Kennedy would begin to have a life so quickly. "What's he look like?" She realized they were whispering.

Kennedy said like Matt Dillon if he dressed like Eminem. She always had liked dark-haired guys, Carter commented. How had she ever wound up with Berkeley Butler?

Kennedy tore off the hat and bunched it between her hands suddenly. She pushed a hand through her hair, not as if she wanted to arrange it, but as if she couldn't believe it was even there it bothered her so much. "Berk's been in the house."

Carter bit her lip. "Berk broke into our house once before."

Carter watched as her twin began to rapid-blink—the response Kennedy only had when under stress, times she'd had to get up and speak in front of the class. Suddenly, Carter wondered if she'd misjudged her sister. Berk had always been a master manipulator.

"He broke in before? What do you mean?" Kennedy asked. She looked shaken.

Carter had a flash of the comforter being lifted off her sleeping frame, how at the time she thought groggily it must be her sister, since Kennedy had snuck in with her when they were younger, if she had a secret, a dream she wanted to tell. Instead, she'd felt the bed move under the weight. Male weight. She'd lain there, frozen, as she heard his breath and smelled the burnt scent of him. She'd chosen to play dead, fast asleep, hoping whoever it was would leave. He swiped her hair off her neck and put his lips against her skin as her heart hammered in her chest.

She smelled booze. *Please don't be my father,* she thought, and she was horrified that she could think it. *Please don't be an intruder.*

A hand came around and stroked her nipple over her long cotton shirt, as if he had radar in his fingertips that determined the location of her areola, could tell where its exact point was even in the dark. Carter's whole body went rigid with anger.

"Get out," she whispered, her voice louder than she expected as she summoned every bit of strength she had, hoping she wouldn't wind up strangled or raped.

"I thought you'd be happy to see me," the man breathed in her ear. It was Berk Butler.

"I'm *Carter,*" she hissed as she started pushing him away.

He didn't move his erection from her back immediately, nor his hand from her chest. If anything, he twisted his fingers a bit, and she heard herself gasp involuntarily. Only one boy had ever touched her breast before, and that was Isaac Richmond that time on the quad. It wasn't fair.

"Get out before I scream."

"So uptight," he slurred. On wobbly legs, Berk rose off the bed. She could see him now clearly in the dark, his broad shoulders outlined by the blue light coming in through the partially opened blinds. He backed away, his hand out in a stop sign. "Which room?" he begged.

"Get the hell out of our house!" Carter heard her voice harden in a way she didn't know she was capable of. She smashed herself into the farthest corner of bed and wall, feeling tears glaze her cheeks, and relieved he couldn't see them.

She heard him out in the hall, whispering *Kennedy*, then, when no response came, creeping down the stairs. She listened as the back patio door clunked softly in its frame. She had thought about waking her mother but opted to lock herself in the bathroom instead, falling asleep on the tile after wondering a million times whether he'd meant to be in her room and if so, whether she might have done something that would encourage it. She remembered how she'd stared at Kennedy the next day, not sure how to bring the words to her lips, feeling for some unknown reason ashamed of herself.

Looking back on it now, she saw that as an illogical feeling. She'd done absolutely everything right, and she'd short-circuited his advances. Today Carter realized she ought to have felt proud and powerful.

"I'm sorry I brought that piece of shit into our lives," Kennedy said when Carter finished recounting the incident. As the door to the restaurant opened and Gerry entered muttering, Kennedy leaned in. "We can't talk right now."

They both watched him come in. He looked exasperated—still jangling his car keys in his hand, bopping them up and down as if they would turn into a yo-yo. Parking always stressed him.

He ordered a Kentucky Gentleman, and Carter said, "Dad!" which prompted him to change the order to a Bloody Mary. Kennedy could drive, he said as he took off his coat. She didn't have a license, Carter argued. It would be a parole violation. She'd done her written portion that week, Gerry argued.

Carter wanted to ask more about Berk Butler, why Kennedy thought he'd been in the house, but she knew they couldn't talk about it in front of Gerry.

The server came with drinks and they ordered food. She asked for the shrimp salad, and Gerry said, "Eating meat now?"

"Oh." Carter peered down at the menu. "Well, it's just shrimp."

As a lawyer, no contradiction escaped him, except the ones he didn't want to talk about. Carter watched Gerry sip his drink. Instead of debating the ethics of pescatarianism, he blurted out, "I'm going to sell the house."

"What?" Carter peered at him.

"The house. I've decided to sell."

"Now?"

Kennedy, who was sitting on the same side of the table as he was, knocked Gerry's silverware off with her elbow. She leaned down and picked it up. When Kennedy handed it to him,

Carter could see she had an unsettled look on her face. "Do I have to go with you, like I'm twelve?" she asked.

"We'll check with the lawyer."

"Where are we going to live?"

Wherever, Gerry said, someplace smaller. He would have sold right after the reno but it hadn't been the right market. He tossed the celery stalk with a red splatter onto his plate and sipped his drink. It was a terrible market now, and getting worse, but neither twin reminded him of it. "Besides, she's already taken down all her posters," he remarked to Carter.

Carter looked at Kennedy, who nodded reluctantly.

"I made a mistake keeping that place." He finished the drink. "You can stay in the past so long it comes back."

In the past, Carter might have reassured him, felt somehow that it was her job to tell the white lies required to maintain a good face and keep a meal going without friction. But now she didn't care. She looked at Kennedy, whose eyes bugged. Her sister had come home after all these years, and now he was going to take it away. Vintage Gerry: you could put it on a rack and charge sixty bucks. He claimed to care about others, but at the end of the day it was only ever about what he wanted.

"Is this because of what you just told me?" Carter forgot her sister's earlier command not to ask about Berk. Kennedy kicked her softly under the table. The salad came, Gerry's chicken and grits, Kennedy's corn bread and chili, interrupting the conversation. Carter reached for the shrimp first.

"The parole specifies I need to live with someone who owns their own home. That's why I can't live with her," Kennedy said.

"You would live with me?" For a grim moment, Carter was cheered by her sister's vote of favor. Then she turned to Gerry. "What about Mom? Don't you care about her memory? It was her house too."

"She used her last breath to dictate a divorce petition," he said to Carter with a dismissive hand wave. "She couldn't wait to leave." To Kennedy: "I can own another home, you know. Pick one. I'll buy it tomorrow."

A sly look came over their father's face. He turned to Carter. He propped his chin up with one hand and raised an eyebrow. "How about I get one of those luxury units in Shockoe Slip, that big glassy tower, you know the one, right on the James. How would that be?"

Carter blinked.

"You've been inside them. Do they sell those in two-bedrooms, or only one?"

Carter pushed another shrimp into her mouth to avoid answering. She hadn't seen or heard from Everett, but it was obvious that somehow her father knew. Had he had him secretly tailed, the way he did to Berk after he got out of prison, keeping tabs on him as if there was something more to be revealed? Carter glanced at Kennedy, then looked down at the tablecloth. She felt light-headed as she chewed and swallowed.

Kennedy was the one to pick up the thread. "There wasn't anyone there, Dad." Her voice was forceful—the way it always was a little too confident when she lied. "The alarms were on."

"What are you saying?"

"Maybe you're seeing things."

"The leaf."

"A leaf's a leaf," she said.

"You were the one who suggested we call the police. Why's that? What'd you tell her before I came in?" Gerry's voice climbed. A sweat had broken out along his hairline. "You think someone was there too. Admit it." He dabbed his forehead with his napkin, then shoveled two forkfuls of grits into his mouth in quick succession, as if he wanted the meal to finish quicker. He turned for the waiter as he passed and handed him his glass for a refill.

"Dad."

"*What?*"

Carter and Kennedy radioed each other across the table. *Say something. But what? Challenge? Defuse.*

Carter laughed. The couple at the table next to theirs stood up, and at first Carter thought it was in response to the argument. Then she turned to follow their gazes. Outside of the large front window, it was snowing, chunky white flakes falling. People were turning to look, worriedly, or to ooh and ahh. The hoods of the cars parked along the curb were already covered.

Gerry turned from the view and glared at Carter across the table.

Kennedy pulled her hat back on, lower, as if she could hide inside it.

"Why are you laughing?" Gerry asked Carter. "What's wrong with you?"

"I'm on Lumalex. I can't—it's funny. It's all so awful it's funny."

"Are you high? You mess up your life again, I'm not bailing you out this time." Gerry fumbled the words in his anger. He dropped his own fork this time and a server came over to replace it, even though no one was eating anymore.

Carter leaned back against the banquette seating. "You want a mess, Gerry? I fucked Everett Kimberson. Whatever you think they took from us, we deserved it."

Gerry's face flushed. He picked up the napkin again and mopped at his brow.

"I'm not even good enough for him. That's the funny thing. I love him, and it doesn't matter because I'll always be your daughter, your sister." The words were coming out in between gulps for air.

It felt like everything in the world had stopped moving except the snow falling outside. But when Carter looked around she saw that none of the other diners were looking at them as she'd expected them to be. An old woman was showing off pictures of a grandchild. A man and a woman two tables over looked like they were on a brunch date. A big guy dining alone was flipping through the weekend newspaper to the sports. A little girl had her face pressed to the glass and her mother was scolding her not to put her tongue on the window. The problems they were airing were only theirs.

"What are you doing?" Kennedy said. "Do you hate me?"

"I wanted something that was mine. Something not wrecked by this family."

Carter watched as Kennedy stood up shakily and made her way out of the restaurant. Carter looked at the crumpled napkin in her lap. She recognized for the first time since she'd started the Lumalex that it was still possible to feel sadness. She knew she'd hurt her sister deeply. Outside, the snow swirled. Carter watched as Kennedy lifted her face to it, an absolute lack of expression on her face, like a dog sniffing the wind trying to decide which direction to go.

Chapter 28

THEY AGREED THAT THE DOOR would be closed. Kennedy had folded away her clothes and cleaned the room in case someone should open it, but it wasn't as if they'd had time to paint. It was the one room in the house that was rough around the edges. The carpeting had aged. The blinds were outdated. The shapes where the posters had been still stood out darker than the rest of the sun-faded wall.

Kennedy was sitting outside in the Japanese garden, smoking—even though her father had asked her not to—when the first waves of viewers for the open house arrived. She watched them pass on the other side of the glass. After an hour or so, the double door slid open and a young man with dark dyed hair stood there. "Oh my god, this is amazing." He looked at her instead of the garden. "Are you her?" he asked.

She put out the cigarette in an ashtray on the table. "No. I'm the other one," she lied.

"Can I take my photo with you anyway?" He removed a slim Canon PowerShot camera from his suit jacket pocket. He was already positioning himself beside her. "Daisy, come here!" he called to someone inside.

"Why?" Kennedy asked.

"I read all about her. Daisy!" he hollered toward the house.

Up close he smelled of coffee and rancid cheese, his vintage suit jacket possibly never sent to a cleaner. Kennedy stepped away from him down into the garden, even though she was only wearing her shoes, not her boots, and the snow they'd had the week before had left everything slushy, muddy.

"The house is nice. Why don't you go see the inside and leave me alone?"

The man held up a finger and tapped the air with it as if she'd shared a secret with him that he thought was right on the money. His nails were painted dark blue. "I'm going to see her room. Thank you."

Kennedy swallowed. She watched him head back inside with his camera, then sat back down. Who came to an open house with a camera? All the photos and details of the house had already been posted online. Even though her butt was getting cold from sitting outside, she waited fifteen minutes, and when more people came out to look at the back area—a couple asking about the pond and its upkeep—she snuck inside and found Gerry with the real estate agent in the dining room by the coffee tray.

"Who are these weirdos?" Kennedy whispered in his ear.

"I've already been asked twice if the murder weapon is hidden here," Gerry hissed, his complexion ashen.

There was a snap of a large camera shutter. Kennedy and

Gerry both looked toward the kitchen, where a lady in her for-
ties was using a bulky pro camera to photograph the knife
block and the slot for the missing knife. She was a curvy
woman with dyed black hair in pigtails and a dress with a skull
design on it. Kennedy at seventeen might have admired her,
but Kennedy now elbowed Gerry.

"Is she allowed to do that?" Gerry asked Miranda, the real
estate agent.

Miranda smiled nervously. She didn't look like a real estate
agent so much as a kindergarten teacher. She had blond-brown
hair that she wore loose over her sweater, much longer than
most women in their fifties; a daisy-patterned skirt; and a "fun"
necklace made from colored ribbons and glass beads dangling
over her chest. Kennedy guessed she'd had no idea what she
was dealing with when she took Gerry on as a client and booked
the open house. "I suppose it can only help find a buyer—they
all seem very excited, don't they!"

"Yes, but excited by the wrong things," Gerry muttered.

"Let me see what I can do." Miranda went over and steered
the woman toward the refrigerator and the stove, opening them,
an overwide grin on her face. "All new appliances and the owner
is open to including them. Wouldn't you love to make dinner
every night in this kitchen? That countertop is real marble."

A man in a suit interrupted Miranda to ask about the furnace. They spoke for a moment, then he moved on—down to
the rec room to get a good look at "the bones of the house."

The goth lady lifted her camera and took a shot of the contents of the fridge. She reached in and moved some jars around,

as if searching for something in particular, then lifted the camera and shot again. "Are there closets?"

"Lots of closets!" Miranda exclaimed, taking her by the elbow and guiding her into the hall.

"Can I get shots of all of them?"

"Oh good god, get me a drink," Gerry said in Kennedy's ear.

"No way," Kennedy said, watching as the man who had spoken to her on the back deck posed on the couch in the family room. "You brought these people here, you stay sober and deal with it."

"We could both leave."

"That's a thought. Do you trust them here alone?"

"Just one drink."

"Fine, but you call me Carter today. If they think I'm me, it's all over." Neither of them had spoken to Carter since the restaurant.

"Deal."

Kennedy went into the kitchen and fixed a vodka soda for Gerry. She put it in a tall glass so it would just look like he was drinking fizzy water. As she stared at the glass, she remembered that it was how Carter used to do it when they were young—so no one would know he was drinking at times when others weren't. Kennedy had always felt hot shame when she saw her sister do it.

Kennedy hid the vodka behind the cereal boxes. While she was in the kitchen, she grabbed the knife block and stashed it in the bottom cupboard behind some pans. She returned to the refreshments, where she'd left Gerry, but he was gone. An old woman carrying a Chihuahua in her shopping-bag purse was there, nibbling the scones they'd put out.

"He doesn't bite," she informed Kennedy, and Kennedy accepted the invitation, reached out and touched the dog on its bony head.

She couldn't imagine an elderly person wanting to own such a large house but at least the woman didn't seem like the murder fans swarming the place.

"How long have you been here?" the woman asked. Her short hair was white and she had on a cardigan and a cashmere coat that she'd undone.

"Um, since '87. We lived in the city before that."

"No, I meant how long have you been out?"

Kennedy took her hand back from the dog. "Um, no, I'm Carter."

"People who say *um* are nervous." The lady selected another scone. It crumbled in her hand and she fed part to the wiggly dog. "I've been following local crime for years. I still say it was the Butler boy, but maybe you could tell me better?"

"Excuse me," Kennedy said, and grabbed the drink off the table and went upstairs to find Gerry. Even before she could get to him, she saw that her room had been opened, the door slightly ajar. The man who had asked about the furnace was at the top of the stairs engaged in a discussion with his wife about whether the house was priced right for them. He was ticking things off on his fingers. He seemed serious enough about the place that he'd probably been the one to open it.

Kennedy squeezed past them with a fake smile. She was

about to go to her room and look inside when the goth woman at the end of the hallway said, "I wouldn't go in there."

She was lining up a close-up shot of a framed photo on the wall of Carter and Kennedy at a duck pond when they were ten. Kennedy remembered only that shortly after the photo was taken an angry goose had chased her and she'd wound up running through the pond and getting her tights soaked. She'd been wet and miserable for the rest of the day trip.

"What do you get out of this?" Kennedy asked.

"It's history. Don't you like history? They said you did, in the articles. That it was where you met her. History class." The woman faced her and let the camera hang more loosely around her neck now.

"It was English class. Carter had history with her." Kennedy realized after she said it that *she* was supposed to be Carter.

"Are you going to be interviewed on *Crime After Crime*?"

"What?"

"Interviewed," the woman said, drawing the word out as if Kennedy hadn't heard her. "I read online that they were looking at your case."

Kennedy felt her brow furrow. "I don't know what that is."

In her father's office she could hear Gerry's voice rise: "Please don't touch that!"

The woman lifted the camera again to take a photo of Kennedy.

Kennedy bolted for her bedroom.

"Really, don't—" the woman started to say, but it was too late. Kennedy had already rammed the door open.

A man in a blue polo shirt sat on the bed, his back to her, as if he was staring out her window. Maybe he wanted to see what she saw when she woke up in the morning. Kennedy had known the room would get opened at some point, but she'd thought the curious would pop their heads in, then politely duck out. She hadn't been prepared for the kind of people who would come to gape at the place where they lived. She was already a couple steps into the room—about to ask him to leave—when she heard the man breathing fast. She saw his penis before she saw his face. There it was, white and wormy, the head cupped in his wobbling hand, the rest hidden in his khakis. He gazed over at her: he had a skinny face, his jaw clenched with concentration. He looked like anyone, some man who worked in an office. She didn't want to be there when he finished, leaving a mess on her bed. She didn't want him to look at her. She ran, brushing past a guy in a ball cap in the hallway, spilling half her father's drink as she sped downstairs.

On the front lawn she found herself still holding on to the glass. She drank what was left and fought back tears. She was about to go back inside and tell Miranda to call the police when a compact car crept up and parked in the line of cars at the end of the driveway. The engine cut and Marly Kimberson stepped out of the vehicle.

MRS. KIMBERSON CAME UP the walk slowly, looking the house up and down as though Kennedy weren't even standing there. As she got closer, Kennedy saw that Marly's mouth moved though she wasn't speaking, more like her tongue was searching the space inside. Marly stopped a couple steps away. She peered up at the façade.

"Mrs. Kim—" Kennedy began, an apology the only thing to do in this situation. But Marly didn't let her finish.

"Wow, I thought this place was hot shit back then. I thought, 'Look at my daughter. She's really made it. She's always had a good head, always had the grades, but now she's got a job in a law office, hanging out with these people. She's going places! She could get into a real college, have a real life!'"

Marly was speaking but almost not to Kennedy. She knew Mrs. Kimberson had gotten pregnant at eighteen. She'd been a mom and worked at the outlet mall that opened, the kind where you had to drive from one end of the parking lot to another just to go to a different store. Kennedy stared at her. She'd aged an unfathomable amount, lines around her eyes and lips, and her shoulders slightly bent. Up close she looked older, closer to sixty-five than the fifty Kennedy knew her to be.

"I'm going to buy this house," Marly said. Her voice was the same as Kennedy remembered from after-school afternoons at the Kimbersons', but now there was none of the warmth in it.

As if unable to process what she'd said, Kennedy tried again, "Mrs. Kimberson—"

Marly pulled her head back and lifted her chin. She hefted her bag farther up her forearm. "I'm going to buy it so I can burn it to the ground."

Chapter 29

GERRY OVERHEARD SOMEONE say something about the furnace, and someone else something about closets. He left the dining room before Kennedy could come back. He shot up the stairs quicker than he had in years, intending to get to his office and secure the closet there in some way—whether by stationing himself in front of it or moving a piece of furniture inside, wedging something against that panel so that no one dared open it, either for morbid curiosity or to check out the water heater.

He couldn't believe he'd been so naïve about what the open house entailed. The real estate agent had said he and Kennedy needn't even be there—and he could see now that he'd been right to stay. As awkward as it was, it would have been chaos without them. He supposed he hadn't moved the copy of *Sex* or the note because there was no better hiding place. The safe, maybe. But a little part of him worried that he might summon *her* by touching it.

At the top of the stairs, he halted. Some movement in the bedroom at the far end caught his eye. A small twist of a shape, a flash of auburn hair. And for a second he stood still, waiting, holding his breath without realizing it. He thought it was her again, in his bedroom. Then the shape appeared, barreling along the corridor, directly at him.

Gerry pressed himself against the wall, and the shape—which belonged to a girl of about eleven, someone's daughter—flew past him down the stairs.

"I found the room I want!" she hollered to her mother. "It has a balcony. Come see!"

Gerry crossed into the office. There was a young man in there, standing near the file cabinet, the exact item of furniture Gerry might have moved inside the closet had he found the room empty. The guy looked about the twins' age, a worn LA Lakers ball cap shielding his forehead. He was fiddling with his jacket cuff, and for a second Gerry had a flash he might have taken something, pushed something up inside it. But when he spoke he had a pleasant manner, as if to balance out his leonine face.

"My father never put whiskey in his either," the man said, nodding at the glass decanter sitting there. "Does anyone put whiskey in these things?"

Gerry shrugged to try to seem unconcerned, though his gaze went to the closet door. He was grateful to see it was shut. "Who has time? It's always gone too fast for that."

"Ah!" the man exclaimed, bopping his cap. "That does sound like him too."

Now Gerry wasn't sure what to do with himself. He hated having his purposes undermined by casual conversation. How long until the young man left and he could do what he'd come upstairs to do? There were two more hours left on the open house. But the guy was already sticking out his hand and saying a name, Josh something. And now Gerry was shaking that hand and supplying his own name. There would most definitely be a conversation of some sort about the house and its history, or when the roof had been done. Josh was there from California, he said.

He put on his best smile, just in case the young man really was a serious buyer. He hoped Kennedy would bring his drink upstairs. He'd thought he'd heard her voice out in the hall.

Josh pointed out the copy of *One Flew over the Cuckoo's Nest* he'd spotted on Gerry's shelves. "Great book," he said.

His wife had given it to him. Gerry had never actually read it but didn't let the kid know. It had been one of the films they saw together in the early part of their relationship. Obviously it had meant something to her. To him, it had meant leaning into her hair, which smelled as sweet and fruity as Pez candy. It wasn't a typical date movie. Afterward Laine talked about how the masses would always be sedated and the message was to cast off authority before it was too late. *Be good, follow the rules—why?!* Her passion attracted him, though half the time he had no idea why she was so fired up. When he thought on it now, it was easy to see where the girls got their rebellious streak.

"The guesthouse out there"—Gerry pointed—"it's heated. Could easily be turned into another office. I thought of it myself once upon a time—for more solitude, back when my two daughters still lived at home." He was getting excited now, thinking he might get an offer.

Josh peered down at the indicated guesthouse, which was somewhat bigger than a shed but not as large as a coach house. Gerry had had it built in '88 to accompany a pool that they somehow never got around to putting in. Laine had run a small business out of it for a while, trying her hand at millinery of all things. It had been a restless year, he remembered, a year when the two of them could feel the dissatisfaction settling in like a permanent layer. Gerry stared out at it himself, somewhat wistfully, as if it were a structure representative of more peaceful times. They should have put in the pool, he realized. Laine and the girls would have enjoyed it, and her body at forty was still taut and golden, something he recognized now that he couldn't see then . . . in his youth. His rapidly aging youth. *You always believe yourself older than you are.* He smiled sadly.

"You know, Mr. Wynn," the young man said, "there's something I should tell you."

He turned to see that the guy had picked up the silver letter opener from the desk. He was peering at it absently, to distract himself, it seemed, uncertain how to say what he wanted to.

"Go on," Gerry told him.

"We've spoken before. I told you I came here for work and that's true. I phoned a couple months ago from the show I work on, *Crime After Crime.* Then I came and left my card for you. We want to have you on."

Gerry tried not to clench his teeth. He couldn't believe the man who stood before him could occupy his space so easily, not even a shameful expression in his tone or his face. "I'm not interested," Gerry snapped. Then he thought better of it, softened his manner. "Never wanted anything but a nice life, a private life."

"I understand." The boy rolled the opener between his fingers.

"Don't touch that!" Gerry yelled. He hadn't meant to raise his voice so much. The boy dropped the letter opener on the desk.

"Sorry," Josh said. "I don't mean to invade your privacy. I just thought that you might be more receptive to coming on the show now that we've met. Now that you see who I am. I find your side of things interesting. Could give you a chance to talk about what you went through. There are some who feel your daughter was bullied into the plea by the lawyers. I know it must have been hard."

Gerry walked around the desk. He grabbed the guy by his jacket to physically remove him, but the boy flinched and held his hands up.

Gerry stepped back. He knew better than to assault someone in the media. It would only be worse down the line. His hands dropped to his sides. "*You know it was hard.* Really, what do you know?!"

"Please, Mr. Wynn. I don't mean any offense."

"Go," Gerry rasped. "Look around all you like. Just don't kid yourself that you're one of the good guys. And don't contact me again."

The boy unpinned himself from between Gerry and the

window and placed a hand on the desk, as if he might hurdle over it.

"Listen, I'm sorry," he said, patting Gerry's shoulder with his other hand. Then he dodged around Gerry and out the office door. Gerry heard something fall off the desk in his haste.

When he was gone, Gerry looked at his hands and saw his fingers shook with anger. The nerve of these people, the disgusting entitlement, thinking they could come in here and somehow immediately understand. Determined to complete his task before some other insane interloper could arrive, he removed the decanter from the file cabinet and wrestled the black metal piece of furniture into the closet. It covered the latch to the cubby. He breathed hard. He walked over to the desk and began to rearrange items there. What else had the TV writer touched? He flung open the drawer and surveyed its contents—had he taken something? Then Gerry stashed some personal items inside: a paperweight, a miniature clock, a pottery dish Carter had made as a girl where he kept butterfly clips. Where was the letter opener? It had been right there. Gerry bent to look under the desk. He'd heard something fall when Josh left. He began to inch his hand farther back, but a pain deep in his chest stopped him and he straightened up.

Gerry sat in the leather chair, breathing furiously.

In the Japanese garden below he saw movement, a flit of orange. He gazed out and watched with horror as Haley Kimberson's mother appeared, arms crossed, meandering between the dwarf cedars. Her short, bright hair, a scowl on her tight face. He closed his eyes. Was he seeing ghosts again? The truth was he didn't think anyone had been in the house that time, and that terrified him more than if someone had. It was the reason he wanted out quickly.

But it seemed unlikely he could conjure Marly Kimberson, especially when she was still alive. Even if he was delusional, could he imagine her in such detail? he asked himself. His mouth felt dry. He knew he was shaky and thrown off by the encounter with the TV kid. But when he opened his eyes, Marly Kimberson was still there—turning now and trudging back toward the house. He saw Miranda Peters, the real estate agent, speaking to her from the deck.

"Mr. Wynn! You'd better phone the police." The boy from the television show was back in the doorway.

"Good idea," Gerry said, uncomprehending that anything further could have gone wrong. He reached for the landline phone that sat on the executive desk. "Wait, what in the hell are you talking about?" Gerry asked, realizing there was no way the guy could see Mrs. Kimberson out there, and that he probably didn't mean to have himself removed from the premises.

"A man in your daughter's room. He was . . . getting off."

The operator came on and asked Gerry what his emergency was. But there were too many for Gerry to know how to answer.

ON THE WYNNS' BACK DECK, a place she'd never been before, Marly Kimberson stood with her arms crossed. Miranda the real estate agent was trying to coax her back inside, speaking to her gently and in a high pitch as if she were a puppy. Gerry knew her fangs, stood at a fair distance. Gerry didn't trust Marly Kimberson—who was to say she hadn't brought a gun with her even, inside that unbleached canvas tote bag?

"I'm not leaving. I have every right to be here," Marly said, her voice forceful.

"Of course, but you've seen most of the house and we're going to wrap up now," Miranda tried to reassure her.

"Over my dead body are you going to buy this house!" Gerry boomed.

"Dead bodies. You want to talk to me about dead bodies." Marly marched up to Gerry. She didn't touch him, just stood in front of him and stared him down.

"Please," Miranda was saying. "An open house is not the time for this."

She'd managed to move Marly and Gerry into the kitchen when Kennedy came across the sitting room, the front door behind her open. "Dad!" she called. "The police are here."

Gerry glanced over at her and noticed Josh was still inside. He had some kind of device strapped to his wrist. He was filming their conversation.

"Hey!" Gerry yelled, and the guy let his sleeve fall back over his wrist, the tiny camera covered from view.

Josh bolted past two police officers who asked Kennedy what the problem was.

"A man—" she said only, not willing to put the act into words. Gerry would have sent them after Josh, but Kennedy pointed up the stairs toward her room. "A man."

Chapter 30

EVERETT STARED AT THE GAME BOY in the back of the drawer before pulling it out. It was one of the few items he had taken from his childhood room besides his clothes to bring with him to the condo. Haley had bought it for him—the year before she'd met the twins. She'd saved her money from baby-sitting jobs and given it to him for his birthday. His birthday was lodged in the week between Christmas and New Year's, which meant he'd never gotten a birthday party in his life. At that age he had no real understanding of what the handheld video game cost, but he knew she only made $2 an hour, $3 if she could get a gig for one of the better families over in Blue-heart. The math added up to love. Everett remembered how hot the plastic used to get in his sweaty hand. The sound of Tetris bleeping to life. The cord was there, wrapped around it-self. There was never any real reason to pull out a Game Boy. *Except when you miss your sister.* Everett walked over to the wall by the bed and plugged it in. His cell phone rang.

"Hello, Everett." Dee Nash had a slow, gentle way of speak-ing similar to that of a school counselor or the social workers

Everett had been sent to after his sister died. "I want to say you did really well at the preinterview."

"I don't know if I said the right stuff."

"From what I saw, you're honest. That's all that matters."

"Are you—did you get the results back from the sample?"

"It's sixteen years old. There are only a couple labs that can do it, and there are backlogs. It's going to take time." She let him digest that, then said, "I was wondering if you might be able to put together some things for us to shoot. Photographs, objects that belonged to your sister. Anything that might be meaningful or give people an impression of who she was."

"Y'all want me to bring them to the hotel?"

"We have a temp office," she said, and gave him an address.

"I really thought you were going to shoot at the house at some point."

"We still need your mother's permission, and—" There was a long pause and at first Everett thought his cell had dropped the call. "You know, for some folks, anger is a way out of grief, a way back into the world. If necessary we'll use the street shots we took of her place. What you can bring us, we'll shoot here. Yearbooks, schoolwork, photos, anything that's not too much trouble."

Everett's mother wasn't like Gerry Wynn. She hadn't kept Haley's room pristine, waiting for her return. There was no returning. She'd cleaned out the room as soon as she was able, chucking things into boxes without even looking, saying, "What does she need this for now, when she's with God?"

He knew she cared but that she simply hadn't known what

to do with her feelings. The Kimbersons weren't wired to express things. Still, Marly hadn't gotten rid of everything.

"You're doing hard work, and when we put the story together, even if nothing new emerges, I think it will be good for you."

Everett wasn't so sure about that, but he thanked her and said goodbye. He'd tried not to think about the possibility the placental tissue could show DNA that matched his father's.

When the Game Boy had charged, he sat down on the edge of the bed and played Tetris for an hour or more. He watched the blocks on the screen fall and lock into place, rectangles and wedges, shapes like L's and T's. He spun them to get the best position, build a solid wall. The thump of them hitting and clicking wherever he directed them to: it was easy to feel at peace while the digital tune chimed happily.

"Where do you go?" he said to a falling piece.

EVERETT WAS GLAD to see Marly was already up and dressed when he arrived at the house hoping to talk to her, and maybe sort through some old things.

"I saw her the other day," Marly told him before he'd taken off his coat.

"You go to that cemetery too much," Everett said, hanging his winter jacket on the hook on the wall. "I don't want to see you be like those people in the lawn chairs."

"I am one of those people. What are we supposed to do, sit

on the ground? But it wasn't the cemetery. I saw her here. In the backyard." Marly took a sip of coffee.

"Ma, what are you doing to yourself?"

"No, no, I was coming in with the groceries and I saw Haley through that window." Marly pointed out the kitchen window above the sink. "She didn't wave or nothing, but I knew she saw me. Then she turned around and walked into the woods."

Everett went over to the window. He couldn't tell her what Ted had admitted in the barn. Not yet. Ted had kept the pregnancy away from Marly because she never had been strong enough. That was true, but maybe his father had other reasons too and that detective at the funeral who called him Deputy Everett had been right about Ted.

"You believe there are souls in heaven." Marly looked at him studiously, as if waiting for him to deny it. "How's that different from ghosts?"

He knew better than to disagree. "You got me there."

"She was just the same as the last day I saw her alive. She had on that blouse I hated. That yellow one, you could see right through it. But she was beautiful, Everett. She was so beautiful. She was my daughter and the woman she never got to be."

"Like, older?" He asked it before he remembered he didn't believe her and shouldn't encourage her. He had wondered so many times what she would be like now. He gazed at the woods. The leaves were mostly down now, a golden-brown sheet wrapping the roots of the trees. The woods ran the northern length

of Longwood and Blueheart—and Haley had been found almost exactly between the two. "You got to take care of yourself,
Ma. Are you eating?"

"I had groceries in my hand. Those were real too."

"Suppose it wasn't a ghost," he said. "I remember watching
that show *Destination Paranormal*. They had an expert on saying ghosts maybe aren't souls. That if someone dies in a traumatic way it's like it's been recorded. Like sound hitting a tape.
That's why when you see a ghost they only do one thing and
repeat it. Maybe it was that. That tape-record thing."

"And it was violence that caused that? Funny." She lit a cigarette and pushed the newspaper around on the table.

"What?"

"That violence would be powerful enough to do that for
eternity, but happiness doesn't cut it."

EVERETT OPENED A BOX in the computer room, which had
previously been Haley's bedroom. He reached in and thumbed
books and knickknacks uncertainly, suddenly having a difficult
time distinguishing between her possessions and his mother's.
He removed a yellow binder. Inside, his sister's neat penmanship
detailed the French Revolution. Tucked in one of the binder
pockets was an ad for United Colors of Benetton. It had been
torn from a magazine. Farther down in the box were drawings
from her early years that his mother must have saved. He found
a mood ring Haley had worn for a few months, insisting it
"knew things," like when it glowed bright turquoise someone

she liked was close by. There was a bottle of men's Eternity cologne with a quarter inch still in the bottom. Haley had dabbed it on because she loved the smell, and wearing men's cologne was considered cooler. Everett uncapped the bottle. It was like looking at his sister's smile.

He stashed a few things in his knapsack, then put the box back and went over to a bureau that had once been in the dining room. Now it was full of stationery, old bills, and uncompleted sewing projects. In a drawer divider, beside sewing scissors and markers, was a stack of patches. Everett reached in and pulled the small tray closer to the front of the drawer. At the back of the divider was the jackknife.

"Goddamn!" he yelled. "Ma! Ma!"

Marly appeared in the doorway. "What, Everett? What?!"

He didn't want to touch it. After all these years, he didn't know if it still counted as evidence. The investigators had turned the house upside down as they searched for the possible weapon—Everett remembered even his bedroom being pawed over and sifted through.

"Oh, that old knife. I found it in the garage four or five months ago. Not too long after you moved out. Swept it up in my dust pile. It was so coated I didn't know what it was. Guess it fell behind that deep freezer we don't use anymore."

Everett reached into the drawer and pulled out the whole tray that held the scissors, buttons, patches, and knife. He set it on top of the bureau.

"And you didn't tell me? Didn't call anyone? *What the hell, Ma!*"

Marly's voice was flat, beaten. "Well, what for? Who knows—who cares—what knife it was?"

"Don't you understand this totally changes the nature of the crime?"

Marly stubbed out her cigarette. "How? It was a violent crime, and it's still a violent crime."

Everett pushed past her in the doorway and went and got a large Ziploc from the kitchen. He returned and shoved the whole tray inside the plastic bag.

"Don't take my good sewing scissors," Marly protested.

Everett grabbed his knapsack from the floor and slung it over his shoulder. He picked up the tray, keeping it level so the contents didn't spill. "When was the last time you even used them?! You stopped living when she left us. I raised myself and tried not to let you die of grief. I was twelve years old the time I threw all your disposable razors out because I didn't trust you. Pa was the alcoholic, but at least he got sober. He opened himself up to change. You, there's no change. You think you see her, talk to her, but do you *care* about her? Or do you only care about pinning everything on the Wynn family? Because let me tell you, there's three individuals in that family and they're not all the same."

Marly had begun to cry. "Why are you talking like this, Ev?"

"Go ahead and cry, Ma. But I have to take this somewhere. I have to see this through. For Haley."

Everett snagged his coat from the kitchen and ran to his car. He was already on the expressway before he realized he'd left the stereo on from the drive over and it was playing *Sister*, by Sonic Youth. It was Haley's CD. The chords to "Schizophrenia" rippled through the interior as the Mustang flew into the left lane, passing the other cars as if they were only phantoms. He felt the tears, the mucus in the back of his mouth.

Chapter 31

WHEN CARTER PULLED UP outside her apartment, she saw what looked like Everett Kimberson's Mustang parked across the street. It was the parking spot she usually tried to get. She passed it and found a parallel spot farther down the block. He wouldn't just come there without calling, she told herself. She reached into the backseat of her car and took out the shopping bag, which was packed with things she'd picked up for Christmas. Even if Kennedy had stopped speaking to her, she couldn't skip buying her something for Christmas. Carter glanced up and down the street as she walked back.

Her place was one of the colonials she'd always hoped for, but the main floor had been divided in half. Hers was the apartment in the front. She got the porch; the woman who lived in the back got the backyard. It was grand on the outside, at least, she told herself. She hefted her bag and grabbed the mail from the box before she stepped inside. There was an acknowledgment of receipt from one of the schools she'd applied to after the lunch she had with Kennedy and Gerry that had left her wondering what she was doing with her life.

She wouldn't know if she'd be admitted for several more months. She had no idea how she would pay for or manage such a thing without Gerry's help. But she'd decided she'd wasted too much time in her life. She had to make the first step and worry about the rest later.

Carter was in the middle of taking off her boots when the doorbell rang. She pushed the one she'd just taken off on again. If it was him, Carter at least wanted to look put together. She turned around and tripped over the shopping bag stuffed with gifts. She gathered the things up quickly and shoved the bag against the wall. When she opened the door, Everett was there. His eyes were puffy.

She felt the air thicken, and if she hadn't been on the Lumalex, she might have called it an overwhelmed feeling. But now she simply breathed back out again.

"I tried to call you from the pay phone at the store on the corner." He jerked his thumb over his shoulder, as if she didn't know where her own corner store was.

She smelled the winter on his collar. The leather was cold, like he'd been walking around outside. He permitted the hug, though she kept it briefer than she wanted to. She had her pride.

"Come in." Carter drew him by the arm into her hallway. "What happened?"

"I guess I left my phone at my mom's." He sank down onto her couch.

"No, I mean what happened?"

"Please don't hate me." Everett's shoulders slumped. He

pressed his hands together between his knees and stared at her floorboards.

"I don't." She sat beside him but wasn't sure if she should touch him again. She didn't know yet what it meant for him to come there. Lines appeared in his forehead, running vertically up from his nose. His nostrils broadened as he drew in a breath. She knew she was supposed to get up, offer coffee, make things easy, comfort him casually, maybe tell him about her life, what she'd been up to. But she couldn't actually talk, couldn't move. All she wanted to do was stare at his face.

"I'm not even speaking to her anymore," she said finally.

Everett straightened and looked at her, silent.

"I told them about us, and Gerry just hangs up on me since then. Kennedy—she'll probably come around eventually. If I keep reaching out, but I don't know why I should." Carter got up and pulled the shopping bag over to the couch. She stacked the gifts. "Stupid, isn't it? That I'd buy them things."

"She's your sister," Everett said. He reached out and thumbed through the objects. He touched a tiny wooden box there.

"That's for you," Carter said. "I don't know why. Turn the handle."

Everett took the miniature handle and cranked it. The golden spool inside turned, the bumps plinking off notes—complicated for such a basic piece of hardware, haunting and sad. Carter watched as his mouth pursed and eyes got shiny. It was Sinéad's "Nothing Compares 2 U." She'd found it among a row of other boxes that played contemporary songs. The Doors, the Beatles, Queen, Celine Dion, Elton John.

"Silly, right?"

Everett swiped at his face with one hand. He laughed. "Makes more sense to me than Rochester and Jane. Why'd she fall in love with him? That part about him regaining his sight at the end is bullshit. Why not let the maimed and afflicted stay that way?"

"You finished reading it."

He nodded.

"So many reasons. He fits the image of the complicated, moody man, right? Then he's handsome, well-off. And some might say they're intellectual equals."

"What would you say?" Everett turned to her with those bright hazel-green eyes. She noticed his hands were shaking slightly where he held the box.

"I would say I was young when I read it, and we latched on to it, called your sister Helen instead of Haley, because it was a thing we could all buy into. I mean, fiction is bonding, more so than reality sometimes. A romantic fantasy, in a curriculum of mostly male characters."

"You always were the smart one," he said.

Carter stared at him. "But if you look at Jane and Rochester it's also the first time in a long while she has a home, a sense of family." Carter stopped talking as Everett played the music box again.

"I know she didn't do it," he said.

She watched his lips saying the words, heard them slowed down. *I know she didn't do it.* That wasn't really what he'd said.

Carter stood up, moved away. "Why do you know that? I

don't even know that and I'm her sister. I'm not sure if Kennedy knows."

"Because *I know*," he said, and she watched him hunch and cry.

THE KNIFE LAY, bagged, inside the tray on his front seat. Everett and Carter both stared at it, his car door open, neither reaching for it. Before he took it out to show her, he'd already borrowed her phone to call and ask Dee Nash if they could meet.

"What does it mean?" she asked. She felt her whole body shaking.

"I think it means my father—" Everett stopped short, unable to visualize what had happened to his sister.

Carter looked up at him and understood now why he'd been crying. It wasn't just about her—their relationship had never been about only them.

"He wouldn't just toss it behind your freezer, would he?" she asked. It wasn't the hiding spot of an adult man who had done the worst thing imaginable. But she knew Haley hadn't liked Ted Kimberson; it was one of the reasons she spent so much time away from home at the Wynns'.

"I don't know. Did she ever tell you about . . . things that might have happened between them?"

"What? Shit, that makes sense." Carter straightened from peering at the knife. She held her coat closed at the collar, suddenly cold. "But I mean, you would know if your own father . . ." She let her voice trail off, uncertain.

"I honestly don't know if I would," Everett said, his voice suddenly sounding bewildered and boyish. "Here's what I do know: the police searched for this, and Kennedy didn't have access to our garage."

Tears came to Carter's eyes. "I doubted my own sister."

She felt him reach up her arms and pull her into him. His mouth went into her hair, then to her cheek. She'd thrown on her coat but not her scarf, and he found that hollow at the base of her throat and put his thumb there lightly. He might have kissed her on the mouth then—she wanted him to—but the rattle and ring of her phone went off in her pocket and she jumped.

She accepted the call, then heard her own tone change, going sharp as tin. "I have to go," she told Everett.

❙❙❙ ❙❙❙

Chapter 32

K ENNEDY HEARD THE MAIL-SLOT SOUND, A faint *ting* and a *whoosh*. The mail truck outside started up again and pulled down the curve and around to the next neighbor's home. She stood up and walked over to the foyer. A letter for her sat on top of a pile of magazines and mail for Gerry.

How can time change everything except the way you shape a letter, the way you hold your hand around an object? Kennedy wondered as she kneeled down and slowly picked it up. It had a post office stamp on it and had been mailed the day before. *Kennedy Wynn*, the envelope said, and the address. All uppercase, tight scratchy letters, like a messy boy trying to be neat.

She felt air pass over her teeth and she inhaled. She felt the edges of the envelope. There was something hard inside, a card. A part of her didn't want to be alone when she opened it. A part of her did. She was grateful Gerry was out. He went out for an hour to the Starbucks, mostly in the afternoons.

She went upstairs to Carter's old room, which she'd begun sleeping in since the open house, as though her own room had become haunted. Carter's bed was newer anyway, she told herself.

She placed the envelope on the bed and went across to Gerry's office to get the letter opener. She couldn't find it. It wasn't in the drawer or on the desk. She thought she might have seen it on the file cabinet, standing upright in that old mug with some pens or something, but when she turned she realized the file cabinet was missing. She opened the closet door. The file cabinet was there, wedged in against the wall. The mug that had been on top of it was gone, and so was the decanter. At this point, she knew she should go back to the letter, but she couldn't help wondering what had prompted him to move the file cabinet there. It was a weird place for it. She pulled out the drawers, riffled through the hanging files. Then she reached out and ran her hand along the edges of the cabinet. Her fingers touched the line in the paneling where it came apart.

She jostled the cabinet over to the side and felt the wall until she found the twist latch that unlocked the panel. She remembered a plumber coming in once when she was an adolescent. She felt the wood open. There was black plastic coating on the other side, but when she looked down she could see that there were several inches of blank space and, at the floor, a book had been set down, leaning between the wood and the plastic. She put her hand down to touch it. She withdrew it. *Sex*, it said. The Mylar sleeve was gone and it was just the engraved silver cover. She went to put it back inside without opening it, but a small one-by-one-inch square of paper fell from the book.

She knew immediately what it was. A note. From her to

Carter, maybe. But when she picked it up, she saw it was folded in a way she couldn't have done, more intricate. Haley had had her own ways of folding: she could do a tiny rectangle with a pull tab; she could do heart shapes; she could do fans. There had been too many notes among all of them to know what it contained. Any notes she'd had from Haley were gone years ago, taken from drawers and put into evidence bags. She crammed it in her jeans pocket. She returned the Madonna book to the wall, popped the panel back in place, shifted the file cabinet back over. She had a vague and queasy memory of Gerry's confiscating it from them.

Back in the bedroom, Kennedy grabbed the letter that had come in the mail. She put her finger into the fold and pulled across the top, tearing it sloppily. It wasn't a card but two Polaroids. She knew when these were from: a few weeks before Haley died.

In the first, she and Haley lay on a futon on their stomachs, propped up on elbows, their eyes wide and spun. Haley was laughing and blurry. Kennedy could see at her throat the velvet stripe of the yin-yang necklace. Kennedy stared at the camera, a trying-to-be-sexy pout on her lips, her cheeks rounder, chubbier than she remembered their ever being. Her hair was violet fading out to pink. One hand was yanking her square neckline down as if to show off her cleavage, though there wasn't much to show. Only the top of a purple bra, its shoulder strap, and the implication.

They had decided it would be fun to taunt him.

She turned the Polaroid over. Berk had written: *More where this came from.*

In the second, Haley had her tongue out, pointed at Kennedy's neck, miming a sexual act more than engaging in one. Kennedy was shirtless, still wearing the bra, but shooting the photographer the finger. Her lips had been painted with Velvet Crush sometime between this photo and the last. The photos said, *Look at us.* And: *How dare you look at us?* If Kennedy hadn't already been shaking she might have marveled at how perfectly they captured adolescent female sexuality. But she was shaking. She could feel a shiver running all the way from the base of her spine to her neck and down the back of her arms.

She could guess what the other photos showed. How had Berk kept them from being claimed by police in the investigation? He'd hidden them—well. Just like the yin-yang necklace. What else had he hidden?

Chapter 33

THE HOMES OF GEORGETOWN all looked like the same dollhouse to Berk. As he drove in agonizing circles looking for parking he realized he hadn't been to DC since Lollapalooza '92 and parking was the main reason. His old roommate Julian had not returned his email so Berk pieced together his address from searches and the White House web page. He knew Julian worked as an aide for the Bush administration, but he wasn't about to stalk him outside the Eisenhower building and get shot.

The two had already connected on Facebook, or rather, Berk had sent several friend requests to Julian after meeting with Dee Nash. The producer from her crime show kept phoning, even after that first meeting. Berk hoped his threats to Kennedy had been heard and that she wouldn't take part in the show but now, just the day before, he'd looked out at the store and noticed one customer in a blazer and baseball cap, taking pictures. If the producers decided to delve back into his relationships with the girls, Berk knew he might not even be pushing apples at Butler's.

Berk ended up paying for parking on M Street and walking

back to what he hoped was Julian's house. He stepped up to the brightly painted red door but before he rang he peered into the front window. A man who looked like Julian, still thin but now with a shaven head, was clearing plates from a large dining room table where an older man sat. He too had a shaven head and both had oxford shirts on.

When Julian came to the door he stared at Berk for a silent minute before he spoke. "What are you doing here?"

"Nice place." Berk looked past Julian and inside the renovated row house.

"It's Allen's. It's mine too, but his."

"Your roommate?"

Julian rolled his eyes at the word *roommate*, but Berk kept going without noticing.

"I suppose rent is high here. Not like at VCU. Man, what did we pay for that dump? Two fifty each?"

"I'm not going to have a reunion on my doorstep. It's after work. We're tired."

"Has anyone been contacting you? About me, or that summer?"

Julian's brow furrowed. "We shared an apartment for one year, and it's been fifteen years since. I'm not who I was then. I'm really not proud of some of the stuff we did."

"You did that favor for me. And it saved my life."

WHEN BERK WOKE UP at his parents' house in the afternoon on July 5, he was still tripping on the Rain Forest acid. Waking in the middle of the hot day, all Berk wanted to do was throw up, then go back to his room and listen to some old Jesus and Mary Chain to come down. When he got up he looked down at the entrance from the second floor and saw three men talking with his mother. Men in bad suits and short sleeves.

Berk quietly walked back into his bedroom and phoned Julian.

"I need you to get the box out of the apartment!" he whispered desperately.

"The box?"

"Yeah, the Polaroids. Don't throw them in the garbage. They'll look there. Just put it, like, on the roof. And flush anything you're holding."

The detectives did not knock when they came into his bedroom to arrest him.

WALKING WITH JULIAN through the cold Georgetown night fifteen years later, Berk realized it was strange what time did and did not do. It made bodies soft and pushed memories further apart, but it did not change relationships. With a few words Julian was following Berk's orders again, walking a step behind him on the street, looking at the ground.

"The way I see it," Berk said, "they'll figure out everyone I knew and drag them in again. Just for a cable show. Kennedy, still fucking up my life."

Julian stopped walking and rubbed his cold hands under his arms. "That girl died out in those woods alone, Berk."

"You think I don't know that?"

Julian stared at him. "I didn't know what was going on that day. If I knew I wouldn't have hidden those things."

Julian had stashed away the photos that day, and when Berk was released after the drug charge, he retrieved them—as Julian quickly moved out. The semester was over anyway, he'd said, but Berk had known something had been broken between them.

"What are you saying?" Berk asked now, lifting his chin.

"I'm not going to keep lying for you. If that producer calls I'll tell him everything I know."

Berk grabbed Julian by his cardigan and pulled him close, almost off his feet. Berk's arms were big from pushing dollies all day. "I got a good life now. Biggest house in Blueheart. Looks like you got it good too. You want to keep it?"

Julian flinched. "I did the worst thing I ever did in my life because—"

Berk felt Julian's gaze on him, lingering as it often had. He let go of him.

"Because of friendship," Berk finished, unwilling to see who Julian was or the different directions life had taken them. "Doesn't that matter anymore?"

Chapter 34

KENNEDY HEARD THE KEY in the lock downstairs. Gerry was home. She hadn't been able to look at the note she'd found in his closet. It rode down the stairs in her hip pocket. The Polaroids had disturbed her enough. She wanted to get out of the house. She had her coat half-on, slung over one shoulder, the other arm reaching back and fumbling as she ran. There were two options—Carter or Nathan Doyle. Carter was clearly the better person to talk to. But it was the middle of the day, and even if she broke her silence with her sister, Carter would be at work. How much of a phone call could she manage?

"Whoa!" Gerry said as Kennedy sped past him. "Where you going? You need a ride?"

"No, I'm good."

"Well, slow down and tell me where you're going. I am responsible for you."

"Oh Jesus. Well, give me the ride then." She found her hat in her coat pocket and pulled it on. She grabbed her purse and slung it over her shoulder.

Gerry held up the keys. He made to throw them to her and

she opened her hand in time to catch them. As she looked at him, she tried not to think about the book in his closet or what he might have done with it. But she could already feel her face burning.

"Practice time. You'll thank me one day."

They wound through the cul-de-sacs, Gerry in the passenger seat and Kennedy clutching the wheel so tightly she didn't know if it was because of her growing fear of Berk Butler or the nervousness she felt in a small space with Gerry. She could feel a patina of sweat forming over her forehead but didn't want to take her hands off the wheel to remove her hat or turn down the dash heat from where Gerry had set the dial. Whenever they were in his car she felt like they were two shoes shoved into a suitcase. Compressed. Even if it was a luxury vehicle. She had once known how to do this, she reminded herself, putting on her signal and moving into the right-hand lane, the expressway ramp coming up in a half mile.

"I was thinking of calling Carter," she said as she veered a bit too suddenly into the ramp.

"Slow down."

"But I have to speed up in a second." She eased her foot off the gas as she took the curve.

"Now speed up."

For a second Kennedy recalled having this exact exchange before, when she was sixteen and Gerry fortysomething, back when they still had a typical father-daughter relationship. The other drivers moved over to accommodate her. At least Virginians were polite.

"Everything I've done for this family. That stupid bitch sold us out," he said as she got the BMW SUV up to speed.

"You can't—" she started, but when she glanced over he had no expression on his face. It was the same look he had when he talked about the weather.

"Just like when she was into the drugs. With you, you were young and didn't know any better. With her, it was almost gleeful. For Christ's sake, she'd seen you go through it and look how that turned out."

"They say you can't learn through others' mistakes," Kennedy said through tight lips. She couldn't help but defend her. Carter had been the one with their mother up to the end. She'd watched her die. It made sense that she would lash out in some way afterward.

"Your mom and I did smoke some grass once, at a party. We both felt good but said we'd never do it again. You girls were just little. Are you checking your rearview and your side mirror? Keep your eyes moving."

Kennedy glanced nervously up, then sideways, monitoring the other traffic into the city. He changed the topic and asked where they were going. Work, she lied. There was a new telephone script and they had to be there early. In truth, she planned to call Nathan from a phone outside the building and see if he could pick her up in his clunky Trans Am.

After a moment, Gerry scrubbed a hand down his face. "I guess I sympathize with how you got so caught up with that son of a bitch Butler, if you felt anything like we did that night we smoked grass. There he was, feeding you euphoria on a paper tab."

Kennedy hit the gas for no reason. "It wasn't like that."

"Easy." Gerry's hand went to the dash.

Maybe her father was right, although she hated to agree with him. Maybe she hadn't been in love with Berk at all but with the feeling of her own body when it was high. The shimmering universe. She recalled the nebulous feeling she had as she lay on that futon in the Polaroid and stared up at the orange spun-glass lamp that hung in the apartment. What did he mean by sending the photos to her?

Suddenly Gerry's hand was on hers, pulling the wheel slightly, realigning her. She put on her blinker for the next exit. They drove in silence. The building where she worked was a plain brick two-story with large windows across the front. It said FUTURES on the front of it in brown lettering that looked tired, as if the future were a pause button. When she brought the vehicle to a stop in the parking lot just off Broad Street, Gerry said, "From now on, it's probably better if we don't talk while you're driving."

She nodded and took out a cigarette that she wouldn't light until she got out of the vehicle. He hadn't opened his door though and she felt there must be something else—something he was waiting to tell her.

"We got a fair offer on the house."

"Not Mrs. Kim—"

"Guy in the three-piece suit. Little redheaded girl flying

around. Wife with the Burberry handbag." He reached into the backseat and pulled out a newspaper. It was open to the real estate section, and several houses and condos had been circled in blue pen. Glancing at them, she saw he was favoring the city over the suburbs. "We have to be careful of neighborhood though. There's so much violence these days. Miranda has some places for us too, ones that aren't listed yet. Add any you think are worth consideration."

"Prison may actually have been less complicated than this," Kennedy said as she stuck the cigarette in her mouth and opened her door.

Gerry got out his side and as they passed each other behind the vehicle, he grabbed her by the arm. "Don't be so ungrateful."

"Dad!" She ripped her arm away from him, then stroked the place he'd gripped her, thinking it might bruise. "I didn't mean anything by it. I just don't understand."

"Was there someone in the house, or wasn't there?"

She put her hand into her pocket and felt the edge of one of the Polaroids. She had once told Berk how to pop the sliding back door, that there was a way to do it using a screwdriver or the blade of a knife even if it was locked, but that was years ago and Gerry had replaced the door with a newer one since then. She shrugged, unable to trust her voice.

"Then you know why. Because *she's* there, her presence," her father said. He got back in the car, and Kennedy jumped out of the way. He pulled out of the lot less smoothly than she had pulled in.

Kennedy stared after the BMW. She thought he meant Laine.

She had assumed the redecorating had been meant to scrub the place of any last fingerprint of her mother's. She walked across the street to a family-run taco restaurant and used the pay phone there. Nathan Doyle's voice sounded sleepy when he picked up. She felt like an idiot for thinking about how warm and smooth his chest was, that thorny bed of roses tattooed over rib and muscle, how the blankets would stink like him, and how she wanted to burrow down and hide underneath them and maybe never come up.

She ordered a taco plate, and under a fuzzy speaker playing ranchera music, she waited for Nathan to show up. She unfolded the note Haley had written more than fifteen years ago. It began:

Dear Kennedy,
I can't tell you whose it is. But I told the tree our initials,
just like in the song. Not quite, ha ha. I'm always getting
things wrong.

Chapter 35

THE BMW LAUNCHED into the grocery store lot. Gerry sped into the nearest parking spot, stopped the car, got out of the vehicle, and headed over to the sidewalk, a long, cold walk toward the store doors. It was one of those strip mall layouts where you had to drive around to get to the nearest ATM before completing your errands—a concrete maze of competing needs. The restaurant where they'd eaten when he'd confronted Carter about Everett Kimberson was in an adjoining strip, up and around the next block of buildings. The numbness in his jaw came back as he clamped his molars together as he walked.

Cars cruised through the lot and the lane next to the sidewalk, disoriented drivers trying to figure out the best place to park. One driver was plodding past slowly when the car jerked to a full stop beside Gerry. He turned and saw the weary face of Marly Kimberson.

Someone was with her in the passenger seat. Gerry tried not to look, hoping they hadn't seen him. But Marly put her fourways on, and got out and approached the building with the

ATM, walking only feet behind him. Gerry continued on, then stopped a little farther away and looked back. There, in the passenger seat, was Haley, her yellow top streaked with dark blood. She glared at him from her stony gray skin. Gerry stopped walking.

Marly finished at the machine and had started back to the car when she spotted him. She got back into the vehicle beside the ghost girl, turned off the four-ways, and advanced. She was muttering—to herself, or to the girl, Gerry wasn't sure. As they passed him, Marly lowered the passenger-side window and yelled, "God sees everything you do, Mr. Wynn! He knows what's in your heart!"

Gerry waited for Haley to disappear. But she didn't. If anything, she turned her face toward him. He stared at her hazel eyes, the black liquid eyeliner on the bottom, the long, pale lashes on the top. She opened her mouth and a snail rolled out the open window and fell at the curb in front of him.

Marly put the window back up and inched out of the lot as slowly as she'd been going before.

As he watched the girl's bright hair winding through the lot, disappearing as the car continued, someone struck him hard between the shoulder blades; it felt like the point of a knife. So hard, he felt it all the way through his body, from back to chest. He folded at the knees and leaned forward, not from the pain but to try to touch the snail shell there among the cigarette butts and pebbles. If he could reach it with his finger, touch it, he would know if it was real. If she was.

Gerry heard a stranger asking if he was all right, but the words sounded like they were sizzling, the hiss of water boiling over in another room. They were not his concern. He stretched for the snail shell; his hand came up short, scratching at parking lot dirt.

Chapter 36

KENNEDY PASSED THE PHOTOS of herself under the table to Doyle. "That asshole I told you about, the one who's stalking me. He sent me these."

She glanced around, over her shoulder and out the window to the street, afraid he might be there somehow.

When she turned back she saw Doyle's gaze had turned hard. He was looking down at the photos. "How old were you here?"

"Sixteen. She was seventeen."

After he'd glanced at them he said, "Don't feel right looking at that."

"That's her. My best friend." She didn't know how much more she should tell Doyle. He didn't sneak another glance at the photos, just passed them back silently. "Berk Butler—he's the one who sent them to me."

"A Butler? Figures. No doubt in my mind he did this," Doyle said of Berk. "I knew a couple of killers inside. I think it changes people. Doing someone in. You can see it in their eyes—they didn't have to weigh anything else ever again because they broke the scale. I look at you and that's not there."

Kennedy unfolded the note. She read aloud from it, her voice weaker than she expected.

I can't tell you whose it is. But I told the tree our initials, just like in the song. Not quite, ha ha. I'm always getting things wrong.

With Berk, we tried, but it didn't work. He gave up after a few minutes. He says that you two have a soul connection, and that he and I do too. He said something about spirits in the material world but I think he was too high. The person most likely to be the father is already a father.

Too afraid to tell you for real, face-to-face, who else might have planted this in me. Please, don't say anything to Carter. I feel too ashamed as it is.

As DOYLE DROVE HER OUT to Blueheart Woods, Kennedy licked her lips again and again nervously. "She appeared to me. When I was jogging, I heard her voice. It was so I would find this."

"That dog don't hunt." Doyle fished a new, tightly rolled joint out of his car ashtray, one that had been waiting there as if he'd known she would call. "Or I have to be higher before I believe in ghosts." He put it between his lips and lit it with an old Zippo lighter.

Kennedy eyed the joint. The sweet richness of pot was too much to resist. When Doyle finished his puff, he handed it to her and then the taste was on her lips, in her lungs. She closed her eyes. They would find the tree, she thought, feeling a buzz of confidence.

After they'd parked, she led him in. The light was melting—buttery, five-o'clock light. Kennedy got out and walked in, singing under her breath, the last words she'd heard Haley say. She hoped that Haley would guide her somehow, that she would feel the physical grip of her, like a hand, know exactly where to step and in which direction.

Chapter 37

W EARING A BLACK BUSINESS SUIT, Dee Nash waited for Everett, leaning against the shabby building where *Crime After Crime* had its production office. When he pulled up she came around to the passenger side and opened the door.

"Well," she said as she reached into his passenger seat and took out the tray, staring at the knife. "There it is."

"What happens now? Do you ask them to reopen the case?" Everett said as he got out of the Mustang.

Dee took the tray and headed toward the building. She was already on her cell phone. "Winter, where are you?" She keyed in a code beside a double door. "Have you looked into our liability insurance yet? Tell me you did, or you're fired."

Everett followed her down a hallway.

"Because it's goddamn important, Josh. This is not a little thing. We're talking about potential evidence, taken from a private residence. Because if this thing opens up again a judge would never allow it, so come up with a better story."

Everett worried they were talking about him, that he had somehow failed as "Deputy Everett" but then wondered how they could already be working on the thing he was bringing them. He'd only called Dee half an hour before.

She held the door with one high-heeled boot for him as she finished the call.

"I do apologize," she said.

She unlocked a door and brought Everett into a three-hundred-square-foot space. It was stacked with gear cases and banker's boxes, and housed one large table and three mismatched chairs. The window looked out on the main street. Everett was surprised that TV could happen in a space like this. He understood why they'd filmed in the hotel. In the small workroom, he could smell himself sweating and realized he'd had a burst of adrenaline after finding the knife. He felt shaky. Everett sat down on one of the chairs.

She folded her hands on the table. "Kennedy pled, and she served the time. No one likes to be made to work, especially when the job's already done. But things are getting serious now. That DNA evidence, we sent it to a private lab. If we get it back in time for the show, then the state will have to reopen."

Everett stared at the table, at the knife inside the plastic sewing tray. "I can accept that it's my father." He felt ashamed and exhaled deeply.

She sat down across from him and fixed him with a steady gaze. "Why do you think that?"

"The knife was hidden, at my home."

"The knife was there. But was it hidden? You're making a supposition. Not stating a fact."

Everett had already told her on the phone where his mother

had found it, dust furred, how she'd wiped it off and thrown it into a drawer. From his perspective it would mean that either his sister lost it there before the crime, or someone in his family put it there. No one else he knew had access to their garage.

"My father did this." Everett rubbed at his nose. It was a new belief for him and he wasn't used to its being challenged. He also still wasn't ready to say the word *molestation* and wondered if that was still the word used. "He did other things. To Haley. Probably more than he admitted to me."

"I'm sorry that happened. That's horrible."

Everett watched as Dee got up and went to a safe in the corner. She bent down and unlocked it.

When she came back, she set a bag down on the table. Inside was a long, thin metal object. Everett stared at it. It looked like a dagger, but not a real one, more ornamental, like a stage play version. It was about eight inches long, silver with a Lucite design on the handle. Dee asked if it meant anything to him and he shook his head. He had never seen Kennedy or Carter with it?

"No," he responded.

Dee sat down across from him again. "This letter opener was made by a company in Columbus called Betterpoint between 1920 and 1980. They're still in business, but not the letter-opener business. Guess people don't open emails with a blade. I feel that it would have been a gift item, something given to Gerry Wynn during his career. A promotion? I can't say for sure, of course."

"How did you get it?"

"That's between me and my producer. Who may not be that for much longer."

"Is . . . Is this—?" Everett felt the words get slippery. His pulse throbbed in his temples. He started to stand up, then sat back down again.

"You can't get too attached to knives. These are both interesting, but there are millions out there. DNA, on the other hand. That's unique to a family: mother, father, child. Carter Wynn. Do you think we could get a sample from her?"

"Carter?" Everett was beginning to feel like he had the time the police questioned him as a kid. They'd given him Twix bars and let him play with their hats and badges, but at the end of the day they were grilling a nine-year-old about his family and neighbors.

"How long were you involved? Now, don't look so surprised, there's that pretty hair behind you right on your Facebook profile." Dee smiled.

He sat there, dazed, for a moment. "Not long," he admitted finally, though everything about their relationship seemed strong enough to bend time.

"Long enough she was angry you're talking to us, I bet. Do you think she would help us?"

Everett touched the corner of the bag and pulled it closer. He asked if it could really kill someone.

Martin Luther King Jr. had been stabbed with a letter opener in 1958, Dee told him. King survived, of course. It was a lady, probably carried the damn thing inside her handbag. So it wouldn't be the first time it had happened. In his sister's case, no one questioned—including Berk or Kennedy—had had cuts on their hands. "That's unusual," Dee said.

Everett held up his hand to stop her talking as a chill ran through him. He didn't need her to explain, didn't want to think about the weapon's becoming slippery, being fumbled in anger. He looked down. The opener had dull sides.

Dee moved to bag up the camping knife, slipping it expertly from the tray he'd brought it in. She took the two blades away, back to the safe. When he saw his evidence that he'd found being filed away, joining all the evidence from over the years—pieces of junk all as subjective as mercury running through your hands—he stood up. "I just want to know who did it. My dad? Kennedy? Kennedy's dad?"

"Here's what we need to do, Everett . . ." Dee placed one hand into the other out in front of her chest like she was making a prayer or a bond with him. "You'll give me your DNA. Then I want you to get her DNA. We test her DNA, it's as good as testing her father's."

"But DNA, that's a little personal."

"No. It can be anything. Hair. Bit of saliva off a glass or bottle."

Embarrassed by his own naiveté, Everett paused, listened to the cars in the street outside the office. He supposed he could ask her, he said.

"Or," Dee suggested, "just invite her over, offer her a drink, and give us the glass after. Familial DNA is acceptable in Virginia."

"You mean, you take my saliva—"

"For your father, and her saliva for her father."

Everett grabbed an empty sample collection bag off the table. "If you want the Wynn DNA, go get it yourself. They're down at the hospital. I'll give you mine, but it is going to say there's a piece of shit out in Shenandoah who should be in jail. Not sitting in a redneck mansion that Haley's murder helped pay for."

"Sit down."

She was firm in her command. Everett didn't realize how loud he had gotten. He sat down and breathed again. Dee opened up a manila envelope and took out a wrinkled photocopy. She handed it to him and asked, "Do you know the name Doug Macaulay?"

"That's the lawyer from her co-op placement?" Everett shook his head as he took the paper. It was a typed letter dated August 1993. He read it and realized only an hour ago he'd told Carter all the wrong things.

Chapter 38

KENNEDY AND NATHAN were walking hand in hand, and she was happy enough for a minute to forget what had happened in the woods.

"Do you feel it? It's good weed," he said with pride.

It was a conversation Kennedy must have had a dozen times, but long ago. Nathan flicked a finger up her wrist and she stopped, pulled him close. They paused to kiss. After a few minutes, Kennedy came out of her pot fog and said this wasn't why they'd come here. Nathan was persistent, continuing to bump and nudge her as they walked, groping her lightly until she said, "We have to find it."

"Don't blame me," he said. For a second she feared he'd bring up the photos she'd shown him. But he didn't. He said: "I can't resist your pretty eyes."

He stepped up on a log and began to walk along it.

She moved ahead of him. December had made the woods a skeletal version of the way they'd been that July. She hadn't told Doyle that this was where she'd actually found Haley, and he continued to talk to her, hazy from the pot, about nothing.

As she and Doyle wandered farther in, the sounds of Smoke Line and the expressway faded, and he turned silent too. Kennedy watched the muscles in his back ripple and thought of that gun tattoo by his hip. *I look at you and that's not there*, he'd said. But what kind of violence was Nathan himself capable of? she wondered. She was still unused to being around men.

Kennedy knew she was feeling paranoid, now that dusk was coming. She suddenly felt as vulnerable as she had as a teenager, when she'd look at a boy and think his hair was like velvet and all the arm hairs and prickly parts of him were beautiful thorns that might catch her. She tried to remember to look for the tree with the initials carved into it. She recalled Haley at one time saying she had a favorite tree, but after so many years all the trees were alike to Kennedy. They were blank faces, and no trunk seemed to hold any special marking. Standing there with the smell of the bark, the dampness, the dull grass and fallen leaves, she felt her sense of time collapse. She could have been sixteen or thirty-one. Kennedy was high in the woods. She breathed deep and the air felt reedy in her throat. It could have been 1993 or 2008. She turned in the silent, dark wood, looking for Doyle but didn't see him or hear him anymore.

SIXTEEN-YEAR-OLD KENNEDY HAD COME to the edge of the woods, where she would need to turn for home, and found herself not wanting to go. She'd pivoted and walked alongside the brushland in the other direction, to where she lay down in long grass and imagined herself swimming in the sky. She was

alone with crickets and other jumping bugs, and an owl creat-
ing a symphony of sound and sparks, until she heard screaming
in the dark trees that sent the bird and the swirling bug lights
scattering. She assumed it had to do with Fourth of July.

She remembered the yellow mist of dawn touching her, lying on her forearms like a whisper, and how she had gotten up
and brushed herself off. Time still existed after all, and she
headed for home, insect bitten and thirsty as the sun was coming up, to find Haley.

But Haley wasn't there, and when she phoned the Kimberson house she wasn't there either, so Kennedy returned to the
woods.

Thirty-one-year-old Kennedy was cold in the woods
and alone, again. She'd found her way to the creek. Where was
Doyle? He'd been walking behind her, balancing on a fallen
tree. Then he was gone. She called out his name, but he didn't
answer. The dead leaves rustled in the wind. She'd been waiting that night too, she thought. Haley walked off singing, and
Kennedy stood in the Mobil parking lot, before starting home
along Smoke Line. She remembered waiting there for someone.
Berk had a pager. Had she called it from the pay phone? Had
she called home? *Numbers, do numbers even exist anymore?* she
remembered Haley's saying.

Kennedy sank to her knees and lay back on the ground, a
little ways from the creek, unable to go exactly there. She stared
up at a darkening sky that was also fifteen years older. *A man*,

she said, out loud or in her head, she wasn't sure. *A man did this. I didn't do this.*

She sat up and removed crisp yellow leaves from her hair, like a dead girl waking up. She understood now why, when confronted with a powerful emotion, Carter was always saying she couldn't breathe. Kennedy crawled, then rose and stumble-ran back through the forest. Her mother had been right to warn her about men. She'd just warned her about the wrong ones.

The knowledge left Kennedy absolutely alone in the universe. She turned, screaming Nathan Doyle's name, but no return call came. Where had he wandered off to and why wasn't he here when she needed him? After a few moments the screams of his name just turned into a long, wordless wail as she tipped her head back—if she screamed, she could breathe—and the pain that had built inside her for years climbed up into the branches of every tree that Haley had loved.

Chapter 39

Berk hadn't seen the girl who looked like Haley since Thanksgiving, but a part of him wondered if he had done too much acid and, like all things nineties, it was catching up to him. He'd looked online and read about a condition called hallucinogen persisting perception disorder, also known as permafried. But he never saw trails or tracers.

He paced around the loading dock of the Butler's store with his clipboard, trying not to think about it. No more phone calls from the TV show had come since his trip to DC to see Julian, and no one strange was trying to contact him through Facebook. He wondered how much worry he was making up on his own. Maybe he hadn't needed to go see Julian, at least not for that reason. If he was making up all his worry about this, he wondered how much had he made up about the night Haley died.

As he counted off crates of Romanesco on his list he paused and remembered that it was a fractal vegetable, each bud a self-similar recursion of itself. He considered the possibility of his life's having been one long repeating dream since that July Fourth. It was plausible but silly, like an idea from one of those stoner books he had packed in the garage, maybe something by Terence McKenna or Jean Baudrillard. Besides, if this life was his hallucination of choice, he had to be punishing himself for something.

He would rather punish Kennedy.

An offer had come in on his house from someone who said they'd looked at one like it over in Blueheart—but wanted it cheaper. Berk's subdivision, Bittercress, had a lower school rating and fewer shops. They were bidding way less than Berk could afford to accept. But Oz was pushing him to take it, at the same time Serenity had told him she was going to visit her mother in Nevada.

"How long?" he asked.

"However long I need."

BERK LOOKED UP from his clipboard to see a tattooed man hop up on the loading dock with one move and advance toward him. He assumed Nathan Doyle was another trucker who'd forgotten to get something signed. "Can I help you?"

Nathan didn't stop walking until his nose was an inch away from Berk's face. "Stay the goddamn away from Kennedy Wynn. Hear me, boy?"

Berk flinched at his breath and spit and stepped back. He glanced around and saw several of his stock clerks aware of the discussion he was having. He knew they'd help if things got heavy. Berk snickered and spat out, "You're about right for Kennedy. Pure trash."

Before Berk could punctuate his sentence, Nathan's fist smashed into his face. Berk saw black and then bright static as he went to the ground. For no more than a moment the static reminded him of the fireworks in the sky when he left Haley and Kennedy in the woods.

As he was kicked in the stomach Berk saw his staff standing around. They did nothing to stop Nathan.

Chapter 40

FOR AN HOUR Carter stared at him. Sleeping. His face was slack, someone at ease. She remembered, when she was young, one of her friends had said he looked like Richard Gere. She'd never seen it. Who had liked Richard Gere? Whatever pain her father was in, his face wasn't holding it. Carter could only watch the evidence of his heartbeat and blood pressure on the machine. The nurses had said a doctor would come and talk to Carter shortly, but no one came.

She hesitated to call Kennedy at work when she knew nothing but the steady blip of temperature, pulse, but in the end, she 411'ed the call center. They said Kennedy had missed her shift.

She was debating her choices when a text came.

Rochester: When you were with your mom at the hospital that night, was your dad with you?

She'd left to come to the hospital after the phone call, and he'd gone to meet Dee Nash to show her the knife. He must have found his phone. How did her parents' being at the hospital back in '93 mean anything? It didn't make any sense to

Carter, and Everett did not, in all honesty, have the acuity of a detective. Carter peered down at the text, then walked over to a row of chairs and sat. The hard plastic beneath her made it easy to recall the hours of waiting on chairs like this one.

She remembered how they finally took Laine in for tests at midnight and there was more shifting from one waiting room to another, Carter gathering up their purses and Laine's clothes and shoes since they had her in a gown. At two in the morning a bed opened for Laine, and Carter was relieved to get out of the hallway, where every stranger who passed by seemed to leave a periwinkle trail behind them, a visual smudge. Gerry came just after they were settled in the room, wearing his work clothes, a stiff white shirt and gray dress pants. She remembered how terrified he looked at the prospect of Laine's being sick. In her mind, she could hear him going over things with the nurses. Then he'd walked over to Laine and croaked, "Get some rest." He told Carter that since there was only one chair in the room, he'd go sleep in the car. He'd be there for them in the morning—page him if the doctor came in. She'd been relieved. She hadn't known how to make conversation with him while high.

Her cell rang, startling her from the reverie. The number showed the name *Gerry Wynn*. His landline. Kennedy.

"Why aren't you at work?!" Carter scolded. The lines *I don't want to be here alone with this. I was alone with Mom. Don't make me do this again* stayed inside Carter. She knew her sister had no idea about Gerry's being there.

Kennedy said, "I have a note from Haley."

Carter was silent, torn between two alliances, wanting to know where her sister had gotten it and what it said. But mostly, wanting her to come, be with her for the first time in a long while. "I'm with Gerry at the hospital. A nurse called to tell me he had a heart attack."

"I don't think I can come."

Carter couldn't tell if it was hesitance or petulance on Kennedy's part. She blurted out, "I need you!" before hanging up on her sister. People in the waiting room looked up, and Carter fled their stares by going again to the snack machine, keeping her back to the room as she glared at the snacks without really seeing them. Everett could wait.

CARTER SAW KENNEDY arrive before Kennedy saw her. She was wearing the pants and belt Carter had picked out for her before she was released from prison. On top she had a men's T-shirt. Kennedy edged through the foyer with halting movements, as if she didn't know whether to approach the information desk or choose a hospital wing.

Carter stood up, wiping the Dorito dust from her fingers uncharacteristically on her pants. Kennedy spotted her and headed over.

"It's Nathan's," Kennedy said defensively when Carter stared at the shirt.

Kennedy's shoulders twitched, in that catlike way she had, like she could feel and hear things no one else could. It was the hug she must have sensed before it landed. Carter grabbed her by the shoulders and pressed her ear against Kennedy's, her elbow wrapping her neck and locking her there.

"I'm sorry, I'm sorry," Carter said.

"Stop it," Kennedy said, and it took Carter a second to realize she meant stop crying, not stop hugging her, not stop apologizing. Kennedy dragged her down into the row of chairs by the hand.

"Everett's the only person that's made me happy in fifteen years. And I know, I know. It's probably because broken things go together." Carter searched her pocket for a Kleenex. "Do you remember when you were young and a boy could look at you and it was so overwhelming you thought you would die?"

"I never felt that way. I just assumed they would look at us." Kennedy lifted the sleeve of the oversize T-shirt and offered it to her sister to wipe her nose on. Satyricon, the logo on the shirt said. When Carter hesitated she said, "It doesn't matter. It's a metal band."

"Gross," Carter said. She managed to find a crumpled ball of tissue in her purse instead.

"I'm not angry about Everett. I'm mad you didn't trust me."

"I know." Carter felt like her face was reddening; she took two deep breaths. She didn't know how to begin to repair the space that had come between them. "I'm sorry about that too. He's talking to a crime show about Haley. He said—"

"Are you going to talk to them?" Kennedy scratched at her cheek. "How many people watch that show, do you think?"

"You would never—" But Carter cut herself off. There was

no such thing as *never* with Kennedy and she knew it. She had owned her part of the crime from the beginning. Touching Haley, trying to make her prettier—more peaceful, maybe—in her death.

"I was thinking about Haley earlier," Carter said.

Kennedy interjected. "There was someone else who could have come to the woods that night. Nathan and I went out there and I remembered: I called someone."

The double doors to the lobby opened and Carter watched as a man was wheeled in a chair through the lobby by an orderly. His mouth was bruised on one side and a white eye patch had been taped onto his skin. He passed them, unseeing. She clutched Kennedy's arm and whispered, "Berk?"

Kennedy turned in time to watch Berk Butler being spun around and lifted into the elevator.

"What did you do, Doyle?" Kennedy said to herself, but to Carter she didn't look all that surprised.

"Dad's stable. Come see him."

Kennedy didn't answer. She took Carter's hand. "I called him that night."

"Berk?"

"Dad."

"That doesn't mean—why wouldn't he ever tell us that?" Tears sprang to Carter's eyes. She cleared her throat. "I don't understand. You're going to see him at the house when he's let out."

"No, I can't. I'll stay at Nathan's apartment."

Carter tried to read her body language. She had stiffened. "What about your parole?"

"Carter? Dad came to pick us up that night." Kennedy took a folded piece of paper from her jacket pocket and passed it to Carter. "And I found this fifteen years late. She must have hidden it in the house for me to find, put it in my bed like we always did."

"That night?" Carter reached for the note. She had forgotten that teenage-girl hands could fold a full sheet of paper so tiny.

Tears came again, steady enough to slide and fall, as Carter saw Haley's name at the end of the letter and read what she should have known years ago. She reread it, then held the note even as she sobbed. Kennedy gently took it from her before it could get wet and was refolding it when a nurse came to them and passed a pamphlet to them: *Coping with Grief and Loss*.

"We also have a chapel," the nurse offered, thinking they'd just lost someone close to them.

Chapter 41

WHEN GERRY OPENED HIS EYES his two little girls were standing at the foot of his bed. Kennedy, he was pretty sure, on the left and Carter on the right. Yes, that was Kennedy, he thought, noting her hair was shorter. He tried to rub his eyes, but it hurt to lift his arms. They weren't dressed in matching outfits as they usually were.

"Where's your mother?" he said, but his hoarse voice croaked. He glanced around and saw the hospital room, a pitcher of water on a rolling table. Neither girl moved to get a glass for him. He struggled to sit up, and Carter held out what he thought was a homemade get-well card. Gerry shook his head. He must have been half dreaming. His girls were adults now, he thought, arguing with his own dream. The nurse had changed the IV bag earlier and he had no idea what was in it—maybe morphine; he knew that inspired crazy dreams. He smiled at the thought of Kennedy and Carter's being young again.

"I hate you," Carter said. She held out the note that Haley had written years before. There was nothing girlish about her tone.

Kennedy touched her arm. Gerry looked at her face, so similar to Laine's when she was their age. He tilted his head and sighed. They were beautiful, his lovely girls, and they were together again.

"Stop smiling," Kennedy said.

Carter held the note up again. "We know it was you."

Gerry shook his head. "I'm so thirsty," he said.

"Gerry!" Kennedy came around the side of the bed and took him by his arm, shaking him briskly. On her face was a hard expression.

He started. "You're real," he said. "Are you real?"

Kennedy nodded. "We are. But you don't exist anymore."

A nurse in pink scrubs appeared in the doorway. She said something Gerry only half heard about getting him too excited. She was at his side now, not his daughters. She pressed a button on the heart monitor. The girls were fading away, back toward the wall under the exit sign.

GERRY WOKE THAT NIGHT to a flash in the corridor. It was immediately clear to him that she had followed him there. The nurses and the doctor earlier had told him he needed to rest. They'd observe him for another day. When he tried to talk, they told him to sleep. Now she was here. He reached up and pulled the tabs off his chest, detached himself from their monitors. The nursing staff would come, but he wanted them to. He wanted them to see.

He gripped the IV stand and rolled it out into the hallway.

Each step he took dragged. His chest and shoulders still hurt, as
if he'd been punched. Gerry looked down the passageway, some
doors open, some closed. The nurses' station was to the right.
To the left, a bright vapor. Like something had been burning.
There she stood. Her eyes were downcast, her lips moving as if
she had been singing to herself before he interrupted her. Her
yellow shirt was tattered. She looked up at the squeak of his IV
stand. She stared at him, her eyes bruised, the orange lashes a
bright contrast. She went back to muttering.

When he got closer he said, "I can't hear you."

He turned and glanced back over his shoulder. Why didn't
the nurses come? He walked a few more steps toward her. The
air between them flickered, a shock like static. Her voice was
almost guitar feedback, the kind his daughters once listened to.

"I knew you would come," she said. "I knew you would
come."

She sounded happy, though her ashy face stared blankly at
him. Her voice was like a recording, playing from the wrong
figure in the wax museums of Gerry's youth.

"Yes, I'm here," he said uncertainly.

"Let's go into the woods. I want to show you something."

"We're not in the woods," he said, and took a step away
from her.

Haley raised her arm to him, held out her fingers, fluttering
them delicately, a girl inviting him to the dance floor. Her
nails were full of dirt and a hole ran through one hand. Blood
flowed down from the wound, a ribbon wrapped around her
forearm.

"I knew you would come," she said, again happily, her voice following the same cadence as before. "I knew you would come."

He wondered what to say to a ghost.

Haley stared at him. "Let's go into the woods. I want to show you something."

The ghost girl turned then. Gerry followed her in his bare feet, his blue cotton hospital gown. The floor beneath his heels was wet with muddy water. As she put her arms at her sides and led the way the blood ran off the tip of her finger. Gerry stepped over the trail.

"I want to show you something." Haley pushed open the stairwell doors and turned back, blinking at Gerry, waiting for him to look. A beetle ran out from beneath her disheveled hair and scurried over her cheek, but she didn't flinch. Gerry peered into the stairwell and saw instead a gas pump glowing in the thick pool of night, the long stretch of Smoke Line one had to drive to get there.

Chapter 42

Even with Doyle sitting across from her in a yellow jumpsuit Kennedy felt the idiot was still worth it. If not for the protection then for his beauty, which he couldn't erase, no matter how many green-ink tattoos and bad decisions he threw at it.

"I am sorry. Real sorry about this," he said, showing her a palm, thumb up.

"Just tell me what happened."

"Got in my head to do the right thing."

"How did that, of all things, ever make it inside your head?" she asked.

"Meth. Needed to level out a bit after the woods. But it's not really my thing. Butler was easier to find than your tree."

Kennedy looked at his knuckles, still bloody and swollen, folded now in his lap. She looked around them, the concrete walls. County jail wasn't high security, and they sat close together on blue chairs. "I'm on parole," she said, talking low. "I can't believe I'm even here. If I'm caught—"

"It's cool. They know me here."

"That's kind of the problem with you."

Nathan leaned forward, his gaze unwavering. "I stuck up for you. Ain't a lotta people doing that. I'm right or am I right?"

"Just tell me what you did for me." Kennedy arched an eyebrow at him. She wanted to hear him tell it.

"I go down to the Butler's. I walk in—no one pays any mind. I look like I should be hauling or delivering. I get right in Berk's face and tell him what my business is with him."

She already knew how it would go but asked anyway. "Then what happened?"

"Rich boys fall fast. Best punch there is." He made a small clocking motion with the bruised hand. "So he's on the ground with all this old rotten broccoli and I'm kicking him and yelling so everybody can hear, 'You killed that little girl, didn't you? You killed her.'"

"He didn't. He's an asshole, but he didn't kill anyone."

"Still the most fun I had since I got out. 'Cept being with you."

"How long are you going to be in here?"

"Six months for parole violation. Can't do nothing about that. More if he charges. But he ain't going to charge."

"Of course he will. He'll put you away and me too."

Nathan shook his head and winked. "I told the police about those photos. Said that's why my blood was up. They were real interested so they're going to be swinging by his place soon."

"All thanks to your good citizenship?"

"You better believe it."

Chapter 43

CARTER PULLED UP in front of the pizza place. Nathan Doyle's apartment was upstairs. Kennedy had been living there since he went into county for assaulting Berk Butler. The rent was paid for the remainder of the month, and Kennedy said the place fixed up better once a mop had been through it and a few home items had been purchased from the nearby Target. Carter had offered to let Kennedy stay at her apartment, but when Kennedy said no, she didn't argue. She knew they didn't need to be slid in beside each other like books on a shelf. They were still repairing their relationship. They were similar people, but they weren't the same. Time had made sure of that.

Kennedy must have been watching because she was already coming out of the building. She ran to the Honda and got in. "We're really going to do this?" Kennedy asked as Carter drove. Then she answered her own question. "Yeah, let's do it."

"I'm so mad I can't form sentences." Carter braked early for a yellow light.

"Try this: Red leather, yellow leather. Red leath—"

"Don't tease me!" Carter accelerated as the light changed.

"I'm not. How's Everett?"

Carter nodded. "He says good luck."

Carter and Everett were navigating the new lines of their relationship, one that allowed them to go out in public together. Earlier that week, they'd taken a walk through the Maymont estate, in the geometric Italian gardens, before returning to their much less organized lives. Not much was growing yet, but Everett had been sweet, laying a finger on that spot on her neck that made her squeeze inside. Neither of them had asked when they would tell Marly.

Kennedy pointed. "That's it," she said, indicating the address that she held on a contract in her lap. Carter parked the car in the lot between the bingo hall and the drab single-story office building where *Crime After Crime* had set up.

Carter opened her door and got out of the Honda, spreading her scarf over her neck and chest, not because of the cold but to hide in that moment. She felt a brief welling up of panic but didn't want Kennedy to know.

Kennedy opened her door and stood up, one hand on the roof of the car, the other on the door. "Give me a good line in case I clam up. Something you would say. Something poetic and smart."

"You won't," Carter said. She waited for Kennedy to shut the door, then clicked the key fob and the doors locked. "Catharsis begins with paperwork. They'll probably have you speak to the lawyer before they take you to the actual interview site."

As Carter trailed behind Kennedy she took in her stance,

her neck and shoulders straight with resolve. She wasn't blind angry, as Carter had been; she was determined. Seeing it gave Carter her own sense of strength.

Josh Winter was ready for them when they opened the door of the small office. He asked if they had their paperwork and the twins nodded. He snapped on a pair of blue latex gloves and picked up a swab test.

Carter opened her mouth and Josh ran the swab inside, then recapped it in its tube. Kennedy opened her mouth, and he repeated the procedure.

"What if it turns out we're not sisters?" Carter said to break the tension, and Kennedy laughed.

The producer snapped off the gloves and led them into the main office, where Dee Nash was waiting.

Dee came over to Carter and Kennedy. Her gaze shifted between them, but she seemed to know Kennedy. She took her hand first. Dee's handshake included holding her grip longer than necessary and with both hands, as if meeting a dignitary. Then Kennedy sat at a table with the producer, Josh Winter, saying she understood as he briefed her on how the interview would proceed, initialing the papers he pushed across the surface. Carter had been right. They asked Carter again if she would consider being interviewed, but she shook her head. "Kennedy will be better at it."

"One more thing," Dee said. "If you have anything from

that time, photos, or maybe objects that were passed between you and Haley Rae Kimberson?"

"I'll see if I might have something like that," Kennedy said, but she glanced briefly at Carter, and Carter felt their radio again. She could see from her sister's face that she had thought of something specific.

Chapter 44

KENNEDY STARED INTO THE BATHROOM mirror as the makeup artist danced a soft brush down her cheek. Out in the hotel suite the crew fussed, moved lights around, and wrestled with disagreeable gels. When Kennedy had arrived in her chosen outfit—boot-cut jeans and an old crushed-velvet jacket over a T-shirt—Dee Nash had said, "We have to help you out," and sent a production assistant to the Carytown boutiques.

The assistant came back with two on-brand dresses—charcoal and black—and a marigold-yellow blouse with a bow. Kennedy had never learned adult fashion the way other women were able to: that day-by-day learning that accrued while childish phat pants gave way to hip-huggers, then to perfect slacks. Kennedy chose the black dress—it was the easy one—but the TV host shook her head and said, "Trust me. Go with the blouse."

Kennedy met Carter's gaze in the mirror. She nodded in agreement. "We'll look better in it," Carter said.

Kennedy glanced in the mirror once more as she was called to the interview set. With her hair fuller, face defined, and thirty-one-year-old body a strange revelation to her, Kennedy realized she looked exactly like Carter for the first time since they were sixteen.

THE PRODUCER AND THE HOST had assured her there was no need to be nervous, but as Kennedy sat in the armchair, she couldn't help but feel guilt. Whatever she said now would be what she said forever. She hadn't expected there to be more than one camera, an audience of men in cargo pants, moving cables and fixing her mic. How could she feel guilt when he'd let her sit in prison all those years?

Dee smiled, then her face shifted to serious. "What do you remember about the day they took you to jail?"

"Loneliness." The word came out before Kennedy even thought about it.

"Talk about loneliness."

She had never felt entitled to her feelings, and now she explored them tentatively with a stranger: "I was sixteen and I went from a world with my twin sister, seeing our friends every day, to sitting in white empty rooms for a year. I was in isolation until I was eighteen."

"What did you think about?"

"Nothing. Nothing for those two years. Looking back I would say I went crazy. When I went to the general population it was better. I was scared too, but no one knew who I was."

"You weren't 'Dead Kennedy' to them?"

"I wasn't."

"Did you think about Haley?"

Kennedy paused, searching back to a time she'd tried to forget. "Not then but later." The host looked at her, waiting for more, but nothing more came. Kennedy wore dress clothes but they covered years of battle armor. She wasn't sure she could give it all up yet. She kept her back straight in the armchair, her chin tilted up slightly to ward off the presumption of fear.

"You don't remember the evening of her death, still," Dee said. "But at your sentencing you claimed you were innocent while accepting the charges."

"The prosecutor was going to get a conviction any way he could."

Kennedy was retreating to defense talking points and unsure that what she needed to say would come out. Dee took it back to the personal. "Tell me about your friendship with Haley."

"We were best friends, quick. That's how it happens when you're young. She went to our school, but she was not from the same world as most of the families."

"Rich girl. Poor girl."

"Exactly."

"Did you give her things?"

"Sure. We bought clothes together. My sister and I took her to concerts. I mean, we had things she didn't. That was obvious."

"What did she give you? Why the friendship?"

"Haley was free in a way I couldn't be, because of how my family expected me to be. Haley would do and say anything. She wasn't afraid of anyone."

"Like Berk Butler?"

"That's true."

"He's denied that he ever had a relationship with Haley and said the night of her death he dropped you two off at a gas station, then drove miles away from the scene."

"They definitely had a relationship that spring and summer."

"Did Haley tell you that?"

"I was passed out in his bathroom after a party. I heard sounds in the other room and I woke up. Haley was making out with Berk and his roommate Julian. I told her to stop, and she invited me in to join. They had taken E. I didn't know what that was. I had never seen two boys kiss before. When the three of them got naked I went back to bathroom and locked the door."

The producer dropped his coffee with a splatter and both host and interviewee turned to look at him. He signaled Dee over to the monitors while two PAs dove with paper towels to soak it up from the carpeted floor.

Angrily, Dee got up and covered her hot mike with her hand, though Kennedy could still hear her ask, "The fuck was that, Winter?"

The producer whispered back: "Who's Julian? I don't have a Julian in my notes."

"I'm ready to keep this interview going. Are you?"

A PA handed Dee a manila envelope. She came back and took her seat. "I apologize," she said to Kennedy. "There was a sound issue. It's amazing what editing can do."

"I'm worried about that." Kennedy glanced toward the other room, where her twin sat on the edge of the bed, watching the shoot.

"Keep being honest and you won't have to be." Dee looked over at Josh. The producer nodded back and they were good to go. Dee returned her attention to the subject. "Without going into details, you would say that Haley was sexually active?"

"She would finish a phone call with a boy and she would hold up her pinky and say, 'Got him. Wrapped right here.' But looking back I think it was the other way around a lot of times. That confidence I loved about her. Maybe it was her fear of not being liked."

"You thought Berk liked you at first. Did you think Haley had stolen him? Were you angry?"

Kennedy paused. She knew her feelings were showing on her face. "I thought he took advantage. They were older. And I knew Berk could be persuasive. I felt he was the one responsible, not her. She was my friend but he was—he was supposed to love me. I loved him, and I had told him so."

"Did Berk know Haley was . . . with others?"

Kennedy took a breath. "Not until later. Haley liked people. She was giving."

Dee began to slide paper out of the envelope. "I have here a deposition given by Doug Macaulay. A late business associate, a friend of your father's."

"And my mother too." Kennedy felt her forehead wrinkle. Laine had alluded to her infidelity once with Carter, who had immediately told Kennedy.

"This was taken by Macaulay's own attorney just after your plea. It was given to the state police and never entered into evidence. He had a belief that your father, Gerald Wynn, and Haley Rae Kimberson—"

Kennedy nodded. "Had a relationship?"

"Um, yes." Dee shifted in her chair.

"That she was pregnant when she was murdered?"

"Goddammit. Cut." Dee slapped the letter and envelope on her knee and stood up.

"You told me to be honest," Kennedy pleaded as the producer, Josh, rushed over and crouched before her.

"We need to build up to this," Dee snapped.

Josh asked quietly, "Kennedy, where is your lawyer? I think we should get them."

"I don't have a lawyer. I hate lawyers."

The producer took off his ball cap to wipe his forehead. He was nervous as he spoke to Kennedy. "We don't have all the evidence to back the, uh, assertion, that Wynn, your father, was a suspect. Maybe we should have a talk off-camera."

"Keep the cameras on," Kennedy said, suddenly feeling a hot flush of anger on her cheeks. She'd been waiting fifteen years for people to listen to her.

Josh looked back at Dee. After a moment Dee sat back down in the chair. Josh walked into a different room in the suite while dialing his phone, probably calling the network lawyer.

"We'll try it this way. Kennedy. Did Berk Butler have anything to do with Haley's death?"

"Yes and no." Kennedy glanced at the camera. They were still filming.

"Talk about yes."

"He kicked us out of his Jeep in the middle of the woods. We were just girls and we were high."

"You were doing acid?"

"I had never been that high before."

"And he had given that drug to you?"

"All the time that spring. But this time, it was more powerful than we expected."

"And when you say 'no' you mean that he did not kill Haley?"

"That's right."

"Do you know who is responsible?"

"Yes."

Dee met Kennedy's gaze and leaned forward slightly. She wasn't going with the producer's way of doing things. "Can you tell me?"

Chapter 45

GERRY WAITED IN THE HOSPITAL lobby in the wheelchair. The doctors had signed off on his paperwork and he could go home, but he needed a ride and an escort. He'd called the landline half a dozen times and Kennedy wasn't picking up. That didn't surprise him since she hadn't come to sit at his bedside the whole time he'd been there. But Carter—she had that cell phone in her palm twenty-four/seven, never ignored it more than an hour. He tried to remember what they'd said to him when he first awoke in the hospital. Thinking about it gave him a headache that made his eyes water.

After two, Gerry asked the staff what he could do and they said they could arrange a home care worker to take him. He said all right, then waited another ninety minutes for one to appear and take him back to Blueheart in a cab.

Her name was Selena, and she told him he'd be just fine. He told her he was not fine at all but stopped short of saying he was a man with a broken heart. Back at the house, it was obvious that Kennedy had cleared out. Her closet was empty and the house was still.

He could have informed Kennedy's parole officer she was no longer living with him, but that would have been too much. Gerry was afraid of what his daughters could do now.

A few days later—no calls returned—he felt motivated enough to get out of bed and go into his office to move out the filing cabinet from the closet. He was not surprised to see the panel left askew. Inside, his hand reached into the crack and found nothing. He peered in: the book and note were gone.

AT FIRST, Gerry wanted to think his neighbors were looking at him because of how he'd changed after the heart attack: ashen complexion and his skin loose from losing fifteen pounds. But then he noticed it was other people too—people he didn't know. Eventually he accepted why the baristas and parking lot attendants were assessing him with concerned stares as he ran his errands.

He was sitting in the recliner in the family room when he saw the special report on WRLH promising "a new lead in the fifteen-year-old Kimberson murder."

A reporter in a trench coat stood at the end of the Wynns' street in the drizzle: "The show *Crime After Crime* has been developing a story on the Wynn-Kimberson murder. A tragedy that touched all of us at WRLH back in the nineties."

Did they keep the family photos all this time? Who are they getting those from? Gerry asked himself as the camera cut from the man on his street to a montage of images: photos of the girls in tenth grade, Haley Kimberson's funeral, Kennedy leaving court. *God, she was so young.*

The anchorman was saying: "A source has told us the police were given groundbreaking physical evidence in the case."

"A source," Gerry said to himself as he stared in disbelief. What in the hell could it be?

THE NEXT MORNING, Gerry received a call from a detective. He wanted to talk about the case. There were some new questions. Gerry explained he had just had a heart attack and the detective said he could wait. *Take your time and feel better.*

Gerry had been alone at the house since the hospital, except for Selena, who would stop in every day to make sure he was eating and taking his medication. She brought a portable blood pressure checker and the squeeze of its band was the only contact he had most days. Kennedy had gone, and Gerry left it alone. Maybe it was better she was gone: Haley Kimberson never would have been part of their lives if not for her. Gerry wouldn't have set up the internship for her at Macaulay's office, like his daughters asked. He wouldn't have stopped by there to see how the girl was doing. He might have been angry at Laine, sure, but nothing would have happened.

After that first call from the detective, the phone kept ringing. The next call was from the real estate agent. There'd been a retraction of the offer on the house—the couple had changed their minds.

"Won't they lose twenty thousand dollars in fees?" Gerry asked her.

"Yes, but they're still taking it back," Miranda said.

After a few requests from media, Gerry started to let them go to the voicemail. Selena asked him why he didn't ever answer and he replied that they were all telemarketing. By the second week, Gerry unplugged the phone entirely. He guessed 1993 would come back to screaming life soon. He had, he thought, started seeing plaid shirts and baggy jeans again.

He hadn't seen her ghost since the hospital—a hallucination from the medication, he told himself—but it didn't matter. He had started to see Haley everywhere in every girl, as if a wind from the past whispered his sins into their ears. They just knew.

Then it happened. He was in a restaurant in Blueheart when he saw Kennedy's face in a commercial for an upcoming episode of that crime show with a title crawl, *Kennedy Wynn Talks for the First Time.*

He set down his fork and coughed salmon into a napkin. He paid up and left immediately. He realized she was gone forever and he would have to start protecting himself. On his way home, Gerry pulled the SUV over to the side of Smoke Line. He had an idea of what this new evidence could be.

"THAT'S DEFINITELY A JOB for a chain saw," a tall clerk in a red smock explained to Gerry.

"Wouldn't that be noisy?"

"It'll be quicker," he said. "With an ax you'd be there all day. What kind of tree is it?"

"Black tupelo."

"I'm twenty and I wouldn't try to take down a tupelo with no ax."

Gerry glanced at the kid's physique. In spite of the smooth, youthful face, he had a corded neck, evidence he spent as much time working out as he did at his job. "A chain saw it is," Gerry agreed.

The clerk leaned in and spoke quietly, as if to avoid being caught by a manager in the act of losing a sale. "You know you can phone guys in town to take a tree down. Wouldn't cost much more than a chain saw."

"Oh, it's for destruction of material evidence. So I should take care of it myself."

"I see." The clerk didn't see, or thought Gerry was joking. "I'll meet you at the front till."

GERRY WALKED DELIBERATELY into the woods. He was winded, but he found himself unwilling to give up. He put a hand out to touch a tree as he passed it, then another, and another. His gaze scanned the ground, the tree trunks, the detritus left behind by hikers or high school kids, or thrown from windows of passing cars. The air was cold and the ground was hard. It smelled of pine and peat as Gerry headed deep into the woodland, searching for the exact type of yellow leaf, but for the tree too. He knew the area that it must have been near.

The wind had picked up and the hemlocks swayed. Walnut trees rattled. He turned to his right and faced the wind. Flying at him were dozens of small yellow and red leaves. Black tupelo. He could hear the brook, its sound thick, rasping as a voice. He breathed heavier and heavier, a distinct pain creeping through his jaw and down his arm. Here, it was here fifteen years ago.

GERRY HAD BEEN DRUNK on the Fourth of July when Kennedy had called him from a pay phone speaking nonsense.

"We've walked into the flower called Nowhere. Come find us," Kennedy said.

He had fallen asleep at his desk earlier. The blotter held a mouth shape. Through a whiskey headache Gerry tried to make sense of Kennedy. What was wrong with her? Was she drunk too? "What do you mean nowhere? You have to be somewhere."

But Kennedy didn't seem to process what he'd asked. "Dad, you have to come get us. Haley's pregnant. I can see her baby growing inside her right now."

"Pregnant? What's going on?"

"Haley is life. Did you know that?"

"Where are you?"

"Come get us! The green demon can come back anytime."

He heard Haley laughing in the background before she took the phone from Kennedy. "We're at a space station. It's a mobile one."

Mobil. He knew the one. The gas station on the old road just past the woods. He felt for his wallet, looked around for his keys. He surmised Haley was drunk too. And talking about being pregnant. Jesus Christ, what was her game and what else was she telling his daughter? He grasped in that instant she did not understand how serious it could be. Gerry picked up the decanter and poured the last of the amber liquid into a coffee cup that may or may not have been clean. He swallowed it down. He grabbed the letter opener from the top of the cabinet and ran downstairs.

When he woke up the next day he practiced saying it over and over again. *That didn't make it premeditation.* His daughter had been incoherent. There was a green demon, whatever that meant. Drunk, he'd rationalized that when you go into the woods you bring a weapon. When he'd backed the car out of the garage, he was lucky not to have scraped it.

He'd been on the links that day with a group that included Macaulay. It was pure humiliation. Every jocular word seemed calculated to gouge under Gerry's skin: *Wynn, you are the worst shot since Hinkley; Wynn, that's my ball you're putting and you haven't even bought me dinner yet; Wynn, I slept with your wife and made her come like the Tivoli fountains.* That last one was imagined, but still, Gerry had had enough and come home to find the house totally empty—a surprise. He knew the girls had planned to go out that night to the fireworks. Laine must have taken them. Her car wasn't there. No one had left a note or a message. He considered himself lucky and imbibed some more; the evening fell away until the phone call.

Haley is life.

He drove past the gas station four or five times in frustration. The girls had wandered since the phone call, he guessed, so he stopped the car just down the road, got out, and stood in the night air. It was cooler than he'd expected and smelled of damp earth. It was a few moments before he heard a girl laughing. He followed it off the road and into the woods. Haley was lying on the ground and holding her hands up at the sky, flicking and stretching them. "Haley, where's Kennedy?"

"I haven't seen her in like five years."

"She just phoned."

"She left after she asked me if I loved Berk and I said I love everyone. I love her. I love you. Why can't we love anyone we want to? Let's go into the woods. I want to show you something."

Her hazel eyes were totally dark, the pupils dilated.

"Get up. You're high, aren't you?" Gerry took Haley by the hands and dragged her upright. "Do not ever tell my daughter about what happened. Her future is everything and you're not going to fucking ruin it."

It had only been a moment in his car—he'd been five-o'clock drunk after a meeting with the men at Macaulay's firm and had offered to drive her home. They'd pulled into these woods, like teenagers, which of course she was—but now he could see he would lose it all. Everything he'd built would fall away, and in the end, Macaulay and the other men would be his judges. He could already hear them laughing, as they had on the course.

"Don't you love me anymore, Daddy?"

Gerry pushed the small girl against a tree trunk. Her head snapped back with a crack against the hard surface. She stumbled and then she touched the back of her head. Her fingers came back bloody.

"This is the mark of Cain now. Everyone is going to know."

What he heard was not a girl's shame but the threat that she would tell.

GERRY DID NOT REMEMBER if he cried while dragging Haley's body to the creek, but he knew he had to get her away from the crime scene. The creek would wash evidence of him away, the lawyer part of Gerry argued. He remembered the boots—just like Kennedy's and Carter's, piled up beside the door—when his sticky hands let her feet fall with a splash into the water.

As he stumbled out under a streetlight to his car, he saw blood had gotten on his clothes. He thought he could erase her, be done with the mistake, but instead it was everywhere. He was afraid to go home, so he drove straight to his office, where he had a clean suit. Getting out of the car, he saw a blood smear had transferred from his pants to the upholstery, so he decided to leave the Acura in the office lot. He could drive the Cadillac until he had time to clean it.

He rinsed his hands in the men's room, then cleaned the letter opener. On the bathroom counter, his pager began to vibrate as loud as a siren. Gerry turned off the taps and stared at the buzzing device. He leaned over to see the illuminated screen: Longwood Hospital. *They found her already*, he thought. *She can't still be alive?* When he picked up the pager, it showed a text: *Family emergency, please contact*, followed by a number. He was back in his office before he understood it was his own family, not hers, contacting him.

He took the letter opener and rammed it in the back of his desk drawer. An office would be a separate search warrant. Absolutely, Gerry thought. He snatched up the clothes he'd worn earlier and balled them into a bag. When he arrived at the hospital he would lob them into a dumpster in the back parking lot before going inside to find Carter and Laine. In the moment he was proud of himself for thinking of such a good place to dispose of them. No one would notice bloody clothes at a hospital.

After the police started questioning Kennedy, he thought there was no way charges would be brought against her. But as both sides dug in, Gerry sat silent and did math that was secret to him. *This family needs me. Without me it falls apart. Kennedy, if she pleads to manslaughter, that's what? Five years. She doesn't remember anything from that night. She could still go to college.*

GERRY WAS ALREADY WINDED when he found the tree. He sat down on a fallen log and stared at the initials while trying to catch his breath. As bright as that July Fourth night was, he had not seen them.

The woods were colder, damper at this time of year than he'd expected. Although it was four o'clock, the sun was white and fogged. He stared at the tree, the rough heart hacked into the surface.

H.K. + G.W.

A statement. His girls were always trying to make statements—politically, aesthetically, their fashion, their food choices at the dinner table. But they'd never carved them into wood. How long did that take, and did her hand cramp or develop blisters? It had taken her longer to do this, he knew, than what had transpired between them. She would have told, he assured himself, and he'd have lost everything. She was still telling now.

Gerry stood up and slipped on the work gloves and safety glasses the hardware clerk had thrown in for free. As Gerry approached the tree, he realized how big it was. He supposed you were meant to take a tree like this down with multiple cuts, but like hell he was going to climb it and slice off the branches. That would take all day and require more serious gear.

Which way did a tree fall? Gerry left the path and squished toward the trunk in his overshoes. The tupelo looked like it leaned slightly, so he'd make the wedge on that side. He pulled the ripcord and his chest muscles screamed. The cord snapped back and the engine went quiet. He pulled the cord again, this time watching how far he extended his arm. The machine came to life. Gerry looked up at the tree and then down at the trunk. He made his first cut through the bark. It spat chips and the blade seemed to go in. After a few inches of cutting the vibrations made his hands numb and the saw stopped. It was at too steep an angle. Gerry wrenched it out, then looked at the tree again.

All this for four letters. He then realized he could just take off the bark and a bit of the tree around the scratched-in heart. He yanked the chain saw on again and he put his feet down in the earth for balance before raising the teeth up to the bark, turning the tool upright. He would peel it like skin off a carrot. The saw skittered across the bark and began to chew out the letters. Still, time had deepened Haley's four-letter story into the tree. He had just brought the blade back against it when he saw the girl, moving through the woods, a gold-yellow blouse that seemed to float.

Chapter 46

Even though Kennedy's heart felt like it was pummeling the inside of her chest, she eased Nathan Doyle's beat-up Trans Am along Silver Creek Lane, following the posted speed limit, no matter that the car stood out in the neighborhood like a scout from an invading army. A cast-iron pot leaf swung from the rearview mirror.

To her relief, the driveway was empty.

Kennedy disabled the alarm to the house. She glanced around, then, without stopping to take off her boots, took the stairs two at a time. Her hand went to the drawer and her fingers slipped under the wool of old sweaters. They closed over the small disc and its velvet cord and she was downstairs in a moment, the yin-yang necklace clutched tightly in her hand. She could imagine this piece on camera, among the photos the *Crime After Crime* crew had filmed. It was the most personal part of Haley she had; it had lain at the base of her throat all that spring.

Back in the Trans Am, Kennedy wove around Stonemeadow and eventually came to Smoke Line. Here the speed limit increased. The large trees of the woods flashed past her, and the rearview ornament rocked on its chain. Then Kennedy slowed, in spite of the posted speed of fifty. Up ahead was Gerry's BMW, parked beside the ditch. She scanned the nearly leafless woods and spotted him just as he edged between a row of trees. He was lugging a chain saw. Kennedy snapped on her blinker and gradually pulled over, parking her boyfriend's car behind her father's on the soft shoulder.

"What the fuck are you doing?" she whispered under her breath. She got out of the vehicle and closed the door gently. She didn't head in immediately, unsure if her curiosity mattered as much as her safety.

After a few minutes she followed the sound of the buzzing.

She stopped when she saw Gerry. He was hacking, vertically, at the tree, like someone with no understanding of physics, like someone crazed. Strips of bark were raining down. Wood chips and sawdust fogged the air all around him. She was pretty sure a chain saw wasn't meant to be turned in that direction, as if it were a sword.

She was at the edge of a clearing, off to his right by thirty or forty yards. For a second she couldn't breathe. She knew where they were. The creek was off to the left, by a half mile.

She recalled walking through that clearing the morning after the trip, calling for Berk and Haley—the herbaceous scent of wildflowers and dewed grass seemed like a bright color to Kennedy, *Buchnera americana*, or the bluehearts that the suburb had been named for, purplish and waving—before she found her finally, unmoving and emptied. She'd known her friend was dead when she approached her, Kennedy supposed. She just hadn't wanted her to be.

Kennedy must have made a sound, because her father turned his head then suddenly. The chain saw continued its furious drone, metal teeth fighting the tree.

Kennedy froze, felt her breath hitch.

Gerry locked eyes with her but didn't seem to recognize her.

Tentatively, she took a step toward him and her dad twisted, looking not at his task but at her. She heard more than saw the chain saw skitter across the surface, that change in sound. His forearms jerked with the force of it and then the blade jumped— landed at his throat.

"Dad!" Kennedy yelled, and ran toward him. He was already on the ground, the machine sputtering nearby against the dirt and then into silence.

Kennedy heard him gasping as if there was no air, only blood. Gerry looked up at her, her hands pressing to the wound to hold it closed.

"Please, don't," he said, the words hardly audible, as if he thought she was there to kill him, or possibly, Kennedy considered later, as if he didn't want to be saved.

⫼ ⫼ ⫼

December 20, 2008

I'M AFRAID I SAVED HIS LIFE out of habit. Carter and I were always saving Gerry, like wives did for monstrous husbands in the gothic novels we used to read. But a softer side of me wants to believe it was because there was a part of him that needed to live to see what he'd done. That's why I'm now sitting in his hospital room, to be here for when he wakes and finds out what's left of him.

My creative writing instructor at Heron Valley, Christina, used to say, "There are many truths. Which one do you choose?" She would cock her head, the tight, dark bun she always wore on top of her crown, seeming to point only out the window, never toward an answer.

I choose this: I helped him even though I hate him.

He is unconscious in bed, his head held somewhat lopsided above the red gash closed by a dozen staples on his neck. Two heart attacks and a chain saw couldn't kill him though. I don't know how he will do against facts and truth. When his eyes open and he sees me, legs curled up and under my jacket, I suppose he'll try to speak and I'll have to tell him, *Don't even try.*

You have no voice left. He might start to sit up and then realize his hand and leg are cuffed to the bed's railing.

WHAT DOES FORGIVENESS MEAN when you're faced with someone whose crimes are as hideous as Gerry's? We always thought of ourselves as being worldly and tough, but we were just little girls; I can see that so easily now.

Asleep, his expression seems soft, medicated. That will fade.

There are many things I want to say to him when he wakes. I want to be his narrator and tell him what the next years of his life will be like. I know what it involves.

The state will bury him with multiple charges; the worst will be murder in the first degree and others will rhyme with blatutory tape. Possibly his friend Jim Stone will come out of retirement and act as his lawyer to see him through the bail hearing. But it won't matter. Gerry will sit in the courtroom dissociated from his surroundings, his wound permanently tilting his head one way. The state will threaten him with the death penalty—and brag that they'll get it—but Gerry won't plea.

He might have given up on me, but he's never given up on avoiding responsibility—and he'll continue to do that. He could throw me away for fifteen years because it was the idea of the Wynns, not the Wynns ourselves, that he loved. I understand that, and maybe even as kids we knew it. We were rebelling, not against things but toward something real, like love and truth.

In spite of his best efforts, bail will be denied. Privilege has limits.

The media will swarm and ask Carter and me to speak. Carter will brush past them, no comment. But I'll stop, turn, and say one thing and one thing only: *I inherited my father's sins. It's time to give them back.*

Kennedy Wynn
Longwood Hospital

Chapter 47

Dee let Everett tell Marly before they handed the test results over to the police. His mother wouldn't have believed it otherwise, that Gerry Wynn had been arrested. Everett decided to let Ted find out on the evening news.

As Everett told her the story, trying to remember terms like *mitochondrial* and *Y chromosome*, Marly continued to flit around her kitchen, putting together a Sunday roast. "Kennedy didn't do it!" he finally shouted.

Marly set the roasting pan down, faced him, and said, "Well, at least a Wynn still did it."

He decided to wait a bit before telling her about Carter and him.

In the car outside his mother's house Carter had refused to get out. "It's the only way," Everett reasoned. "She has to see us together. Some things can't be denied."

Carter was shaking as Everett took her by the hand. They walked to the front door. He knew that even on her antidepressants, she still had these little moments of panic, where the world felt too threatening to her. The person she had been supposed to rely on the most, her parent, had betrayed her—and Everett knew exactly how that felt. So when she cried, or became nervous, he just held her, as closely as he could and for as long as the situation allowed. He hadn't spoken to Ted in months and didn't intend to.

Everett nodded, and she raised her finger and pushed the doorbell. He watched as Carter touched her hair, a nervous girl about to meet the parents for the first time—even if it had been years of acquaintance.

"Why you ringing your own bell?" Marly shouted from inside. He had called ahead and she expected him, and someone he wanted her to meet. He'd said, "You know her already," but he hadn't said who, and Marly had guessed a couple names of Longwood girls.

When she saw it was one of the Wynn twins standing beside her son, and his fingers feathering hers, she glared.

"Ma, this is Carter. She's my girlfriend." Everett put on a half smile and leaned in to embrace Marly. He could feel the fear in her small frame, but she clutched him back for just a moment in a way that said her anger would fade.

When he pulled back he could see fifteen years of hate and obsession flickering on fast-forward and reverse. But there was no final explosion. No tape snapping. After a moment Marly said, "I suppose you should come in."

It wasn't the most pleasant afternoon any of them had ever spent, but Everett told himself it would get easier in time. Maybe.

Chapter 48

CARTER PAID TO LIGHT a candle in memory. Under the long rows of columns and the vaulted ceiling of Notre Dame, she shed silent tears. The high stained-glass colors blurred. When she looked over at Everett, she saw him still staring up at the ceiling, gawking.

He lit his candle, but neither of them said, "For Haley." They didn't need to. They watched the soft flicker and placed their candles in the row of others. As she and Everett moved reluctantly away, making room for other tourists, their two lights for Haley became anonymous, but Carter knew they would always burn.

They walked along the gray Seine afterward, the February day overcast, and Everett kissed her gently as the rain began to fall.

Everett had wanted Italy, but it was only a vague romantic notion that drew him to that idea. Carter had chosen Paris, and he had given in easily. She and Haley had learned about the French Revolution in history, pushing their desks together to work on projects. Carter had been involved in French Club and promised Everett she could remember enough of the language to navigate the city.

Everett had asked to visit Jim Morrison's grave, and Carter had tried not to roll her eyes. He was his sister's brother, after all.

BACK AT THE HOTEL, Carter showered to take the chill of the rain off. When she got out, Everett was sitting on the bed, staring intently at his laptop screen.

"What is it?" she said. She knew the episode of *Crime After Crime* had been supposed to air while they were away, and she'd timed their trip so they'd be out of the country. They had seen the preview before they left. It included voiceover, and a clip of Haley's yin-yang necklace swinging from an anonymous man's hand, an actress a bit too old to be a teen Kennedy wearing a velvet dress and Docs and walking slowly through Blueheart Woods.

"Dee just sent me a link where we can watch it online," Everett said, that vertical line dividing his forehead as she knew it only did when he was tense.

Carter stared at the image of her childhood home on Everett's laptop. He opened the image to full-screen mode. The house in Blueheart Woods, with its circular drive, its multiple peaks, the "suicide doors," as she and Kennedy had called them, being as they opened onto not quite a balcony, in the upstairs front bedroom. The lettering onscreen floated over the grass: *July 4, 1993. Blueheart Woods, VA.* The grass was ratty, though, and you could tell the footage had been taken in the wrong season.

"Did Kennedy watch it?" he asked.

"I don't know." Carter exchanged the towel for a robe, then found her phone and sent a message to Kennedy. She sat down next to Everett on the bed.

On the screen there was an unsteady home video of Haley Rae Kimberson at ten. The footage was aged, amber. She was wearing short Adidas shorts, skipping rope in the Kimbersons' driveway.

Carter drew a breath. To see her friend, alive, happy.

"I'm the toddler in the background," Everett said, his chin jutting forward.

"I don't know if I can watch it."

Everett took her hand and she realized she would stay, she couldn't not be beside him for it.

Dee Nash appeared onscreen, wearing a burgundy pencil skirt and a black blazer. She stared into the camera with an intensity that asked you to lean closer, listen—even from across an ocean.

Carter imagined the show playing on TVs in Laundromats and bars across the United States. People looking up at Kennedy's face, then back down to fold towels. She was in close-up now, her name across the bottom, the beginning of the interview they'd shot at the hotel. They were done hiding, Carter realized. Even though the house in Blueheart sat empty, Kennedy had been living in Nathan's vacant apartment, and Carter at Everett's. When she returned home, they would go back to their lives, and people would, or wouldn't, recognize them. Carter got up and paced to the window, stared out at the lights of the Fourteenth Arrondissement below. She drew a shaky breath and let it out into the blue night.

When she came back to his side, the monitor showed the photo of their father holding a baby on each arm. It was surreal to look at him now.

"I'm on the right," she told Everett. "The quiet one."

She knew because her mother had told her. She had used color-coded pins on their diapers, white for Carter, blue for Kennedy. Kennedy's eyes were shut tight and her mouth was open, as though she were crying loudly. It had obviously been taken in their first week at home. Her skin was soft and pink, new.

‖ ‖ ‖

March 1, 2009

Yesterday morning I boxed old files of Gerry's and shredded receipts, took the books down from the shelves, and ran a long-handled duster over the surfaces. It was clean because he had always paid for a service—but I wanted every skin cell of his gone. When I phoned the Macaulay niece who still lives down the block and asked if she had any advice for where to donate the law books, she told me it was likely that most were outdated. Prison has made me think time stopped. The suburbs too. But nothing ever stops.

I tied a faded paisley bandana from one of my bedroom drawers over my hair while I cleaned; I wanted the air in this place to shine. I sprayed and swiped at the mirrors, watching my face convert—wet and blurry, then coming clear. I'm in Nathan's metal shirt. He'll be out in a couple months, but I haven't decided what place—if any—he'll have in my life. Or anyone, except Carter.

I still have the feeling that I know when Carter is happy or sad. When I woke this morning, I felt it. Knowing where my sister is in the universe is like walking through a familiar room that's pitch-black and not bumping against any of the furniture.

This morning I phoned a charity that takes job interview clothing for parolees and asked for a pickup.

When I carried his clothes downstairs my hand lingered on a sweater of Gerry's. It was the one he wore the day he came to get me from the jail, but I refuse to allow myself nostalgia, not for him. I lugged the stuff outside and left the bags and boxes, piled neatly against the house on the walk.

DEE NASH VISITED earlier this week. She was on her way to a shoot in Baltimore. I could see how fascinated she was by the house as she walked through it, like she was meeting a friend of a friend she'd been told stories about for years.

"All by yourself here?" Dee asked.

"It's everything I know."

"If he's found guilty you can sue the state," she told me.

"They already offered a settlement. Fifty thousand per year of imprisonment."

"Smart of them. But cheap."

"I'm grateful, you know."

Dee turned from the window where she'd been looking out at the Japanese garden. She smiled. "Good goes both ways. Thanks to your episode, we got renewed."

THE REC ROOM will become a music room. That's the plan. Next week the piano will arrive. I've been spending a lot of time in there with my old Gibson Epiphone. There's a melody

I've been trying to find. It begins slowly, then becomes hard quickly. Like me, I guess. Where it goes after that I'm not sure.

Today while playing I heard a sound upstairs. A door shutting.

I set the guitar down and called out, "Hello?"

When I peered out the window the bags stacked outside for the charity were still sitting there. When I went to my own bedroom, I pushed open the door, and stepped around the paint can and brush and tray that were sitting there. The room is now a bright cherry-blossom pink.

"Are you here?" I said to the empty room.

That moment the evening was falling. Some CDs and books on my shelf had slid over, as if a hand had riffled through them, knocking several down on their sides. The copy of *Jane Eyre* I stole from the high school sat on the plastic-draped bed, its pages rustling slightly, as if someone were skimming through them.

"Don't leave me, Haley. I like to have you near me."

It's what Helen told Jane, before she died at the Lowood School. When I said it, the book stopped flipping, as if someone there had paused, looked up. I crossed the room and shut the window, returned the paperback to its place on the shelf. There is no ribbon of hair in it, and there is no time for me to be a girl again. There is only time now to be a woman.

—*Kennedy Wynn*
Blueheart Woods

Acknowledgments

Thank you to my editor, Danielle Dieterich. Her commitment to this book and care for every page guided me to a better novel. Gratitude also to Sally Kim and everyone at G. P. Putnam's Sons for making my novel this beautifully designed book. Thank you to my literary agent, Ryan D. Harbage, who pushed me creatively, and his co-agent, Christopher Hermelin, at Fischer-Harbage Agency. Thank you, Rob Hart, who read this book in an early draft and offered much encouragement. Thanks to Karen Dionne, Bryn Greenwood, and Karen Thompson Walker for their kind words.

Thank you to the twins who talked to me about their own experiences, including my brothers Erik and Ross Schultz, my friends Matthew and Mark Thibideau, and Mari Sasano. Thanks to my brother Dave, my lone sibling who is not a twin, who shared valuable insight from his work in corrections.

There are friends and colleagues who have helped with this novel even though they might not have known it. For the words, coffees, support, and inspiration: Jim Hanas, Cecilia Corrigan, Darley Stewart, Brian Gresko, Tobias Carroll, Paul

W. Morris, Rachel Fershleiser, Alice Kaltman, Andy Gershon, Duncan Birmingham, Kirsten Kearse, Jenny Grace Makholm, Cat Behan, Craig Stephen, Sarah Van Sinclair, Faye Guenther, Dan Robinet, Rob Winger, Michael Holmes, David Caron, Jack David, Éric Fontaine, and Rachel Morgenstern-Clarren. A special thank-you to my friends since the 1990s, Rebecca McClelland and Dawn Lewis. They were and are daughters of the kaos.

Thank you to Michelle Lyn King, Kyle Lucia Wu, Amy Shearn, Kathryn Mockler, and everyone at *Joyland*, a journal and an idea that gave me my career and my community.

I'm deeply indebted to my son's school, his teachers, and therapists, who have been critical to my understanding of autism. As my son continues to develop and overcome his challenges, this ultimately allows me to worry less and write more. Thanks especially, Michelle Flax, Lynne Kalvin, Jennifer Shonkoff, and Katie Yanguas. Thanks to our friend Kristine Musademba, and to Keen Kids athletics program, and the Extreme Kids & Crew group. Thank you to the Davis and Schultz families for your enormous help.

This book exists because of Brian J. Davis, my partner in life and work. He is my everything. He accepts no compliments but always gives out the right ones when I need them. Thank you to my son, Henry, who inspires me every day to live bigger and try harder.

I am grateful to my mother, who instilled the love of story in me from an early age. When I first began writing, she gave me great advice: "Just don't let it be boring." Thanks and love.

little threats

emily schultz

Discussion Guide

A Conversation with Emily Schultz

PUTNAM
— EST. 1838 —

Discussion Guide

1. *Little Threats* is told from the point of view of several different characters, and through interviews, writing assignments, and memories. How did experiencing these different viewpoints change your reading experience? Was there a specific character that you felt most connected to?

2. Kennedy must discover what it means to be an adult after spending her formative years in prison. How does she transform over the course of the novel? What would her adulthood have looked like if Haley had never been murdered?

3. Take a look at the different sibling relationships explored in *Little Threats*, comparing and contrasting the connections between Haley and Everett, Carter and Kennedy, and even Berk and Wyatt. How do relationships with siblings shape us?

4. *Little Threats* is set in 2008, but the crime at its heart took place in 1993. Did the culture of the 1990s have an impact on the crime? How does the 1990s era impact the characters in the present-day? Discuss the interplay between past and present in the novel, particularly looking at the characters who are trying to bury their pasts.

5. Discuss the impact that class and socioeconomic status have upon both Haley's murder investigation and the punishment

(or lack thereof) of those responsible. Consider the different ways that money and symbols of wealth are discussed by the various characters.

6. Throughout the novel, how did your suspicions about the identity of Haley's murderer shift and change?

7. Though Haley is not alive during the events of the novel, she is very much a character. In what ways is she represented on the page? Which characters act in her interests? How does Haley transcend the typical definition of a "victim"?

8. Why do you think that Carter and Everett are drawn to each other? Do you think they would have formed a relationship if they had not been connected by the crime? What do you imagine happens to them after the novel's end?

9. Each of the characters in *Little Threats* carries guilt over Haley's death in different ways. How does guilt manifest in each of them? Why do certain characters find ways to cope with guilt, and others crumble beneath it?

10. Discuss the moments when different characters believe they see Haley's ghost. Do these moments have anything in common? What do you think triggers these sightings?

11. There are many variations on relationships and power and age in the book. Is this something we see differently now than we did in 1993, or 2008?

A Conversation
with Emily Schultz

What inspired *Little Threats*?

I always knew that I wanted to write about a group of people years after a crime had happened. In my own life, I've seen people go through extremely traumatic events and how each reacts and learns to cope is very different. I also wanted to write about the '90s, and twins—my brothers are twins. And this story of people years after a murder seemed to be able to support all these subjects I wanted to write about. I've always found a novel is almost like a band writing a song. It starts as a few notes, then a melody emerges, and it comes together when it does.

***Little Threats* is very different from your debut novel, *The Blondes*—was the writing process different?**

I'd like to point out that *Little Threats* also begins with hair! So there is at least that throughline. But it was very different in that *The Blondes* was told entirely through the voice of one character, Hazel, as she's on this journey through a very strange pandemic. The process for *Little Threats* was all about settling on the voices of the story.

During editing, we decided to only give POVs to the characters who had been through the 1993 events: the two families and Berk. Limiting the writing to them let me focus on what made me want to start this novel: what happens to people after the crime you read about in the news is no longer front-page.

Why did you decide to veer toward the suspense genre? What genre would you classify *Little Threats* as belonging to?

This is my first psychological thriller, but my late father, who was an English teacher, read three mysteries a week and always wanted to write one. Because of that he was a supporter of all my writing: poetry, literary fiction. I wish he could have read this one to tell me how I did.

I think I moved to the mystery genre because something has happened: Women are taking up this genre as our own, as writers and readers. We get to express our darkest thoughts here—what we're most afraid of—in ways we couldn't in other places. For me, I would say what's more terrifying than your very first boyfriend showing up unannounced in your backyard years later? Once I had that scene between Kennedy and Berk, I knew I had to tell the story.

I think how women read mystery is different than how men read it. For us, these are cautionary tales. While we're being entertained we're also processing our own experiences.

The culture and chaos of the 1990s is at the heart of the novel— why were you drawn to write about this time period? What were the 1990s like for you, personally?

I started off the 1990s very young, in my teen years, and ended that decade as an adult. That meant I made both the best and the worst decisions of my life in that decade. I always wanted to write about the music, novels, and films of that period because for me they were so exciting. It was a time of intense optimism and also subversiveness. Depending who you were, 1993 was peak grunge, or riot girl. Activism was everywhere. Hip-hop was also exploding, and by 1995 we were moving into electronic music and rave culture. I remember 1993 very clearly because it was the first year I lived in a house with my friends, away from home. Berk's apartment is going to be familiar to anyone in college at that time, but I wasn't able to put in everything—I had to tailor it to these specific characters' experiences.

Are any of the events in the novel based on your own experiences?

When the character of Berk made his way into the book I recognized where he came from, and I started to understand Kennedy better. Like Kennedy, my first boyfriend was in his twenties when I was sixteen. I spent an unreasonable amount of time after it was over focused on a person for whom I was little more than a conquest. Those early relationships are formative and really shape the way you look at the world, whom you trust or don't trust, whether you are capable of love and meaningful connections. For a very long time, I was not. It was a consensual relationship, but the power imbalance affected my confidence for years.

I want to think I've forgiven that person in my life. I could say nice things: He introduced me to the Beats and encouraged me to write. But I admit it was really easy to write Berk as a jerk—the sly, flirty comments that also undermine, and the things he brags about. It was freeing to write Carter as someone who sees through him, even though Kennedy doesn't. The Berk Butlers of this world used to be a rite of passage for young women and men, and now we're looking at that differently. Another thing I learned is that I'm far from the person I was at sixteen. In all those ways, *Little Threats* is my most personal book to date, but it's also the most fictionalized. I'm not very good at memoir or essays because I do need the freedom of fiction.

Little Threats is narrated from multiple points of view—did you find that some character perspectives were easier to write than others? Did you have any favorites?

It was trickiest to write Gerry because I've never been a fiftysomething male lawyer. But it's just like in acting. You happen on one thing and it becomes the key to the character. Once I put him alone in that house, changing the linens, it opened up his world for me. He really is all about the house, the suburbs, and trying to keep life the same. Writing Everett felt natural because his life is probably closer to mine: I'm a country girl. His relationship with his mom, Marly, was also something I wanted to explore because it is complex. She's stuck in the past and she needs him to stay with her but also wants